Deadly Pages

Leslie C. Norins, M.D., Ph.D.

with

Thomas Hauck

ISBN-13: 978-0-9974698-0-6
Library of Congress Control Number: 2016905794

Medvostat LLC
4301 Gulfshore Blvd. N., Suite 1404
Naples, Florida 34103
USA
www.DeadlyPages.com
info@DeadlyPages.com

Smallpox declared eradicated.
> 1980. Announcement by World Health Organization.

The production line at the newly constructed Building 15 at Koltsovo was capable of manufacturing between eighty and one hundred tons of smallpox a year.
> 1999. *Biohazard* by Ken Alibek and Stephen Handelman (Random House).

"Probably the greatest threat that we have in bioterrorism is use of the smallpox virus."
> 2015. D. A. Henderson, MD, MPH. *The Deadly Smallpox Virus* (History Channel Documentary-YouTube). Dr. Henderson, Dean Emeritus of the Johns Hopkins School of Public Health, directed the international effort that eradicated naturally occurring smallpox throughout the world.

Biological and chemical materials and technologies, almost always dual use, move easily in the globalized economy, as do personnel with the scientific expertise to design and use them.
> February 9, 2016. *Worldwide Threat Assessment of the US Intelligence Community,* James R. Clapper, Director of National Intelligence, Senate Select Committee on Intelligence.

"The major threat our citizenry faces: a 'successful' (as defined by the aggressor) cyber, biological, nuclear or chemical attack on the United States."
> February 27, 2016. Warren Buffet, iconic investor, Annual Letter to Berkshire Hathaway Shareholders.

1.

"His suffering is over," said Martin Riker as he looked at the body of the man on the hospital gurney. "No one should have to die like that."

The face of the corpse was a hideous mask of red pustules. Underneath the sheet his hands and feet, too, were covered with the ugly boils.

With his gloved hand, Riker—his own body encased head to toe in a protective biohazard suit—picked up the man's driver's license and looked at the photo. "He was a handsome guy," he said. "Only twenty-eight years old. Prime of life. What a waste." Riker slipped the license back into the little plastic bag marked with the logo of Mt. Bedford Hospital, New York. He looked again at the man lying before him. In that face he saw thousands of years of human suffering and a disease that over the centuries had killed hundreds of millions of people.

He—and nearly every other scientist—believed the virus had been eradicated.

In the degree to which it ravaged its victims, the disease was indiscriminate; while many died, others recovered, their faces and bodies savagely scarred as a testament to their suffering. In this man's case, the affliction had brought agonizing death.

Riker turned away. There was nothing more that he could do for this patient.

"At least he gave us some information," said Jim Gilmore as they removed their biohazard suits in the clean room.

"A lucky break for us," replied Riker. "Perhaps we can follow that slender thread and find the cave where the monster lives. If we can't, we're going to see many more victims just like this man." Riker glanced at his watch. It was seven o'clock in the evening. Back home in Florida, Thanksgiving dinner had been enjoyed, and by now his sister and his kids had washed the dishes and scrubbed the pots. They were probably watching a movie or a game on television. His mind drifted back to how he had come to be in this place of death when earlier in the day he had been minding his own business, happy at home with his family.

Six hours earlier, the doorbell to Riker's home had been rung. Riker's sister Jeanne answered the door. For the past year—ever since Riker's beloved wife had passed away—Jeanne had been helping him organize family events with his grown children. She had hurriedly removed her apron and wiped her hands on a kitchen towel. After a quick glance in the hallway mirror to ensure her hair wasn't mussed she had opened the front door.

Her expectations were rewarded. "Nancy, sweetheart, come in," she said. She turned and called up the stairs. "Martin! Nancy and Roger are here—with the baby!"

"I'll be right down," he had replied from upstairs.

"Your father's on a video call with some of his old army buddies," Jeanne said to her niece. "Probably trading war stories. Now let me look at you! Don't you look wonderful! How was the drive?"

"Not bad," said Roger, who was carrying the car seat in which the baby was dozing. "Traffic on the interstate was surprisingly light, considering it's Thanksgiving Day. We left Tampa at ten and shot straight down I-75. We only caught one bad traffic jam in Sarasota."

He looked at his phone. "And now it's a few minutes before one. Samantha slept most of the way."

"Let me see her," said Jeanne as she carefully pulled away the little pink blanket from the child's face. "She's so precious! I swear she's got your eyes, Nancy. But I think the round shape of her head must come from Roger's side of the family."

The sound of footsteps on the stairs signaled

Riker's arrival.

"Hi, daddy," said Nancy. "Well, we made it! Our first Thanksgiving with Samantha."

"It's great to see you both," smiled Riker. "Roger, is there anything we need to bring in from the car?"

"Yes, there is," replied Roger as he handed the car seat to Nancy. "We've got the baby bag and a box of things for you." He turned and, followed by Riker, walked out to the car, which was parked in the circular turnaround in front of the house.

"How are you doing?" asked Roger.

"As well as can be expected," replied Riker. "When Rebecca and I bought this house, we expected to live the life of the typical early-retirement couple—you know, go out every night, visit museums, buy a boat. Then she died, and not only did I lose the woman I loved for thirty years but I lost my best friend. Suddenly I felt like a leaf in the wind. I didn't know what to do with myself. It's taken me a while to feel anything like a normal human being." He took the baby bag from the back seat. "I'm glad that you and Nancy decided to come. Jeanne told me that you were thinking of staying home because Samantha was sick."

"She's got a cold," replied Roger. "A few days ago she started getting fussy and her nose was running. She was irritable and had a hard time falling asleep. We had just gotten her to sleep through the night, and taking a step backwards from that milestone was a most unwelcome development. We took her temperature and it was almost one hundred degrees."

"It doesn't sound too serious," said Riker as they walked back into the house. "Most babies get half a dozen colds a year. They're a nuisance, but it's all part of building up their immune systems."

"This morning her temperature was normal," said Roger. "But her little nose is running like a faucet—I feel so sorry for her! Driving in the car helped. It's funny how babies always fall asleep when you drive them in a car. A friend of mine had a baby who was so resistant to falling asleep at night that he'd take him out in the car and drive around until the kid conked out in the car seat. Then he'd carefully bring the baby—and the car seat—into the house."

They met Jeanne and Nancy in the kitchen.

"Looks like we've got everything under control," said Jeanne. "Ever since he was a kid, Martin's been a good cook—all I have to do is help out. We're going to have roast turkey, of course, with stuffing, green beans, sweet potatoes, pearl onions, whole cranberry sauce, and those squishy dinner rolls that everyone loves so much."

At that moment Samantha awakened and let out a plaintive cry. Her mother picked her up and tried to soothe her. She reached into her pocket and extracted a tissue, which she used in an attempt to wipe the baby's nose. The tissue quickly became a sticky mess. She tossed it into the trashcan under the sink.

"It's amazing how much glop can come out of such a tiny nose," said Roger. "I guess it looks worse than it really is. We try not to get freaked out by every little thing. We have friends who give us all kinds of advice about how to keep kids healthy. You wouldn't believe what some people say. One friend of ours—who shall remain nameless—asked us if we had disinfected the house. She said that babies need a germ-free environment, and that any contact with any bacteria is bad. She constantly scrubs her house and she uses gallons of antibacterial lotions and soaps.""Your friend is making a terrible mistake," said Riker. "Tell her that friendly bacteria keep us alive. We can't live without them. Your antiseptic friend has about four pounds of bacteria happily living in her digestive system. They come from the environment. Babies are born without gut bacteria, and they have to ingest them. Most are delivered by the parents. Does your friend kiss her baby? That's good—because with every kiss she's giving her baby important bacteria that will take up residence in her gut and help her digest her food. Anyway, the common cold is caused not by bacteria but by a virus. It's a whole 'nother animal. Or, to be precise, group of animals—there are over a hundred viruses that cause one. Trying to kill them all is a very bad idea."

"As I'm sure you've realized," Jeanne said to Roger, "My brother loves to talk about germs. Once you get him started, there's no stopping him."

Roger turned to Riker. "Nancy told me you were with the Centers for Disease Control and Prevention in Atlanta."

"After I graduated from college," said Riker, "I joined the Army and managed to claw my up to the rank of lieutenant, serving at the Army Medical Research Institute of Infectious Diseases. When I got out I went to work for the CDC. As deputy chief of the Epidemic Intelligence Service, I spent the next twenty years chasing microscopic enemies around the planet. These were the *really* bad guys—Ebola, dengue fever, HIV/AIDS, malaria, salmonella, tuberculosis. The war against killer bugs never ends. It makes you appreciate the good bugs—like the one hundred trillion bacteria that live inside you. Anyway, I spent most of my adult life living out of a suitcase, and it feels good to stay in one place for a while. I missed too many of the big events in our kids' lives. Maybe I can make up for some of that with our grandchildren."

"Grandchild," corrected Nancy. "Only one so far."

"I need your brothers to get with the program," replied her father. "I don't mean to preach to the choir."

"What are they doing for Thanksgiving?" asked Nancy as she stroked her daughter's head.

"Tim is visiting his girlfriend's parents in Baltimore, and Addison is staying at school—he's going skiing in Colorado with some friends."

"I think Samantha is hungry," said Nancy. "I'm going to take her into the living room and feed her."

"Give her a good dose of maternal bacteria," said Riker.

"No problem, dad." She rolled her eyes.

Taking a cutting board, a bowl of green beans, and

a knife, Riker went to work trimming the ends of the beans.

"Do you miss it?" asked Roger.

"Miss what?" replied Riker as he chopped.

"Your job. Chasing bad bugs."

"Nope," he said with certainty. "I've seen enough squalid villages, polluted rivers, swarms of mosquitos, and dying children to last a lifetime. There are seven billion people living on this planet, and at any given time a few billion of them have some sort of terrible disease. When you live in the United States you don't see it. We don't have the same experience with tropical diseases that plague most of mankind. We have clean water, electricity, good hospitals, and a culture that— for the most part—embraces science. Well, I've done my part. I've made my contribution to the world. Now I'm enjoying myself in this little corner of paradise. Here in Naples there's no malaria, no Ebola, no tuberculosis, no leprosy, no guinea worm—well, you get the idea. It's nice to think that if I fell into Naples Bay I wouldn't come out with a terrible waterborne illness, or that when I turn on the tap in my kitchen, what comes out won't give me dysentery. It's comforting to know that if a mosquito bites me, I'm not going to get malaria. It's time for others to take up those battles."

Riker felt a vibration in his pocket. He pulled out his phone. He frowned.

"Who is it?" asked his sister.

"It's the CDC," he said as he pressed the answer button. With the phone to his ear he walked from the kitchen into the front sitting room.

"Hi—Martin Riker here," he said.

"Martin, it's Jim Gilmore."

"Jim, how are you? I'm sorry that you're working on Thanksgiving Day. No rest for the weary, huh?"

"No rest for the weary. Martin, something has come up. Do you have a minute?"

"Sure, okay." He sat down in the overstuffed wingback chair next to the faux fireplace.

"We have identified a case of smallpox."

"Smallpox? Are you kidding?"

"I wish I were," said Gilmore.

"Jim, the last known case of smallpox was in October of 1977, in Somalia. I was *there*, for Chrissakes. It's been completely eradicated. How can you be sure?"

"We're absolutely certain," replied Gilmore. "I'm calling you from New York. We've got a patient at Mt. Bedford Hospital—a Syrian national. His name is Akram Aflaq. He was admitted last Friday. He's got smallpox. Absolutely no doubt about it. He has all the classic symptoms and redundant blood tests have confirmed the presence of variola DNA."

"Major or minor?" asked Riker.

"Major," replied Gilmore.

"Then normally he'd have a forty percent chance of dying within seven days of the appearance of his symptoms. When was he infected?"

"Here's what we know. On Sunday the fifteenth of November he flew to New York from Athens. The next day he went to a clinic in Chelsea with a fever and body aches. They sent him home and told him to stay in bed and take aspirin. The rash appeared on Friday the twentieth, and he went back to the clinic. This time they sent him to Mt. Bedford. On Tuesday night the first pustules appeared on the tongue and in the mouth. They quickly spread to his face and then to his hands and feet. The diagnosis of smallpox was confirmed and he was quarantined. We hope it was not done not too late to stop others from being infected."

"What's the treatment?" asked Riker.

"Just the usual—the fluid and electrolyte balance is being monitored and maintained to avoid dehydration, and he's being given medications for fever and pain. He's also being given Cidofovir, but we don't expect much. His case is very severe. He's in bad shape."

"Does the press know?"

"Not yet. We've managed to keep a lid on it."

"Good," said Riker. "The last thing we want is a

panic. Thanks for the heads up, but it sounds like you guys have everything under control for the moment. Thanks for the call. Keep me posted on how the situation develops."

From the other end of the line came silence. Then: "Martin, I didn't call you just to keep you in the loop. This is serious. We need to figure out where and how this guy got infected. No one can do that but you."

"What are you saying?"

"I'm saying that you need to come to New York *right now*. Before this guy dies. You need to help us track this thing back to its source."

"Oh, come on, Jim, I don't think that's necessary. I've been out of the game for over a year. Surely there are plenty of people who can handle it. The patient was probably visiting Somalia and picked up a latent virus from a remote village. I'm sure he's a dead end. A freak anomaly."

"It's not that," said Gilmore. "Aflaq is semi-conscious now, but when I saw him a few hours ago he said just one thing to me. He said, 'Mahadi—the GSD—they want to kill me.' That's all."

"The GSD?" asked Riker. His stomach began to tighten.

"Yes," said Gilmore. "'Mahadi—the GSD—they want to kill me.' He kept saying it over and over again."

"How long does Aflaq have to live?"

"The doctors give him no more than a few hours. Martin, this story is bigger than some random recurrence of a virus we thought had been eradicated. Aflaq is talking about the Syrian secret police wanting him dead—and by tomorrow he's probably going to *be* dead. This could be very serious. It's a matter of national security."

For a moment Riker sat in his chair. He looked around the room with its comfortable furniture, little tables of personal mementos, books filling the shelves, colorful paintings and family photos on the walls, and the glass-front case with his high school and college football trophies. What the hell was comfort worth, anyway? Since when was the soft life so good? He wasn't ready to be turned out to pasture!

Riker glanced at his watch. "Okay," he said. "It's one o'clock now. I'll be there by six o'clock tonight." He hung up.

With a mix of keen anticipation and deep anxiety he went into the kitchen.

"We're on track to be eating dinner at two o'clock," said Jeanne. "Maybe you'd like to show Roger the neighborhood? It's a beautiful day and you haven't been outside."

Riker looked at the loving and expectant faces of his sister and daughter. He reached out and stroked the tiny fuzzy head of his granddaughter. A lump gathered in his throat.

"Is something wrong?" asked Jeanne.

"I have some difficult news," said Riker. "I'm leaving for New York."

"Oh," said his sister. "You mean tomorrow?"

"No, I mean right now. There's a big problem that I have to sort out."

"Right now?" said Nancy. "Daddy, do you really have to?"

Riker thought about all the times in the past that he had to go away and miss family events. He had sworn to stay home for his family. Now he was breaking that oath.

"Yes, I really have to."

"Why?" asked Jeanne. She put down the radish she was cutting and gave him a hard look.

"There's a man in New York who's very sick," said Riker. "I can't tell you what he's got. He's from Syria. He's tangled up with the General Security Directorate—the Syrian secret police. I need to find out why he's sick."

"When will you be back?" asked Jeanne.

"I'm sorry, I can't say," he said. "I may have to go overseas. Wherever the investigation takes us."

Jeanne smiled. She knew there was no point in questioning her brother. It wouldn't change anything.

"All right," she said as she wiped her hands on a towel. "While you go upstairs and pack, I'll make you a turkey sandwich."

2.

After catching a flight from Southwest Florida International Airport in Ft. Myers to La Guardia, Martin Riker had taken a cab to Mt. Bedford and rushed to the infectious disease wing of the hospital. There he was greeted by Jim Gilmore.

"Let's get you suited up," Gilmore said as he led Riker to the clean room. "The patient is in bad shape. He won't live long."

"Has he said anything else?" asked Riker as he donned the white plastic suit with its attached boots and gloves.

"No," replied Gilmore. "Only that Mahadi wanted to kill him."

Once safely protected, Riker and Gilmore went to Aflaq's bedside.

"Mr. Aflaq, can you hear me?" said Riker.

Aflaq nodded weakly.

"Mr. Aflaq, why does Mahadi want to kill you?" asked Riker.

Aflaq muttered something.

"Did you hear what he said?" Riker asked the doctor who was attending the patient.

"No—but you know how it is with these suits we're wearing," the doctor replied. "You can't hear a damned thing."

Riker leaned closer to the dying man. "Mr. Aflaq— tell me, why does Mahadi want to kill you?"

"It's all because of Sabeen," he whispered.

"Who? Sabeen? Who is Sabeen?" said Riker.

The man convulsed. The doctor shooed Riker away from the bed. Other nurses appeared. The monitoring machines beeped like angry bees. After a flurry of activity the doctor shut off the buzzing devices and stepped away from the bed. The room was quiet. The doctor looked at the clock on the wall. "Death came at seven fifteen."

Riker looked down at the ravaged face. "I thought that no human being would ever see those terrible smallpox pustules ever again," he said quietly. "I thought we had eradicated this ghastly disease forever."

After he and Gilmore had returned to the clean room and taken off their biohazard suits, they went to the office of the chief of the hospital's infectious disease unit.

"Dr. Winthrop—it's good to see you again," said Riker as he and Gilmore sat down. "Although I would have preferred different circumstances."

"Indeed, Martin, this is quite a shock," she replied. "The last thing I expected to see in my hospital was an otherwise healthy young man from a non-tropical region present himself with full-blown smallpox. And then to have him succumb so quickly—we think that he may have had a congenital immune system defect. The autopsy will tell."

"Let's talk about containment," said Riker. "Do we know with whom this man has been in contact?"

"We're developing a list," replied Dr. Winthrop.

"How about educating the staff here at the hospital?" said Riker. "Most of these folks have no idea what smallpox is. They've never been trained."

"We've developed a quick PowerPoint presentation that all employees will be required to attend," said Dr. Winthrop. "It provides the basic information. I wrote the script myself." From her desk she picked up a document, which she scanned. "We tell them what used to be common knowledge: while smallpox is a contagious disease, it's not difficult to protect yourself if you take the proper precautions. Vaccination in advance used to be the way, but general vaccination was discontinued in 1971. The virus that causes smallpox spreads through person-to-person contact and saliva droplets in an infected person's breath. The virus also can be spread through direct contact with infected bodily fluids or contaminated objects such as bedding or clothing, and even scabs that fall off infected lesions. It's occasionally spread by virus carried in the air in enclosed settings such as buildings, buses, or trains. But, unlike Zika, for instance, the smallpox virus is not known to be transmitted by insects or animals—we humans are the only natural hosts."

"Good," nodded Riker.

"We explain that the disease has an incubation period of between seven and seventeen days after exposure," continued Dr. Winthrop. "During that time, victims do not have any symptoms and may feel fine, and are not contagious. The first symptoms include fever, head and body aches, and sometimes vomiting. This is called the prodrome phase and may last for two to four days."

"Aflaq was at this stage when he presented himself to the clinic in Chelsea on Monday, November sixteenth," said Riker. "He had been in New York for only one day."

"Unfortunately," added Gilmore, "and while you can't blame them, no one at the clinic recognized the symptoms of smallpox. No one there has ever seen smallpox and they don't teach it in medical school. It's considered extinct, so they don't bother. The doctor on call thought he might have had chicken pox or even herpes simplex type 2, which shows similar symptoms."

"Plotting backwards in time," said Riker, "I'd say that Aflaq was infected during the first week of November. Nearly two weeks later he flew to New York from Athens. Do we know where he was before Athens? Do we have his passport?"

"It's on its way to the CDC along with the rest of his personal effects," said Dr. Winthrop.

"Okay," said Riker. "We can get images from the CDC. We need to know his connection to Mahadi, we need to know who or what Sabeen is, and we need to know how long he was in Athens and where he was before that. How about vaccinations here in New

York?"

"Our immediate staff, including myself, were vaccinated yesterday," said Dr. Winthrop. "We also vaccinated health care workers at the clinic. Here at Mt. Bedford we're extremely fortunate to have a supply of the three available smallpox vaccines, which are highly effective in combatting the disease. As you know, smallpox vaccines are made from live vaccinia viruses that protect against smallpox disease. They do not contain the actual variola virus, the causative agent of smallpox. The three smallpox vaccines that we and other agencies have stockpiled are ACAM2000, Aventis Pasteur Smallpox Vaccine (APSV), and Imvamune. The primary response strategies for achieving epidemic control are containment activities including vaccination, combined with close monitoring of the people on our list."

"How about people who are immunodeficient—such as those with HIV/AIDS?" asked Riker.

"Because of a high likelihood of a poor immune response and an increased risk for adverse events," said Dr. Winthrop, "smallpox vaccination is avoided in persons with severe immunodeficiency who might get overwhelmed by the weak vaccine virus, such as people infected with HIV and those with other severely immunocompromised states requiring isolation, such as recipients of organ or bone marrow transplants. We've identified a dozen such folks and are closely monitoring them."

"Okay," said Riker. "Where did Aflaq live in New York?"

"He rented a room at the Onyx Hotel on Twentieth Street," replied Dr. Winthrop.

An hour later—after he had checked into the Marriott in Times Square—Martin Riker walked into the lobby of the Onyx Hotel. It was an interesting choice for a guy from Syria arriving in New York from Athens. A storied place, the Onyx was a legendary haunt of poets, rock stars, junkies, and dreamers. It was here that the novelist Robert DeJong wrote his underground classic *To the Ends of Time*, about a cross-country trip he and his buddy Ray Pilsner took to find the perfect peyote buttons. It was here—in room 304—that punk rocker Charlie Chrome killed his girlfriend Suzy Forester, and then later killed himself with a heroin overdose. The hotel had been memorialized in paintings and novels, poems and popular songs; one of the earliest tunes about the place had been "The Onyx Hotel Blues," popularized in the nineteen thirties by Paul Blackman and His Red-Hot Jazzmen. The lyrics described a guy whose girlfriend was a hooker who operated out of the hotel. In the last verse he shot her before going to the hotel bar for a drink.

Its ten stories and sixty-five rooms had plenty of stories to tell—but Martin Riker was interested in only one.

He approached the once elegant but now shabby desk with its marble top illuminated by old-fashioned crystal wall sconces. The clerk behind the desk eyed him warily.

"My name's Martin Riker," he said. "I'm investigating a man named Akram Aflaq. I need to get into his room." He tossed the search warrant on the desk.

With a frown the clerk put on a pair of wire-rimmed reading glasses. He picked up the warrant and carefully unfolded it. Riker got the impression that this guy knew how to read such things. Over the years he'd probably had dozens of them tossed on his marble countertop. "I haven't seen him in a couple of days," said the clerk. "He owes on his bill. Is he in trouble?"

"No, he's not in trouble. But he's not coming back. He's checked out. Show me his room charges."

Without showing a trace of urgency the clerk went to his computer and printed out a sheet, which he handed to Riker. The bill showed nothing special in the way of extra charges—just a couple of nips of whiskey from the minibar at eight dollars apiece (you could buy them across the street for three dollars) and one pay-per-view porn film on cable TV.

"Anybody ever come here with him?" asked Riker. "Any visitors?"

The clerk shrugged. "We don't get nosey with our guests," he said. "But the answer is no, I never saw him come in with anyone."

"Have the maids been in the room to clean it?"

"Sure, I assume they have," replied the clerk.

"I'm going to need their names and contact information," said Riker. "Let's have the key."

The clerk handed him the key to room 438. "Fourth floor," he said.

"No kidding," replied Riker.

He went to the elevator and pushed the softly glowing button on the wall. The antique arrow showed the elevator's progress as it descended from an upper floor. When the arrow reached "L" the doors lurched open. Standing in the elevator were two men. One of them was very old. Without a word the men stepped out and walked to the front door of the hotel.

"I'll be damned," said Riker to himself as he stepped into the box. "That was Howlin' Jefferson, the blues singer. I thought he was dead. Glad to see he's still around." He pushed the button for the fourth floor. The doors eventually closed and the elevator rose. They opened again to reveal a dark hallway. The carpet had once been wine-colored, and fifty years earlier the wallpaper with its fancy gold stripes had been first-rate. The air smelled faintly of mold. Room 438 was to the right, at the end of the hall. Riker slipped the brass key into the lock and turned it, and with a satisfying mechanical "thunk" the bolt slid back and he pushed the door open.

From his pocket Riker took out a pair of latex gloves.

Indeed, the hotel maids had cleaned the room. The bed had been made and the towels were fresh. An open suitcase sat on the folding metal stand provided by the hotel. Riker carefully picked through it: a few shirts, two pairs of pants, some underwear, sneakers, a paperback copy of a detective thriller. No documents or identifying items. He went to the plain wooden dresser. The drawers were empty. In the closet he found only a suit jacket and an overcoat. Aflaq had been travelling light.

In the bathroom Aflaq had the usual toiletries—toothbrush, toothpaste, shaving gear, deodorant, contact lens solution, a bottle of ordinary American aspirin.

Riker returned to the bedroom. Next to the bed, leaning up against the night table, was a black leather courier's bag—the kind you can carry with a strap on your shoulder. The bag was of good quality and well worn. Riker placed it on the bed, undid the metal clasp, and opened the flap. Inside was a newspaper. Riker unfolded it. His rudimentary knowledge of Arabic told him that it was a copy of *Al Ba'ath*, the mouthpiece of the ruling Arab Socialist Ba'ath Party of Syria. On the front page of the paper was a big color photo of Bashar al-Assad, the president of Syria. He was smiling. As usual, Assad was sporting one of those timid moustaches that resemble something a twelve-year-old boy would try to grow. "Just shave the damn thing," muttered Riker. The date on the newspaper was Thursday, the fifth of November. This would have been around the time Aflaq had become infected.

A second newspaper was in the bag. Riker pulled it out. This one was published in English—*Kathimerini,* a daily newspaper published in Athens and distributed with the *International New York Times* in Greece and Cyprus. Its political leaning was center-right. The date of the issue was Sunday, the fifteenth of November—the day Aflaq had flown to New York.

There was a dog-eared travel magazine. It included a profile of the Onyx Hotel, complete with a selection of its most infamous stories. *That accounts for our man's choice*, thought Riker.

Digging deeper into the bag, Riker pulled out a cheap pre-paid Tracfone. Riker flipped it open. It looked new. There were no photos on it and no phone numbers stored. The battery was fully charged.

Riker went into the bag's interior pocket. He pulled out a boarding pass.

It was for flight FDK601 on FlyDamas Airline, one of the few commercial carriers still operating out of Damascus International Airport. The boarding pass was dated Thursday, the fifth of November. The destination was Beirut, Lebanon. Aflaq had probably bought the copy of *Al Ba'ath* at the airport in Damascus. Because the airport was still under government control, openly carrying the pro-Assad paper would have been helpful.

That was all. Except for a cheap ballpoint pen and a legal pad with nothing written on it, the bag was empty.

Riker took out his phone and punched a number. "Jim? I'm in Aflaq's room at the Onyx Hotel. Not much here except a magazine and two newspapers, and a boarding pass that tells us that on the fifth of November our guy hopped a flight from Damascus to Beirut. From there he made his way to Athens and then to New York. At the hospital, did he have a phone on him? No? Strange—I found a phone in his travel bag, but it's a cheap prepaid throwaway. There's nothing on it except the record of two phone calls that he made here in New York. Both were made to the same number—212-555-9835. I'm going to find out who's on the other end of the line. And get a team up here to clean out the room. I photographed the boarding pass and the newspapers. Thanks."

On his own phone Riker tapped out the number from Aflaq's phone. After three rings a man answered.

Riker introduced himself. "I'm a doctor," he said. "I need to talk to you about Akram Aflaq. To whom am I speaking?"

"This is Jalal Kamer," said the man. "Is anything wrong?"

Riker asked where Kamer was at that moment.

"I work at a produce market on Fifty-third Street and Second Avenue. DeAngelo's. I'm here until ten o'clock tonight."

Twenty minutes later Riker got out of a cab in front of DeAngelo's Market at 348 East 53rd Street. A red-and-white-striped awning sheltered the door, which was flanked by generous bins of fruits and vegetables.

Riker went to the cashier and asked for Jalal Kamer. The cashier pointed to a man stacking boxes in an aisle at the back of the store. Riker approached him and showed his identification. Kamer put down the carton he was unpacking and wiped his hands on his apron. His wide brown eyes showed suspicion but not fear.

"Have you had any personal contact with Akram Aflaq in the past three weeks?" asked Riker.

"No," replied Kamer. "A few days ago he called me and said that he was in the United States. He said that he had to get a job and make money to send home. I told him I had a few contacts who could help him, and I invited him to come here, to the store. But I never saw him. What's this all about?"

"Why did Aflaq come to the United States?" asked Riker.

"He told me that he needed to get away because someone was trying to kill him," replied Kamer as he arranged oranges on a shelf.

"Why was someone trying to kill him?"

"He didn't say."

"But he asked you about working here in the United States?"

"Yes."

"Where did Aflaq live in Syria?"

"Just like me, he grew up in Latakia. It's a port city on the Mediterranean Sea. As far as I know, that's where he's been living. I left Syria four years ago, when the troubles started. I knew it was going to get bad. But Akram stayed. He wanted to help the regime defeat the rebels. I told him he was crazy and that Assad would never last. But Akram was always on the side of the government. That's why it surprised me when he called and said he was in New York. I always thought he'd be on the front lines, fighting for Assad."

"Do you have an address for Aflaq in Latakia?"

"Let me think—it's been a while. It was near Haroun Square. He had an apartment on a little side street, where he lived with his mother. She's elderly. I can't imagine why he left her behind. Akram was a responsible guy—he had a good job and didn't drink or smoke."

"What was his job?"

"He had a party position—you know, with the Ba'athists. Something to do with communications. We didn't talk politics much because we disagreed. In Syria, you're very careful about what you say, even to your friends. We talked about other things—music and girls and sports."

"Okay, thanks," said Riker. "You've been very helpful."

3.

"You say you want to travel to Syria?" asked Angela Powell. She circled around her desk and stood before the window, which provided a view of the Ronald Reagan Washington National Airport just across the Potomac River and, to the north, the skyline of Washington, D.C., with the gleaming white Capitol building at center stage.

"Yes—it's absolutely necessary," replied Riker. "Last night I treated a man from Syria who had recently arrived in New York. He had smallpox. His disease was too far advanced and he died before we could save him. His last words were that someone named Mahadi wanted to kill him, and he also mentioned the name Sabeen. I went to his hotel room and found a boarding pass for a flight from Damascus to Bierut. He took this flight a day or two after he had been infected."

"So you're reasonably sure he was infected in Syria?"

"Reasonably sure, but not certain. Last night I interviewed a friend of his in New York, and the guy confirmed that our man—Akram Aflaq—lived in the port city of Latakia. He lived with his mother, and he was a government sympathizer."

"And the diagnosis of smallpox is certain?"

"The blood test has been confirmed by the CDC."

Powell went from the window to her desk and sat down in the leather-upholstered swivel chair. Her portfolio as a case officer for the Defense Clandestine Service (DCS)—an arm of the Defense Intelligence Agency (DIA) that conducts clandestine espionage activities around the world—included approving, funding, and supervising the activities of special adjunct agents like Riker. These were people who worked outside the normal intelligence communities of the FBI or CIA but who possessed highly specialized skills that made them indispensible on certain classified missions.

"Let me be clear about this," she said. "You need to get into Syria to find out how a man contracted smallpox there—a disease that is not even supposed to exist any more. I'm sure you're aware that even though you're going as a civilian doctor, the Syrian government under Bashar al-Assad is not going to cooperate. In fact, if they find out that you're snooping around in their country, they'll either arrest you or throw you out. Any local assistance you receive will need to be carefully arranged with covert agents."

"I understand."

"Okay," she said. "Your passport and travel papers are up to date?"

"Yes."

"Because the Syrian border agents are totally dysfunctional, we'll smuggle you in with a forged visa. Just for the record, I assume you know the State Department's travel warning regarding Syria. I'll refresh your memory." She picked up a sheet of paper and read: "'The Department of State continues to warn US citizens against all travel to Syria and strongly recommends that US citizens remaining in Syria depart immediately. The security situation remains dangerous and unpredictable as a violent conflict between government and armed anti-government groups continues throughout the country, along with an increased risk of kidnappings, bombings, murder, and terrorism.' And so forth. What this means is that if you get kidnapped or killed, we're not going to jump in with both feet to seek justice. What we'll do is very quietly track the perps and nail them with a drone when the time is right.

"As I'm sure you're also aware, the US embassy in Damascus has suspended its operations and therefore cannot provide protection or routine consular services to US citizens in Syria. The government of the Czech Republic, acting through its embassy in Damascus, serves as protecting power for US interests in Syria. But they can't do very much—it's really just a diplomatic courtesy."

Powell took off her reading glasses and set them on her desk. She looked down and seemed to become lost in thought. Riker sat quietly. Powell gently drummed the blotter with the fingertips of her right hand. Then she nodded to herself, as if she had reached a decision in her mind. She looked at Riker.

"This office recognizes the national security value of your mission and will support it in every way that we can, including funding," she said. "There is one more thing that we must do, however. If—or rather, *when*—your presence in Syria comes to the attention of the regime, they're going to check up on you. They will assume you're a spy unless there are indications otherwise. I'm going to have a guy in our communications office write a couple of fake articles with your name on them. These articles will express support for the embattled regime of Bashar al-Assad, arguing that because of all the actors in the region it's best positioned to provide desperately needed stability. In essence, you'll be agreeing with the Russians. We'll post these articles online and make sure that anyone who searches for your name will find them."

"But al-Assad is a butcher who barrel-bombs his own people!" protested Riker. "You're going to make me out to be his supporter?"

"Yes," replied Powell. "Don't worry—as soon as you get back safely we'll take them down."

"But files on the Internet can last for years," said Riker.

Powell narrowed her eyes. "That's my offer. It may save your life. Take it or leave it."

Riker had no choice. Too many lives were at stake. If there was a program to re-introduce smallpox into the world, it had to be stopped at any cost—even to his own reputation.

"It's a deal," said Riker.

"When do you expect to leave?"

"As soon as possible," he replied. "This is a ticking time bomb. It may go off at any time."

Once in a while—most often when national security is at stake—agencies of the federal government are capable of accelerating their bureaucratic pace and moving with a surprising speed and agility that's reminiscent of a gracefully pirouetting elephant at a circus. It was this capability for fast action that propelled Martin Riker, like a stuntman shot out of a cannon, across the Atlantic to Israel. The flight from Washington, D.C. to Tel Aviv took twelve hours, and with the additional eight-hour time difference this meant he arrived in Tel Aviv on Saturday at eight in the morning local time. After a few hours rest in a hotel he took a shuttle flight to Haifa, where he was greeted by Lieutenant Abel Kerman of the Israeli Navy. Lt. Kerman drove Riker to the naval base, where he was shown to his quarters to cool his heels until sunset.

Out of curiosity, Riker Googled himself. He was both horrified and strangely reassured to quickly find a number of authentic-looking articles with his byline that professed support for the al-Assad regime because it was a stabilizing influence in a chaotic region.

At seven o'clock Lt. Kerman fetched him and brought him to a pier. Before them was a sleek aluminum patrol boat. It looked like a swordfish—long and sharp and fast. On its stern was the name *Gershon Zak*. "Back in the late nineteen-forties," said Lt. Kerman, "Gershon Zak was the head of the Sea Service, which became the Israeli Navy." Lt. Kerman and Riker crossed the gangway from the pier to the ship. "The *Gershon Zak* is a Super Dvora MKIII," continued Lt. Kerman. "She's twenty-seven meters in length—that's about eighty feet. Top speed is classified, but I'll tell you that she can outrun just about anything on the Mediterranean except a racing boat. Propulsion is provided by twin diesels, but the key is the articulating surface drive."

"What's that?" asked Riker.

"The boat has twin propellers, but instead of being fixed to rigid shafts that project down into the water, the props are attached to horizontal shafts that stick out of the back of the boat. These shafts have joints, like your wrist. The boat has no rudders. Direction is controlled by pointing the props to one side or another. Plus, they can be lifted nearly all the way out of the water. The ASD system enables operations in extremely shallow water, such as beaching operations during military missions or humanitarian relief missions where the goal is to deliver medical and food supplies or rescue injured persons."

Riker stepped onto the deck.

"Colonel Riker, welcome aboard the *Gershon Zak*," said a smartly uniformed officer with three gold leafs on his hat. "I'm Aluf-Mischne Moshe Silver."

"Thanks," said Riker. "*Aluf* is Hebrew for 'champion.' *Mischne* means 'secondary.' That would make you the captain of this vessel, if I'm not mistaken."

"Quite right," smiled Capt. Silver. "It's my job to get you to Latakia in one piece. Our *rav-samal*—chief petty officer—will show you to your quarters. We shove off in five minutes."

Riker was taken below to a tiny officer's cabin. It had a sink, a chair, and a fold-down cot. There was no porthole. After a few minutes the chief petty officer came back and asked Riker if he'd like to go up to the wheelhouse. Riker gratefully accepted the invitation. The wheelhouse wasn't much bigger than the cabin, but at least you had a magnificent view of the sharp nose of the boat and the Mediterranean in the golden glow of sunset.

"The distance to Latakia is about three hundred kilometres, or one hundred and ninety miles," said Capt. Silver. "In Florida, this is slightly more than the distance between Tampa and Naples, where you live, if I'm not mistaken."

"Yes—that's where I live," replied Riker. The captain's thorough knowledge of his background was both reassuring and unnerving.

"Our running time to Latakia will be five hours," added Capt. Silver.

Riker did a quick computation in his head. Their speed would need to average nearly thirty-four knots, or forty miles per hour.

"I know what you're thinking," laughed the captain. "No, we will not be operating at top speed. And while this vessel is very fast, it can't compare to the Norwegian Navy's new *Skudd*-class corvettes. They can hit sixty knots. No other warship can outrun them."

The captain ordered the vessel to get under way. In a few minutes the boat accelerated towards the open sea. From his position in the wheelhouse Riker felt as though he were flying over the water. On the port side the sky blazed red and gradually turned purple. To starboard he saw nothing but darkness and a faint glow on the horizon.

"We've got to give Bierut a wide berth," said the captain. "It will add to our travel time, but we don't want any diplomatic incidents."

It was just before one o'clock when the *Gershon Zak* slowed and Riker noticed the ship's orientation to the stars overhead was changing. They were heading east, toward land. Strangely, he saw few lights. "This is the way it is now in Syria," said the captain. "A state of total war. You don't see many lights at night. It used to be when you came along the Syrian coast the sky was ablaze. Latakia was a beautiful resort town, the playground of the rich. The Cote d'Azur—on the northern edge of town—was really spectacular. Politically, Syria was always repressive. When Assad came to power many people thought he'd be a reformer. He had a beautiful wife—Asma al-Assad. While she was born to Syrian parents, she was raised and educated in the United Kingdom, and graduated from King's College London with a bachelor's degree in computer science and French literature. It was in London where she met the future president, when he was studying ophthalmology. After briefly pursuing a career in international investment banking she moved to Syria to marry al-Assad. Everyone thought it might be the dawn of a renaissance in Syria. Instead it became the start of the new dark ages."

In the blink of an eye, it seemed, the boat had pulled up against a decrepit pier. "This is where you disembark," said the captain as he ushered Riker to the gunwale. A ladder was thrown over the side. In moment Riker was standing on solid ground. Like a ghost, the *Gershon Zak* backed away from the pier and in a moment was gone, leaving only a faint glimmer of its phosphorescent wake.

4.

From the end of the darkened pier Riker walked toward the shore. Before him loomed the gloomy bulk of the Latakia Sports City, which in happier times had been a bustling center of swimming, tennis, and other sports. It was sandwiched between the big oval of the old horse riding arena to the south and the Sports City Stadium to the north. Riker crossed Sports City Road and entered a weedy parking area. It was nearly empty except for an idling taxicab—an old Toyota sedan. The roof light was switched off, indicating the cab was unavailable. A man was sitting in the driver's seat, reading a newspaper. Riker approached the cab. He stood next to the driver's window. The driver, a Syrian man of about forty with a neatly trimmed moustache, casually powered down the window. "Welcome to Latakia, Mr. Riker," the driver said. "Where to?" His accent sounded like an Arab cab driver in London.

"They didn't tell you?" said Riker.

"The Shahbandar," said the driver.

"Yes—let's go," said Riker as he opened the rear door and tossed his knapsack on the seat. He circled around the car and got in the front passenger seat.

"Tell me your name," said Riker.

"Hussein."

"They told me you were clean shaven."

Hussein smiled. "My wife hated my moustache, and so for five long years I shaved every day. Now we are separated and I can do what I want."

Putting the car into gear, Hussein cruised slowly out of the parking lot and turned south on Sports City Road, the wide boulevard that arced around the harbor. The neighborhoods they passed through were mostly dark, and the buildings—houses, apartments, offices—loomed like gloomy boxes. Riker found it amazing to think that in those dark buildings lived ordinary people, clinging to a semblance of normal life, fearful that that their protector and patron—President Bashar al-Assad—might lose his grip on power; if that happened, as they had seen so often in other Syrian cities, the hordes of savage insurgents would descend upon them, burning, killing, destroying anyone and everything associated with the dictator whom they despised. While the drama played out, the city of Latakia, like so many other once-cosmopolitan cities caught in violent civil war, could only hunker down, stay alert, and pray for victory for their side.

"It's very sad," said Hussein. "When I was a kid we'd go see football games in the stadium, horse shows, wrestling matches—all the things that kids want to do. After school we'd go to the beach and try to pick up girls. We thought we were very European and sophisticated. I used to wear a speedo—you know, those tiny bathing suits? What can I say? It was the style."

"You're forgiven," said Riker.

"Most of my friends had jobs. My very first job was washing dishes at the Cote D'Azur de Cham Resort—it's behind us, in the other direction, up north. What a beautiful place! I worked in the restaurant after school. I made pretty good money, too. In those days you could make enough to buy the cool things that kids want, like sneakers and iPods. When I was a senior in high school I bought a pair of Air Jordans. They were white and black, with the big 'swoosh' logo on the side. My parents thought I was crazy. 'Why are you wasting your money on stuff like that?' they said. But I was happy, and as long as I got good grades they stayed off my back."

"Parents are the same everywhere," said Riker.

"Isn't that the truth?" said Hussein. "Then the war started. The army didn't want me because I have a heart condition. Daily life changed. Suddenly the stores weren't full, the restaurants had nothing to sell, you couldn't get parts for your car. The tourists stopped coming and now all the hotels are going bankrupt. It's funny how many people pretend that nothing is different! If you ask them how things are going, they say, 'Just fine. Everything is fine.' My parents are like that. I say to them, 'Father, mother, isn't this terrible? Why don't you leave?' They tell me that it's just temporary, and soon everything will be the way it used to be."

"They're loyal to the president?" asked Riker.

Hussein shrugged. "They try to stay out of it. They don't care. They just want to be left alone. A lot of people feel that way. They say, 'Why are people killing each other? What's the point? Nothing good comes of it.'"

"And now you drive a cab," said Riker.

"I do a little of this and a little of that," said Hussein. "Whatever keeps the money coming in."

They passed the Fishing and Tourism Marina, with its sturdy elbow breakwater that had once given shelter to the gleaming pleasure yachts of both rich Latakians and visitors from throughout the Mediterranean—people who would come for a day or a week to enjoy the beaches, shopping, and nightlife of this coastal jewel. The marina was dark now, and as the car sped by Riker glimpsed rows of empty berths that once were homes to the luxurious craft of the wealthy.

Then they came upon the vast *Marfa' al Ladhiqiyah*, the industrial port of Latakia, which had been created by the construction of an immense mile-long breakwater enclosing a deep-water anchorage capable of accommodating the largest oceangoing vessels. The tall cranes were dark skeletons, and only a few lights glimmered in the gloomy desolation.

After passing the big rectangular Arab Academy of Science and Technology and Marine Transport building, Hussein turned left on Al Maghreb Al Arabi. A block later, the Shahbandar Hotel appeared on the left—a ten-story concrete box designed in a vaguely Arab-international style and topped by a low-pitched roof that made the building look oddly like a Soviet-era pagoda. Riker had wanted a downtown hotel, and he had gotten one: a functional place for businesspeople to park themselves on a short-term basis while they made their deals and then got drunk at the bar before leaving town. But these days very few deals were getting done in Syria.

"Thanks, Hussein," said Riker as he got out of the cab. "See you tomorrow at nine."

"Okay," replied Hussein with a friendly wave. "And by the way—you know of course, that your room will probably be bugged. Foreign guests and reporters always get a room that's been wired. So be on your best behavior and say only nice things about Syria!"

"I'll remember that," said Riker.

When Riker strolled into the compact lobby with its polished black granite counter garishly lit by fluorescent lights set into the acoustical tile ceiling he felt as though he were entering a strange time capsule. The place looked like a museum display with all its pieces intact, while all that was missing were living, breathing people.

He stood at the registration counter.

"Hello," he called.

From a doorway behind the counter emerged a woman. About thirty years old, she was wearing a dark brown blazer and a white ruffled blouse. Her nametag read Shakira. Her demeanor was one of curious detachment.

"How may I assist you?" she said. Riker got the impression that she was trying to pretend that he was not the first and only person who had checked in during her shift.

"My name is Martin Riker," he said.

"Yes, thank you," she said as she peered at her computer screen. "You're staying with us for a week?"

"Perhaps longer—if that's possible."

She smiled. "Perhaps."

Of course it's possible, thought Riker. This damned hotel is nearly empty!

"You're here on business?" she asked casually.

What an odd question for a hotel clerk. She sounded more like a customs agent.

"I'm a doctor," he replied. "I'm here to do some research on infectious diseases."

She gave him a quick and expressionless smile.

After the usual check-in routine, Shakira handed him the card to room 538. "I hope you will find your accommodations to your liking," she said. "The elevator is to your right."

"Is the restaurant still open?" asked Riker.

"The Yakouta closes at midnight—but perhaps if you hurry they can find something for you," she said.

Rather than go up to his room, Riker decided to go directly to the Yakouta. From the lobby he passed through an arched doorway into a plain rectangular space furnished with rectangular tables topped with bright white cloths. The windows were framed by heavy swagged curtains in faded red velvet, while overhead gleamed twin chandeliers of brass and cut glass. The place looked like the dining room of an upscale retirement home. Riker sat down. There were no other diners. Presently a waiter appeared with a menu. With an oily smile he offered profuse apologies to the effect that most of what was listed on the menu was not available.

"Well, perhaps you can tell me what *is* available," said Riker cheerfully. He did not want to appear to be the Ugly American.

"We have some *mahshi* stuffed with minced beef," he said.

"Okay—that's what I'll have. Do you have any beer?"

"Al-Shark and Barada."

Both brands were products of government-controlled Syrian breweries. Riker had heard that Al-Shark, which had been made in Aleppo, was the superior of the two. He had no idea if it was still being manufactured. Aleppo—Syria's second largest city, with a population of two-and-a-half million people, which was slightly less than Chicago—was smack in the center of the front lines between the government, the various insurgent groups, and ISIS, who held the territory north of the city. The conflict had been marked by the Syrian army's savage use of barrel bombs dropped from helicopters, killing thousands of people. Hundreds of thousands of ordinary citizens had been forced to evacuate.

"I'll have an Al-Shark," said Riker.

A few minutes later the waiter brought a plate with two *mahshi*—zucchinis stuffed with tomatoes, rice, minced beef, and spices. They were dry and tough, indicating they had been made many hours ago, but their blazing hot interiors reassured Riker that they had just been nuked in a microwave and were safe to eat. The bottle of Al-Shark was cold and refreshing.

After dinner Riker retired to his room on the fifth floor. The poured-concrete balcony with its industrial steel railing faced west, and over the neighboring rooftops Riker could see the dark expanse of the Mediterranean Sea—the most ancient of seas, crossed by the ghosts of Phoenician, Greek, and Roman explorers and merchants, medieval crusaders, and twentieth-century mechanized armies. What might these ghosts think of Syria's war? Probably just another bloody and pointless human conflict. Eventually it would burn itself out, as they all do sooner or later. Then only the deep bitter feuds would remain to fester under the surface.

Riker retired to his vaguely damp-smelling bed to watch state-run TV. Within moments he had fallen asleep.

Five stories below, the phone rang in the little office behind the front desk. Shakira picked up the receiver and listened.

"The American had dinner in the restaurant before going up to his room," she said quietly. "Ahmad is coming on duty now. Yes sir, he knows about him. He will keep you informed of the American's movements." She hung up the phone. It had been a long day and she was tired. Her brother was outside, ready to drive her home.

5.

Sunday morning came clear but cool. At eight o'clock Riker had breakfast at the Al Teras, the hotel's informal coffee shop that featured an outdoor balcony overlooking the Al Maghreb Al Arabi. Riker could not help but notice that the morning rush hour looked more like the mid-afternoon doldrums. The pace of the city was slow, almost listless. Its vibrancy had vanished with the crushing weight of a civil war that no one except Assad's hardliners really believed in.

At a few minutes before nine Riker walked out the front door of the hotel. Hussein was waiting for him in his cab.

"I trust you had a comfortable evening," said Hussein as Riker got into the front seat. "Where do you want to go?"

"I'm going to visit a woman named Tamadur Aflaq. She lives at 17 Fandoon Street, which is near Haroun Square."

"I know the street," said Hussein. "It's very near here—only about five minutes away."

Hussein eased the car into Al Maghreb Al Arabi. The sun was out and the sky was a brilliant and glorious blue. While the traffic was light, it looked like any other pleasant morning in almost any city.

A few minutes later Hussein merged onto Ramadan, a main thoroughfare that cut through the heart of the city. He then turned onto Omar ibn Abd al-Aziz Street.

"Almost there," he said. He glanced into his rear view mirror. He frowned.

"What's up?" asked Riker.

Without answering, Hussein made right onto Fandoon Street.

"Let's see..." said Riker as he peered ahead. "It looks like number 17 is a few doors up, on the left. See it?"

"I see it, but we're not stopping," said Hussein. "We've been followed from the hotel. A black car. He's trying to stay at a distance but he's back there."

Hussein drove past number 17, with its blue door and barred window.

"What are you going to do?" asked Riker.

"Lose them. Don't worry—this is only going to be a short detour."

Hussein drove the car to the end of Fandoon Street. They had come back to Ramadan. He turned left and drove a few bocks. He pulled the car up in front of a restaurant.

Riker stole a glance in the outside mirror. A few car lengths behind them, a black car pulled to the curb. The glare on the windshield prevented Riker from seeing the occupants.

"This is a place I know well—some friends of mine work here," said Hussein. "It's actually not a bad place to eat. Go inside. At the back of the restaurant you'll see a sign for the restrooms. You'll enter a short hallway. Keep walking until you come to a door. This leads to the alley behind the restaurant. Go through the door and into the alley, and then turn left. Walk quickly to the end of the alley. At the corner is a bookstore. Go in the bookstore and browse until you see me pull up in front. You will be safe there—the proprietor, Hams Massoud, is an old friend of my family. Okay?"

Riker nodded. He got out of the cab and, without looking to either side, walked through the revolving door into the restaurant. A waiter looked at him expectantly and one or two customers glanced up. Feeling more than a little self-conscious Riker passed through the dining area to the restrooms and then to the door at the end of the hallway. Pushing it open, he found himself in a gloomy, fetid alleyway surrounded by overflowing garbage cans. In the foul air, flies buzzed merrily around the rancid trash.

Here's a public health disaster in the making,

thought Riker as he picked his way through the muck. A big brown rat boldly stared at him before scurrying under a battered dumpster.

At the end of the alley Riker gratefully inhaled the relatively fresh air of the street. He turned the corner and found the Ossama Bookstore. It was a small storefront, with a narrow front door flanked by glass windows showing a dusty collection of mostly Islamist titles.

Riker scanned the street. Seeing neither Hussein's cab nor the black car, he pushed open the door of the bookstore. A bell tinkled. Closing the door, Riker took a moment to let his eyes adjust to the gloom.

A man with a long grey beard sat behind a counter piled high with used books. The man was busy writing something. Riker moved among the overloaded shelves and dusty bins. There were books here, but also so-called antiques—mostly junk, thought Riker, cheap stuff that you would see in a flea market at home. Glassware, vases, water pipes, flatware, dishes, and decorative items from a bygone era. The books— dog-eared and yellowed—were mostly Arabic, but there were English-language titles too: Guide books, histories, art books, a few old novels.

Riker glanced out the filmy window to the street. No sign of Hussein.

"Hello, my friend," came a creaking voice.

Riker turned. The man with the grey beard was peering at him through his wire-rimmed glasses. Riker smiled. "You must be Mr. Massoud. My friend Hussein gave me your name."

"Ah, yes, Hussein. Is he still driving his cab?"

"Yes—in fact he's picking me up in a few minutes."

"I see," replied Massoud. "Well, in the meantime, please look around. I'm sorry that the place is disorganized. These days I'm forced to sell anything that will make me a profit. But at least I'm still here. All the other bookstores in Latakia are gone."

"I'm sorry to say, it's a trend that's happening everywhere," said Riker.

Massoud shrugged. "You do what you can do. On this block there used to be four bookstores. My friend Hassan lasted until just last year. He tried to resist until he finally gave up and started replacing literary books with school and office supplies, astrology books, and children's coloring books. Then he started selling coffee and pastries. Then he got rid of the books and now the only printed materials he sells are magazines and cheap religious paperbacks. With the war, books have become a luxury. When the price of a book becomes the same as the price of a loaf of bread, people have to choose the bread."

"I noticed that your store window displays only Islamist titles," said Riker.

"Of course!" replied Massoud. "I don't want any trouble. If people want other things—Western books— I have them in the back room. But I don't advertise it."

At that moment Riker saw Hussein's cab pull up to the curb in front of the door.

6.

"It has been a pleasure to meet you," Riker said to Massoud.

The old man smiled and nodded. "You too."

Glancing down, Riker saw an old tourist guide to Syria. It looked like it had been printed in the 1980s. He picked it up. "How much?" he asked.

"Three hundred Syrian pounds," said Massoud. This was about a dollar-fifty.

"How about one American dollar?" said Riker as he reached for his wallet.

Massoud smiled. "Only because you are a friend of Hussein," he said. He took the dollar bill, folded it, and inserted it carefully into the pocket of his jacket.

"Good luck, my friend," said Riker as he headed to the door.

Once inside the cab, Riker tossed the tourist guide onto the back seat. "Mr. Massoud needs all the help he can get," said Riker. "What happened to our friends in the black car?"

"I didn't know if they were following *me* or following *you*," replied Hussein. "It turns out they were interested in *you*. After you went into the restaurant, one of them got out of the car and tailed you inside. But unless he knew of the back door, he sat there and waited for you to come out of the restroom, which you never did. Meanwhile, I eased slowly down the street. Then I got out of there. I drove around for a while and then came back to the bookshop. I haven't seen the black car. I don't see any of them around here. We lost them."

"Who were they?"

Hussein shrugged. "Maybe the General Security Directorate. Or the Political Security Directorate. They operate under the catch-all name *mukhabarat*, which covers an array of sometimes overlapping and mutually mistrustful security services. For more than four decades the *mukhabarat* helped to keep Hafez al-Assad in power, stamping out dissent and insulating Syria from the frequent military coups that had plagued our nation previously. Now his son is making good use of them. Or maybe the guys in the black car were undercover Latakia police. These days, who can tell? The streets are full of spies. There is even talk of opposition groups forming their own *mukhabarat*. Imagine that! Spies spying on each other. It won't be long before every citizen of Syria is on the payroll of someone's spy organization. At least maybe then we'll all make some money."

Hussein expertly steered the car through traffic in a circular route back to Fandoon Street. He pulled up a few doors down from number 17. "Okay," he said. "I'll be back when you call. Good luck."

As the cab pulled away from the curb, Riker strolled at a leisurely pace along the sidewalk. He paused at a bakery and looked in the window. He glanced behind him. The few people on the street were moving about normally. He turned and within a few steps had reached the blue door.

While Martin Riker had been to nearly every corner of the globe, seen the most abject human misery and death, and delivered bad news more often than he cared to remember, telling a mother that her son was dead was one of the most painful tasks. All around the world, mothers were the same, and Mrs. Aflaq would be no exception. Riker took a deep breath and consciously relaxed his body. He pressed the tarnished brass doorbell. From inside came the sound of a harsh buzzer. After a moment he heard footsteps. A woman's face peered out of the barred window. She frowned. Riker remained expressionless. The face disappeared and the door opened a crack.

"Who is it?" a voice said in Arabic.

"My name is Martin Riker," he replied in Arabic. "I'm an American. A doctor. May I come in?"

"Why?" said the voice.

"It's about Akram." He had now exhausted most of his working knowledge of Arabic. "You're his mother, aren't you?" he said in English. "Tamadur Aflaq?"

The door opened. The woman peered out. She looked about fifty, with keen eyes and tight lips. Across her forehead were sharp lines, and her hair was greying around the temples.

"Do you speak English?" asked Riker.

"A little," she said. "You have something to tell me about Akram? He's not here."

"I know he's not here," replied Riker. "I'd rather speak inside, if you don't mind."

After she peered left and right, she withdrew. The door swung open and Riker crossed the threshold. She closed the door. Riker found himself in a sitting room. It was simply furnished with a sofa and straight-backed chairs placed on a faded Persian carpet. On the wall were framed portraits of Hafez al-Assad and Bashar al-Assad. The air smelled of cooking—rice and garlic and lamb. The television was tuned to the state-run news channel. The female announcer was describing a tremendous victory for government forces in Aleppo. The woman crossed the room and shut it off.

"Yes, I'm Tamadur Aflaq," she said. "Please sit down." She took her place on the sofa. Riker took one of the stiff chairs.

"Mrs. Aflaq," he said, "I have some very difficult news. Your son has passed away. He died in a hospital in New York."

Her face erupted in grief. "What are you saying?" she stammered in Arabic. "It's impossible! I saw him only a few weeks ago! He was perfectly fine!" She glared at Riker and pointed her finger. "Did someone harm him? Did something happen in America?"

"No, nothing happened to him in America," said Riker gently in English. "Mrs. Aflaq, your son was very sick when he came to America. He had a very serious disease. He caught this disease when he was still here in Latakia. I'm a doctor. I treated him at the hospital.

We could not save him." And now, in Arabic, "He is with Allah."

"What was this disease?" she demanded.

"It was a very serious infection," replied Riker. "A virus. The hospital is doing some tests now. That's all we know."

"Was he murdered?" she wailed. "Did someone poison him?"

"No, no—it was a disease."

"When can he be sent home? We need to bury him here, in Latakia."

"I'm afraid that due to the contagious nature of his disease, that will not be possible," said Riker. For Riker, this was the most difficult part of his task. Telling a mother that her child was dead was bad enough, but telling her that she would never receive his body was worse. Parents crave closure, even if it brings wrenching heartache.

Tamadur Aflaq slumped into the sofa. She stifled a deep sob as she groped for a tissue from the box on the end table. While she dabbed her reddening eyes, Riker said nothing. He noticed on the end table was a small framed photo of three people: Tamadur, Akram, and a man whom Riker assumed was her husband and Akram's father. Like tourists, they were standing in front of an ancient ruin, and smiling. It was a happier time.

At length Riker said, "Mrs. Aflaq, I need to ask you a few questions."

She regarded him warily. "What can I possibly tell you?"

"What did your son do for employment?"

"He worked for the government."

"In what capacity?"

"He worked for the Ba'ath Party. Something to do with security. He didn't talk much about it. I was just happy that he had a good job. He was good with computers. He told me that he was working to protect the party from foreign enemies."

"Hackers," said Riker.

She nodded. "He could have gone far in life. He was always a bright, inquisitive child. When he was little—no more than nine or ten—one day I brought home an old-fashioned radio for him. I thought he would enjoy listening to it. Do you know what he did? He took it apart! And then he put it back together again! But he wasn't like those computer people who don't have lives. Those guys who don't have girlfriends. What do you call them in English?"

"Geeks?" offered Riker.

"Geeks. Akram was a handsome boy. He had girlfriends. Everybody loved him. I asked him when he was going to settle down. He said, 'Someday, mother, someday.'"

Her eyes teared up again and she lowered her eyes.

"Mrs. Aflaq, did he ever mention the name Mahadi?" asked Riker.

Her back stiffened and she gave him a sharp glance. "Bani Mahadi," she said as if she had a wedge of lemon stuck in her mouth. She shook her head. "He was Akram's boss. I would never have said this before, but now I don't care. Akram is gone, so I have nothing to live for. Let them throw me in prison—I'll never apologize. Bani Mahadi is a *pig*. He walks around as if he's the king. No one can stand him. He says, 'Do this, do that,' and people run like scared rabbits. I would ask Akram, 'How can you work for that terrible man? He abuses everyone!' My son would say to me, 'It's okay, mother, don't worry. I won't be working for him forever. I'm on the ladder of success!' That's what he would say—'the ladder of success.' For some reason this grotesque clown Mahadi has the favor of the president. So we all must accept the situation." Her voice lowered to nearly a whisper. "Do you think Mahadi killed my son? That bastard! Is it possible? Then I'll kill him myself!"

"We don't know how your son contracted the disease," replied Riker. "It could have come from anywhere. Mrs. Aflaq, does the name Sabeen sound familiar?"

"Sabeen is not a common name," said Tamadur Aflaq. "The only Sabeen that I know is Sabeen Mahadi."

"Is this person Bani Mahadi's wife or sister?"

"His wife," she said. "I've met her once or twice. She seems very nice. Why she married that horse's ass I will never know. She's much younger than he is. Maybe she was looking for security. Many women are like that, especially during troubled times. They care less about love and more about a secure place in life. Can you blame them? I'm very lucky that Akram's father—may Allah bless him in eternity—made enough to provide for us after his passing, and we also have his army pension. This means that I have no need to prostitute myself. If I live modestly, I don't have to go and find a rich man to care for me. Perhaps Sabeen Mahadi was not so lucky. Perhaps she comes from a poor family. She's very beautiful, though. I can see why Mahadi would want her. Any man would."

Akram Aflaq's last words—that "it was all because of Sabeen"—flashed through Riker's mind.

"One more question," said Riker. "When you last saw your son, where did he say he was going?"

"He said that he was being sent on a very important overseas assignment, and that I may not hear from him for a while," she said. "This was in early November. He packed a suitcase and hired a driver to take him to Damascus. That was the last I saw of him."

Riker stood up. "Mrs. Aflaq, thank you for allowing me into your home. Unfortunately, for the time being I can give you no more information. And I ask that you remain silent. I know this is very difficult for you, but you must not say anything. If anyone asks, tell them your son is out of town. It's for your safety that I ask you this. You never saw me. I was never here. Can you do this?"

"I'll do my best," she said weakly.

Riker knew that eventually she'd start talking—

but perhaps she would stay silent long enough for him to quietly investigate.

"I'll show myself out," he said. "Thank you for your time, and may Allah give you peace."

7.

With his blunt fingers Bani Mahadi reached into the fine porcelain sugar bowl, took out a sugar cube, and dropped it into his coffee. He picked up the matching creamery and poured some half & half into his cup. With a small silver spoon he gently stirred it. The cream and sugar dissolved into a pleasing caramel swirl. Grasping the cup by its slender handle he raised it to his lips and took a sip.

Instantly his fleshy mouth turned down at the corners and his eyes narrowed. He put down the cup on its saucer. He looked across the breakfast table at his wife.

"What kind of shit is this?" he said.

"I'm sorry—what?" said Sabeen as she looked up from the Sunday morning edition of the Latakia *Messenger*. Her face showed a mix of concern and contempt.

"Do you call this sewage water *coffee*?" said Mahadi. "Are you trying to *poison* me?"

"No, I am not trying to poison you," she replied slowly, as if speaking to a child. She regarded him carefully, watching his every twitch and gesture for the telltale signal that he was going to raise his fist against her.

"Well, then, what do *you* call it?" he said.

"My dearest Bani," she said with a benign smile that showed her perfect white teeth behind plump red lips. (Sometimes the loving approach worked to placate him; sometimes not. But it was always worth a try.) "Please try to understand. With the *present difficulties*" (she would never say the word "*war*"), "it's a challenge to get the high quality we expect. We do the very best we can. This coffee came from the grocer, Hasid. He's been able to get good things, but sometimes you have to settle. This isn't the usual brand, but he says that next week he may be able to get more of what we like." Like an actress in a toothpaste commercial she held the smile, hoping the explanation and the smile would be sufficient to calm him.

With his eyes fixed on hers, Mahadi took the coffee cup and held it away from the glass-topped table. With slow deliberation he tilted the cup and poured its contents onto the polished marble floor of the sunroom. The tan liquid spread in a puddle. When the cup was empty he replaced it on its saucer.

With cool detachment Sabeen snapped her fingers. The kitchen door to the sunroom opened and an elderly woman entered. She approached Sabeen with her scarf-covered head bowed.

"Wasimah," said Sabeen, "Some coffee has spilled on the floor next to Mr. Mahadi. Please clean it up."

Without giving the slightest indication that Mrs. Mahadi's request was anything other than purely routine, Wasimah shuffled back into the kitchen and quickly returned with a handful of towels. Circling the table, she got down on her hands and knees and mopped up the coffee. Without making eye contact with Bani Mahadi she gathered the soggy mess and disappeared through the kitchen door.

Bani Mahadi put on his reading glasses—he hated them because they made him look old, but he had no choice but to use them—and picked up a copy of the *International New York Times*, which he had received the previous evening and hadn't yet had time to read. With his free hand he took a spoonful of *mamouniyeh*, the Syrian hot cereal made with seminola, ghee, and pine nuts. He chewed thoughtfully as he read.

Sabeen watched him carefully. Not overtly—she was careful to make sure that he never *saw* her watching him. It was just something that she had learned to do. Call it self-preservation. She watched as he put down his spoon and held the paper with both hands, as if to keep it from flying away. His face—never particularly cheery—grew dark. He grunted and his eyes narrowed into slits, as if he were peering through a keyhole at something ghastly. Then he slowly shook his head.

"The Americans," he said with disgust, "are talking about arming the Kurds. Is there no end to their arrogance? Is no nation safe from their dictatorial meddling?" He slapped the paper down on the table and looked directly at his wife. "The day of reckoning is coming for the Great Satan. Mark my words."

"Yes, dear," she said. She had no idea what he was talking about and she didn't want to know. His work for the government—she knew that he was a Ba'ath Party member and involved in state security, but not much more than that—was obscure but it paid well. Bani and Sabeen Mahadi lived better than ninety percent of their fellow citizens in Latakia, and had access to luxuries that the war had made scarce. Even so, they felt the pinch. The curtains in the sunroom were faded and tattered by the sun, but replacing them was out of the question. The house hadn't been painted in years and the roof leaked when it rained. Every day Sabeen saw in their house the relentless decay of time, just as she saw it everywhere she went in Latakia—fine old buildings that were crumbling, unpainted, with broken windows and hairline cracks in their stucco cladding. Even if the present difficulties were to be instantly and magically resolved it would take years to catch up to where they had been a decade earlier.

As she took a bite of hard-boiled egg, Sabeen's mind wandered—as it too often did—to thoughts of Akram.

Sabeen had not heard from him since he had been sent on some sort of secret mission out of the country. She was worried. Why had Akram been sent? He was just a low-level party functionary who had been trained in computer network security. Or was he a spy? The last time she had seen him, they had met at the villa of her cousin Ghazal Faoud, who understood what it was like to be trapped in a loveless marriage to an older man—not only older, but a brute. The handsome young Akram had loved her tenderly, with a sweet passion that she had never known from the old grump Bani Mahadi. She and Akram had lain together in the big soft bed, talking about what life might be like after the war, but—as always, too soon—their tryst had to end and they roused themselves, got dressed, and rejoined the unsuspecting world. Sabeen and Akram both knew that their affair could get them both killed, but—insanely!—to love him was worth the risk.

It was the next day that Ghazal had passed a message from Akram to Sabeen: Akram was going on a secret mission and he would not see her again for a long time. Sabeen was crushed. Her affair with Akram—her love for Akram—had helped keep her going. It had made her feel that she still had life and vitality, and that sex could be beautiful, and not simply a duty that a wife endured for the pleasure of her wealthy and callous husband.

Just last night Bani had come to her and demanded that she give herself to him. As she lay underneath his sweaty body it seemed to her that he was making a special effort to be rough and degrading. He never asked her how she felt, never said soothing words, never even looked her in the eye. His visit to her bed was brief, blunt, and businesslike. It was almost as if he was paying her for it, and therefore owed her no special consideration.

"Sabeen!" His bark broke her reverie. "You're very quiet this morning. What are you thinking about?"

What a strange question, she thought. *Bani never cares what I'm thinking about.*

"Nothing, dear," she replied. "I'm fine."

She looked at him. To her horror she thought—just for a fleeting second—that he was giving her a sly smile. He looked like someone who knew a deep secret. Was it possible? Could he know about her and Akram? Is that why Akram suddenly left town? Sabeen knew her husband was capable of making his enemies disappear—living in this house she had overheard a sufficient number of phone conversations to understand that he was involved in state security operations. That would explain his recent behavior in the bedroom—how he had been making her perform her wifely duties almost as if it they were a punishment.

She felt a sickness in her stomach.

Her husband looked at her with his peculiar smile, the way a cat looks at a wounded bird.

"I'm sorry, dear," she said. "Actually, I'm not terribly hungry. I hope you'll excuse me." She placed her napkin on the table and pushed out her chair.

"Any special plans today?" he said, peering over his reading glasses with studied nonchalance.

"No," she replied. "No special plans." That's the way it was every day—no special plans. Sabeen was so bored that she could scream. It wasn't even much fun to go shopping anymore—there was almost nothing to buy. They were living in limbo: while the fighting was far away, the national war effort had drained every resource. People like Sabeen were forced to live a grey, inert existence, hoping for victory and a return to normal life. The stakes were very high. For Bani and Sabeen Mahadi, the defeat of the government—for Bashar al-Assad—would mean a gruesome death or, if they managed to escape, exile to Russia.

Putting down his newspaper, Bani Mahadi rose from the table as well. After watching his wife leave the room, he glanced at his watch. He went to his office and took an envelope from the desk drawer. He slipped the envelope into his jacket's inside pocket. Then he went to the garage and got into his Mercedes. Pulling out of the garage into the brilliant morning sun, he headed south past Tishreen University and onto the old Highway 1, which followed the coast to the Martyr Basil al-Assad International Airport—named for the older brother of President Bashar al-Assad who had died in a car accident—and eventually to Lebanon and the big Syrian city of Homs. Along the highway the houses thinned out and he passed farms and fields of olive trees, sugar beets, cotton, and tobacco. A few kilometers beyond the airport, in the coastal suburb of Jableh, he turned off the road, and in a few minutes approached the gate of a nondescript industrial building. An armed guard approached the car and, seeing who was driving, signaled for the gate to be raised. After passing under the gate Mahadi parked by the front door, which was distinguished by steel letters on the wall overhead that read BETA SYRIA PHARMACEUTICAL, LTD.

Mahadi paused before going into the building. He found it horrifying and depressing that only one hundred kilometers to the east, rebel forces—the so-called Free Syrian Army, the Islamic Front, and Jabhat al-Nusra, or al-Qaeda in the Levant—were in control. In fact, what used to be Syria now consisted of a narrow slice of territory along the Mediterranean coast and the Lebanese border. Damascus itself was within reach of insurgent forces! The situation was intolerable. Bold action had to be taken. The world had to realize that Syria was not a nation to be trifled with.

Pulling open the door, he went inside. He was met by another guard, who wore a pistol on his hip. The guard nodded to him before allowing him to pass through set of double doors into a laboratory.

The big space was full of tables, on which were scattered the tools of chemists and microbiologists: test tubes, burners, autoclaves, centrifuges, beakers, microscopes, coils of tubing. Around the perimeter of the room were counters, punctuated by big stainless steel refrigerators, with cabinets overhead. The place looked like a warehouse of used laboratory equipment.

A man walked over. He was younger than Mahadi, with an eager, robust face. "As you can see," he said with a wave of his hand, "To get this facility operational will take a lot of work. But we'll do it."

"My friend Sami," said Mahadi, "It's good to see you. If anyone can get this place in shape, it's you. Is our Russian friend here yet?"

"Yes," replied Sami Noman. "He got here a few minutes ago. He's waiting for us in the office."

"Okay," replied Mahadi. "Let's not keep our guest

waiting."

Walking through the maze of tables they made their way to the back of the room and through a door. They entered a functional office: desks, plain steel chairs, an old desktop computer.

Dr. Luka Radznev, who was sitting at the desk and reading a report, stood when they entered. A tight smile crept across his hawk-like face. "Gentlemen, I can see that you're making progress," he said. "Let's hope we can stay on track."

Once they were seated, Dr. Radznev turned to Noman. "How long will it take to make this facility operational?"

"Three days," said Noman. "Everything we need is here. We have to clean and test the equipment, and then we can begin to grow the cultures."

"I want to make sure you fully understand," said Dr. Radznev, "that we are dealing with one of the great killers of mankind. The smallpox virus is a weapon of incredible power. It doesn't care who its victims are. If any one of us makes the slightest mistake, we could all suffer an excruciatingly painful fate. Okay?"

Noman nodded.

"Where is the sample that I procured for you in October?" asked Dr. Radznev.

"In the containment room," replied Noman with a nod towards a stainless steel door.

"Who has access to it?" asked Dr. Radznev.

Noman shrugged. "Just about everybody who works here. We've all been in and out of there."

"Are you *kidding* me?" exclaimed Dr. Radznev. His hawk eyes flashed. He turned to Mahadi. "Have *you* been in there?"

Mahadi nodded.

"May God have mercy on us," said Dr. Radznev as he shook his head. "Give me the names of those who have been in that room."

"Let me see... Farouq Azmeh, Muhammad Menem, Hashim Hanano, Akram Aflaq, Riad Zuabi," said Noman.

"Are they all here now?" asked Dr. Radznev.

"All except Akram Aflaq," said Noman.

"Where is he?" demanded Dr. Radznev.

Noman looked uneasily at Mahadi. Then he said, "We don't know."

"What do you mean, *you don't know*?" Dr. Radznev said. He was practically shouting.

"He's disappeared," said Mahadi.

"When was the last time you saw him?" demanded Dr. Radznev.

"The fourth of November," replied Mahadi. "He told me he was going on a secret mission."

Dr. Radznev fixed his hawk eyes on Mahadi. "A secret mission?" he said incredulously. "Who authorized it?"

"I have no idea," replied Mahadi coolly. "As you know, Dr. Radznev, there are plenty of people in the GSD who have more authority than me, and I'm not privy to every operation that's authorized at high levels."

"How much does Aflaq know about Project Fire Sword?" asked Dr. Radznev.

"Not very much," replied Noman. "He knows that we have a virus, but he doesn't know the goal of the operation. He probably assumes that we're going to use it against our enemies here in the Levant."

"If he had any idea of how contagious the smallpox virus is, he wouldn't make that assumption," cautioned Dr. Radznev. "The Middle East has become a crowded neighborhood. Your enemies are only a hundred kilometers away. If there was a smallpox outbreak in enemy territory, the chances of it bring passed across the border and into our own people would be very good."

"I'm sure Aflaq knows what he's doing," said Mahadi. "He's a good man."

Dr. Radznev frowned. "Mr. Mahadi, this is a problem. I thought it was a bad idea to provide that sample of the virus to you. You insisted that it was necessary in order for President al-Assad to approve

Operation Fire Sword. So I gave you the sample. Frankly, I don't know what you wanted it for. I don't even know if the president is involved in this operation. But since you've got it, you need to handle it extremely carefully. No one—I repeat, *no one*—is to enter that containment room until we are ready to begin production. Mr. Noman, put a damn padlock on the door. Do you understand? Inside that door is *death*. It is intended for our enemies, not for us."

"Okay," said Noman with open palms. He smiled. "We are more than grateful to have your professional guidance in this critical operation."

"It's for your own protection," said Dr. Radznev. "As a routine safeguard, everyone who has come into contact with the virus needs to be vaccinated immediately. I can do that today—I brought fifty doses of the vaccine with me."

"How does it work?" asked Mahadi.

"The vaccine is made from a virus called vaccinia, which is a 'pox'-type virus related to smallpox," said Dr. Radznev. "The smallpox vaccine contains the living vaccinia virus—not a dead virus like many other vaccines."

"How do you administer it—with a shot?" asked Noman.

Dr. Radznev shook his head. "The smallpox vaccine is not given with a hypodermic needle. The vaccine is given using a bifurcated—that is, two-pronged—needle. The needle's twin prongs are first dipped into the vaccine solution. Then the needle is used to prick the skin a number of times in a few seconds. The pricking is not deep, but it will cause a sore spot and one or two droplets of blood to form. It's usually applied to the upper arm.

"If the vaccination is successful, in three or four days a red and itchy bump develops at the vaccine site. The bump then becomes a large blister, fills with pus, and begins to drain. During the second week, the blister begins to dry up and a scab forms. The scab falls off in the third week, leaving a small scar."

"And this will protect us—even if we've been exposed?" asked Mahadi.

Dr. Radznev nodded. "Yes—if it's given in time. In the vast majority of people, vaccination within three days of exposure will prevent or significantly lessen the severity of smallpox symptoms. Vaccination from four to seven days after exposure will offer some protection or may lessen the severity of the disease. If this man Aflaq had been exposed two weeks ago, it would be too late for him to be vaccinated today. I assume that no one on your team has shown any evidence of an unusual rash or facial pustules?"

"No," said Noman.

"Okay," said Dr. Radznev. "Before I leave here today I will vaccinate you and your team. Now then, let's get down to business. I've been in contact with a former colleague at the Russian State Research Center of Virology and Biotechnology in Novosibirsk—or as everyone calls it, the Vector Institute. As I told you a few weeks ago, for a sufficient quantity of viable smallpox virus, the price is two million dollars. Half to be paid up front, half to be paid upon delivery. Are you ready to make the deal?"

"Yes, we are," replied Mahadi. Reaching into his jacket pocket, he took out the envelope and handed it to Dr. Radznev, who accepted it. "This is good faith money," said Mahadi. "Fifty thousand dollars. We expect to have the deposit of one million dollars in a few days. Because of the present political situation, it takes time to put together that much American cash."

Dr. Radznev opened the flap and pulled out a stack of American one hundred dollar bills. "This is acceptable," he said. "Let me know as soon as you have the full deposit."

They shook hands. Operation Fire Sword had been set into motion.

8.

It was nearly noon when Riker left the apartment of Tamadur Aflaq. He was puzzled by what Akram Aflaq had suggested on his deathbed—that Bani Mahadi wanted to kill him, and that somehow Mahadi's wife, Sabeen, was the cause. Was it possible that Aflaq was having an affair with Sabeen Mahadi? If so, how could this personal soap opera have anything to do with Aflaq being infected with smallpox—a disease that had supposedly been eradicated from the face of the earth?

Riker looked down Fandoon Street. At the end of the block he saw Hussein's cab heading slowly in his direction. A moment later Hussein pulled up. Riker got in.

"Okay, boss, where to now?" said Hussein.

"Let's go back to the hotel," replied Riker.

The cab pulled away from the curb.

Suddenly a black car swerved over from the oncoming lane and blocked their path. Hussein slammed on his brakes and the cab skidded to a halt. He twisted around to look behind him while putting the cab in reverse. "Oh, shit," he muttered.

Turning in his seat, Riker saw that a second black car had stopped behind them.

"We're boxed in," said Hussein. After throwing the transmission into "park" he raised his hands.

Both doors to the cab were roughly opened. Gloved hands reached in and seized both men by their shoulders. With a gun to his head Riker was dragged from the cab and quickly hustled into the black car that was stopped behind the cab. He caught a glimpse of Hussein being taken to the black car in front. A man in a black leather jacket and dark slacks took Hussein's place behind the wheel of the cab.

Riker was shoved into the back seat of the car and pinned between two men in black leather jackets. By their dress he knew instantly that they were *mukhabarat*. He felt a gun at his ribs.

"Keep your mouth shut and you'll stay alive," the man with the gun said in English.

Riker nodded. The other man produced a knit cap, which he jammed onto Riker's head and pulled down so that his eyes were covered.

For five or ten minutes they rode in silence through the city streets. Then the stop-and-go traffic gave way to what seemed like a highway, because the car didn't stop and was traveling at a rapid speed. The car then slowed, made a few turns, and came to a halt. The doors opened and Riker was hauled out of the car and, with a man gripping each of his elbows, marched up a flight of stairs. He was shoved through a doorway. The air in the building smelled like mold and rust. After going up another flight of stairs he was taken down a straight hallway. They stopped. A door was opened—a metallic sound. Riker was marched through the door. His knit cap was removed.

The men left and the door slammed shut.

He was in a prison cell. It was a single cell, and Riker was the only occupant. A small barred window provided light. The cell was furnished only with a steel cot bolted to the cinderblock wall, a filthy mattress, and a bucket in the corner.

Riker turned around. Set into the riveted steel door was a rectangular opening that, at least for the moment, was covered by a steel plate that Riker assumed could be slid open by the guard. Below the opening was a bigger panel set on an axis, which Riker guessed would rotate to deliver food.

Riker went to the window. By standing on his toes he could just see out of it. He saw a brick wall that looked as though it were part of another building. He craned his neck but could not see the sky—only brick.

He sat on the bed. He listened. He could hear no sounds. But wait—yes, there was a sound. He crossed the cell to the door, and put his ear up to the rectangular opening. Yes! Now he could hear it better.

A chill ran down his spine. Breathlessly he listened. It was unmistakable—somewhere, in some distant part of the building, a man was screaming.

With a sick feeling in his stomach Riker backed away from the door. Shaking, he sat on the bed.

This must be a trick, he thought. I've heard about this sort of thing. It's designed to soften me up. These are standard interrogation techniques—you take away the person's sense of control, you isolate them, you scare the crap out of them by suggesting the terrible things that could happen to them. But I'm an American doctor! Would they dare torture me?

Then he reflected on the fates of other Americans who had been held by rogue regimes. He thought about Jason Rezaian, the dual American-Iranian citizen who was stationed in Tehran to cover regional affairs for *The Washington Post*. In 2014, Rezaian was detained for questioning, along with his wife. While his wife was quickly released on bail, Rezaian was kept in the notorious Evin Prison, charged with of espionage, working with hostile governments, and "propaganda against the establishment." He was held for long periods of time in solitary confinement before being released in January 2016 after five hundred and forty-three days in captivity.

Could they really keep me here for a year and a half? thought Riker.

The only answer that came to mind was, "yes."

Riker sat for a while, and then got up and paced. He approached the door to his cell, and then paused to listen. He heard nothing except the distant slam of a steel door. The sound reverberated along the long hallway. He put his ear to the opening. Silence.

He sat down again. The thugs who had brought him to his cell had taken his personal items—phone, passport, hotel key, wallet. He had nothing in his pockets.

They're probably searching my hotel room right now, he thought. But nothing is written down. They won't learn anything about my mission here.

Time passed. He went to the window again. The light seemed to have changed in the way it fell across the bricks, throwing the mortar-filled gaps into sharper relief.

Suddenly he heard the echo of footsteps in the hallway, and the harsh metallic sound of the bolt on his door drawn back. With a grating creak the door opened.

Two *mukhabarat* entered and took him by the elbows.

"Where are we going?" asked Riker as they hustled him out of the cell. Two more *mukhabarat*, each holding an automatic weapon, stood in the hallway.

One of the men stuck his gun in Riker's face. "Shut up," he said.

They marched Riker down the cinderblock hallway past other steel doors with their little sliding windows. A steel door opened, and Riker was led down another hallway, but this one had painted walls and a linoleum floor—industrial, but not naked cinderblock. They came to a door. Riker was shoved into a plain room with a table and several steel chairs. The room had no window.

"Sit down," said the same man who had ordered him to shut up. Riker sat where the man indicated. Another man quickly manacled Riker's wrists to the arms of the chair.

Thus pinned, Riker watched as the men left the room and closed the door behind them.

He sat and waited. Now there was no window to give a clue as to the passage of time—only the monotonous flicker of a fluorescent lighting fixture affixed to the dirty white ceiling overhead.

Riker looked closely at the floor around his chair. He saw no bloodstains. The tabletop was clean. On the chipped and cracked walls hung two dingy framed photos of President Bashar al-Assad and his father and former president, Hafez al-Assad. Otherwise the room was free of any decoration.

I guess they don't beat you in this room, thought

Riker. At least not enough to draw blood.

After a while the door opened and a man entered. He was wearing a dark business suit, white shirt, and tie, and carried a stack of files. Riker guessed he was about forty years old. The man sat down across from Riker. His blue eyes were cold and his demeanor was detached. He shuffled through the papers without looking up at Riker.

Riker said nothing while the man studied the papers.

"Dr. Riker," the man said at length, "How did you enter this country?" His English was good and his voice businesslike.

"By boat."

The man smiled. "So you did," he said. "Don't you think that's rather unusual?"

"Given the present travel situation, it was the best way."

The man gave Riker a hard stare. "This is not a joke, Dr. Riker."

Riker remained silent.

"You are staying at the Shahbandar, yes?"

"Yes."

"And what is the purpose for your visit to Syria?"

"I'm a doctor, and I'm investigating a possible outbreak of smallpox."

"And you think it happened here, in Syria?"

"Yes." Riker told the man that a Syrian named Akram Aflaq had died of the disease in a New York hospital.

"That's why you visited this man's mother?"

"Yes."

More paper shuffling.

"You're a member of the American army," said the man. "A lieutenant, serving at the Army Medical Research Institute of Infectious Diseases."

"Honorably discharged," replied Riker. "No longer active duty."

The man settled back in his chair. His cold blue eyes fixed on his prisoner. "Dr. Riker, I think you're a spy. You have come to Syria to spread lies about the imaginary use of outlawed biological weapons against the criminals who seek to overthrow the legitimate government of our president."

"No, that's not what I'm doing."

The man shrugged. "It doesn't matter. You'll sign a confession. Then we'll put you on trial."

The man abruptly got up, gathered his papers, and left the room.

A few minutes later the four *mukhabarat* came into the room, unlocked his wrist shackles, and led him back to his cell. When they locked the door behind them, Riker was left sitting on his cot, staring at the cinderblock wall.

The light in the window turned golden.

He heard footsteps outside. The panel in the cell door revolved and produced a battered metal tray. On the tray were a bowl and a plastic bottle of water. Riker went over to the tray and picked it up. In the bowl was some steaming goop that looked like dirty rice with bits of meat in it. Riker tasted it with his fingers. It seemed edible, and hot enough to be free of pathogens.

He eyed the bucket in the corner.

If I get diarrhea from this meal, he thought, it's not gonna be much fun. But my choice is to eat or starve.

He sat on the cot and ate the rice goop and drank the water.

The light outside his window became violet. To stay busy, Riker paced his cell while softly singing old Beatles songs.

From the hallway came the sound of footsteps. The door to his cell was thrown open. This time only two *mukhabarat* were there. Without physically controlling him, they motioned for him to accompany them. Mystified at this sudden relaxation of authority, Riker walked out of his cell. The door clanged shut behind him. He walked with the men down the hall and through the door, but this time the men directed him to walk down a set of stairs. He entered a small room. The man in the business suit was there. Without a word he handed Riker an envelope. Riker looked inside. It contained his passport and the other personal items from his pockets.

"This is your lucky day, Dr. Riker," the man said. "I hope we don't see you again." He motioned towards the door. Riker walked out of the room and down a short hall. At the door to the outside, one of the *mukhabarat* motioned for him to stop. The knit cap was produced and jammed onto his head, obscuring his eyes. He was marched outside to a car and put into the back seat. As before, he was flanked by two men. The doors slammed shut and the car drove away.

The sensations of the drive were the reverse of the one that had brought him to the prison. This time the smooth flow of a highway gradually became the stop-and-go of city traffic, and in the city Riker heard the occasional honk of a horn or roar of a motorcycle.

The car came to a stop. The cap was ripped from his head and he was roughly shoved out onto the pavement. The car sped away.

9.

Riker got to his feet and dusted off his pants. He looked around. He was standing in a deserted parking lot near the big commercial wharves in Latakia. It was after sunset and the western sky on the Mediterranean horizon glowed deep red. To the east, a few lights in the gloomy city twinkled.

A car approached. Riker stood and watched it; there was no point in running. The car—a two-door Mercedes sedan in good condition—drew alongside of him. The passenger door swung open.

"Get in," said a woman's voice.

Riker looked into the back seat. It was unoccupied.

"Don't worry, Dr. Riker," said the woman. "I'm taking you back to your hotel."

Riker got into the front passenger seat of the car and closed the door. In the fading light he saw that the driver was about forty years old, slender, with smooth brown hair and almond eyes. She wore a fashionable gray dress that came to just above her knees.

"My name is Amena Qabbani," she said. "I'm an assistant director of the Ministry of Health here in Syria."

"*You're* the one who got me out of prison?" said Riker.

She smiled. "Not entirely. My brother works for the GSD. He told me about you. I convinced him that you were working for us, in counterintelligence. I told him that your mission was to uncover rebel plots that involved biological warfare."

"Thanks," said Riker, "but I need to tell you that I'm incredibly confused. Why would you want to get me released with such a story?"

Amena expertly wheeled the car out of the parking lot and onto Gamal Abdel Nasser. Then she made a right onto Al Maghreb Al Arabi. The hotel was just a few blocks ahead.

"I'll tell you more at dinner," she said. "But first, I assume that you'll want to get cleaned up."

They rode in silence to the hotel. As Amena pulled up to the entrance she said, "Let's not give the GSD spies in the hotel anything more to report. I'm going to the Antika restaurant, which is two blocks down the street. The owner is a friend of mine, and he knows all the local government informants. He'll give us a booth where we can talk freely."

Riker agreed, and after he got out of the car she pulled away from the curb.

Riker went up to his room. On his way through the lobby he passed the front desk where Shakira was peering at her computer. Glancing up, with her mouth she gave him a professional smile. Her eyes were vacant.

On opening the door to room 538, Riker peered in. It's funny, he thought to himself. Every traveler accepts the idea that the hotel maid—a perfect stranger—will enter your room, clean it, and in the process might touch or even move your stuff. This doesn't make you feel as though your personal space has been violated. It's perfectly normal. Heck, the hotel maid might even have a nasty case of the flu, and you'd never know it. But what if the secret police had also been in your room, and searched it? Now you feel violated!

Riker cautiously inspected the room. The bed had been made, just like it would have been in any hotel. There were fresh towels in the bathroom. His suitcase appeared to be undisturbed. His jacket was hanging in the closet.

There was no evidence of a search—but of course, there wouldn't be.

Where was the listening device? In the telephone, the lamp, or implanted in the wall? And how about a camera? Riker shrugged his shoulders. He was like an animal on display in the zoo, and everything he did in his cage was visible to his keepers. This was the new reality. Syria was a police state, and he'd better get used to it.

Riker washed his face and put on a clean shirt and pants.

After descending to the lobby, he passed Shakira at the front desk. He was tempted to stop and tell her where he was going—to save her a phone call, he would say. But he just gave her a friendly smile. She went back to looking at her computer.

Riker walked up Al Maghreb Al Arabi to the entrance to Antika. It was a nondescript establishment, with only a painted metal sign next to plain glass door. He stopped at the door and looked behind him. No one seemed to be paying attention to him, and none of the men were wearing a black leather jacket and black slacks—the ubiquitous uniform of the *mukhabarat*. After pulling open the door, Riker passed through a small vestibule and walked down two steps into a small dining room with perhaps twenty tables and, along the far wall, a row of wooden booths. On the wall above each booth was a colorful Syrian travel poster in a thin frame. The posters, which showed sunny beaches and ancient ruins, looked faded, as if they dated from the nineteen seventies. In one of the booths sat Amena Qabanni. She made eye contact and with a little nod of her head indicated that he had come to the right place. Riker slid into the booth. On the table a red candle in a glass votive flickered.

"Nice place here," said Riker.

"Even today, there are hidden islands of civilization in Syria," said Amena. "You have to know where they are."

"The present situation—" Riker paused to look around the room at the handful of other diners— "is tragic. Syria is such an ancient and beautiful country."

"We can speak freely," said Amena. "The owner has assured me that there are no government spies here tonight."

"But discretion is always wise," said Riker.

"Absolutely," agreed Amena.

The waiter delivered menus, and they ordered dinner and a bottle of wine. When the waiter had left, Riker said, "Do you want to tell me more about how you managed to get me out of prison?"

"I'm not going to say too much more," she said. "Sometimes the less said, the better. My brother became aware that you had been taken into custody. Because you claimed to be a doctor, he asked me what I thought. He assumes that I support the regime. I went online and verified your identity. To be honest, I thought you could be useful to me. So I told my brother that you were in counterintelligence and you were gathering evidence of a rebel plot. I said that of course this was highly confidential and very few people knew about your activities, and in fact many people in government had been led to believe that you were working for the rebels and against the government. This was all part of the necessary cover story."

"So, perversely, if it can be asserted that I'm working deep undercover, the idea that I *appear* to be working for a rebel group—whether it's the Free Syrian Army, the Islamic Front, Jabhat al-Nusra, or someone else—can actually inoculate me against arrest and prosecution by the regime?"

"Yes," she replied coolly.

"It seems like an extremely precarious environment," said Riker. "If just one person gets the wrong idea about me, then—" He drew his finger across his throat.

"The battle lines are constantly shifting," she said. "The city is full of spies for both sides. We both need to be very careful."

The waiter came with their food: for Amena, the lamb *awarma*, with ground spiced lamb mixed with parsley and onions, and served on hummus; for Riker, the *mansaf ghanam*, with seasoned basmati rice and beef cooked and topped with pine nuts. He was impressed by the expert preparation and presentation.

"You know the real reason for my presence here in

Syria," Riker said after a few minutes.

"Something about a possible case of smallpox?" she replied.

"Yes." He told her the story of Akram Aflaq, and how he probably contracted smallpox somewhere in Latakia. But the source of the virus was a mystery. "As you know," he said, "the accepted wisdom is that there are only two places in the world where smallpox still exists. One is the Centers for Disease Control, in Atlanta, Georgia. The other is the State Research Center of Virology and Biotechnology—the Vector Institute—twelve miles outside the Siberian city of Novosibirsk, in Siberia."

Amena nodded. "The Russians have a reputation for aggressively pursuing biological warfare programs," she said. "And they don't necessarily keep this stuff to themselves. In the 1990s, there were rumors that the Russians had given some live smallpox to certain rogue states, particularly North Korea. Of course, in 1998 the Russian director of Vector denied this. Who knows the truth? Russia is a place where deep secrecy is normal."

"Once in a while the window opens and we get a glimpse inside," said Riker. "You remember that in 1992, a Russian colonel named Kanatzhan 'Kanat' Alibekov defected to the United States. He was the deputy chief of Biopreparat, the Soviet network of biolabs for military weaponization of bacteria, viruses, and chemicals for use against, as they said, 'enemy troops and civilians if desired.' Under his Americanized name of Ken Alibek, he wrote a book called *Biohazard*. It was published in 1999. He made some pretty shocking assertions, like this one. " Riker took his phone and pulled up a screen. "Here it is. Alibek wrote in his book, 'We'—meaning the Soviet Union—'explored AIDS and Legionnaire's disease. Both, as it happened, proved too unstable for use on the battlefield or against civilian populations. After studying one strain of the AIDS virus collected from the United States in 1985, we determined that HIV's long incubation period made it unsuitable for military use. You couldn't strike terror in an enemy's forces by infecting them with a disease whose symptoms took years to develop.

"'We had greater success in our work on more traditional killers. One of the most infectious diseases known to man, smallpox, was declared eradicated by the World Health Organization in 1977 in 1980. The last naturally occurring case was reported in 1977, and the medical profession judges the minor health risk associated with a vaccine greater than forgoing vaccination. Today, it isn't possible to get a smallpox vaccination in the United States unless you are a lab scientist or a member of the military. This was for us an excellent reason to weaponize it. Although we officially had a small amount of the virus at the Ivanovsky Institute of Virology in Moscow—matching the only other legal repository of the strain in the United States—we cultivated tons of smallpox in our secret lab in Zagorsk (now Sergiyev Posad), the famous Russian cathedral city a half hour's drive from the capital. At Zagorsk, we experimented with the culture until we came up with a weapons-quality variant. Smallpox was then quietly added to our arsenal.'"

Amena nodded and took a sip of her wine. She set the glass on the table and looked at Riker. "The United States is not immune to mistakes," she said with a smile. "Everyone knows that in 2014, six vials of live smallpox virus were found in an unmarked cardboard box in a closet at the National Institutes of Health. They dated back six decades."

"Yes, and even the CDC got some bad publicity out of that," admitted Riker. "Because only the CDC is the official American repository of smallpox, the vials were then sent there to be destroyed by autoclaving. To verify the process, the World Health Organization has a rule that destruction of smallpox must be witnessed by a member of its WHO staff, probably from Geneva. But at the time of this situation, the WHO claimed that it couldn't spare anybody to send to Atlanta to serve as witness, as all its people were tied up with the Ebola outbreak in Africa. So the WHO was not happy that the CDC went ahead without them."

"I don't know who are more devious," said Amena, "The doctors, who should know better, or the politicians, who care only about power."

"There's plenty of guilt to go around," said Riker.

Riker was impressed by Amena's coolness and self-confidence. During his career he had taken plenty of extended overseas trips, as a consequence of which he had been separated from his wife for weeks at a time, and often his foreign colleagues had been attractive women. In such situations, keeping his mind strictly on business was both necessary and often challenging. Since his wife's death, Riker had been too preoccupied with her honoring her memory to allow his heart—or his eye—to respond to another woman. But it had been a year since his wife had passed away, and time seeks to restore equilibrium. Deep within him, like a glacier cracking and slowly sliding towards the sea, he felt the tug of new companionship. Amena wore no wedding ring—and Riker found himself wondering what that meant.

"You say that Akram Aflaq made a deathbed statement," said Amena. "He said that Mahadi wanted to kill him, and it was all because of Sabeen."

"Yes," replied Riker, coming out of his reverie. "Tamadur Aflaq—Akram's mother—told me that Sabeen was the wife of a guy named Bani Mahadi, and that her son knew them."

"I know who Bani Mahadi is," said Amena. "I've met him a few times. He is a pompous ass. In the eyes of Bashar al-Assad and the regime, Mahadi's only attribute is that he's an Alawite."

"I'm not as familiar with Alawites as I should be," said Riker.

"Simplistically, the Alawites splintered from Shi'a Islam over a thousand years ago. The sect was originally called Nusayri, named after Muhammad ibn Nusayr, who, after the death of the eleventh Imam

Hasan al-Askari in the year 874, claimed he was the imam's intimate messenger. Without boring you with all the details, the Alawite religion is a mysterious cocktail with elements of Shi'a Islam, Christianity, Zoroastrianism, Phoenician paganism, and Mazdakism. They are a minority sect—Alawites represent twelve percent of the Syrian population and are also found in Turkey and northern Lebanon."

"And yet the ruling class of Syria is Alawite," said Riker.

"Yes. The stakes for their survival could not be higher. The fall of Assad would mean bloody hell for the Alawites at the hands of Sunni extremists. With the Islamic State group advancing closer to the Alawite heartland, the next genocide will be of the Alawites, regardless of whether they stand with Assad. Alawites are not only considered heretic, but also an enemy on the battlefield. Therefore, from Assad's point of view it's better that a mediocre buffoon like Mahadi holds a position in government than any non-Alawite."

"May I ask—are you Alawite?"

She shook her head. "I'm a nonpracticing Shi'a. Personally—and no offense to you, if you're religious— I think it's all a bunch of fairy stories. It's hard for me to believe that in the twenty-first century, with all that we know about science and the universe, people are willing to kill each other over these medieval beliefs. It's astounding. I mean, if there is a God or Allah up there, and if he's looking down at these wars and the barbarism, he must think his little creations are crazy lunatics."

"And yet you're an assistant minister of health in Assad's Alawite government."

"I have certain skills and qualifications. And years ago, before the civil war, the Syrian government took pride in promoting women to positions of authority. Even today, the vice president of Syria is a woman— Najah Al-Attar. Assad elevated her from her previous job as minister of culture. It's interesting that unlike Bashar al-Assad, the vice president is a Sunni Muslim, like seventy percent of Syrians. She's not even a member of the Ba'ath Party and is not connected with the security services, the backbone of the Assad clan."

"In the West, we tend to have a simplistic view of foreign conflicts," said Riker. "You know—here are the good guys, whom we like, and there are the bad guys, whom we don't like."

"Sometimes that's exactly what it is," said Amena. "And sometimes it's totally *not* like that! You have to know the difference. Welcome to Syria, Dr. Riker." She raised her wine glass as if to offer a toast.

After putting his glass back on the table, Riker said, "Let's return to our problem. We have an individual who contracted smallpox and died. We believe it happened here, in Latakia. The victim stated that he thought Bani Mahadi was responsible. Of course, he could be totally wrong. Perhaps even if Aflaq and Sabeen Mahadi were having an affair, their relationship had nothing to do with Aflaq being exposed to smallpox. But it's the only clue we have."

"I can tell you that I've never heard any talk about the Syrian government possessing smallpox viruses," said Amena. "The government has lots of terrible stuff—sarin, chlorine, and mustard gas—that it has used against its enemies. But I've never heard of smallpox. If there were a program to use smallpox against Syria's enemies, it would need to be extremely clandestine. Absolutely top secret."

"We can assume that if smallpox exists in Syria— and even right here in Latakia—it had to come from outside the country," added Riker. "The Russians qualify on two important counts: they support the Assad regime and they have the virus. Here's my question: If you were going to launch a smallpox project based here in Latakia, and using Russian smallpox, you'd need a facility. This facility would have to already exist, because you couldn't build it from scratch—not with the intense level of international scrutiny being paid to the government's war efforts. Does any such place come to mind?"

Amena thought for a moment. "The labs at Tishreen University are pretty good, but maintaining secrecy would be impossible. South of town, in the coastal suburb of Jableh, there's a company called Beta Syria Pharmaceutical. They were big before the war, but the place has been closed down for a couple of years. It wouldn't take much to get it up and running as a smallpox factory."

"Can you get me inside?" asked Riker.

"Perhaps," replied Amena, "If you have the appropriate government escort. I'll make a few calls and set it up. I'll contact you first thing tomorrow morning." She signaled for the waiter, and then gave Riker a wry smile. "You'll be pleased that President al-Assad is paying for our lunch today—I'm putting it on my tab."

10.

At nine o'clock the next morning, Amena's gleaming Mercedes sighed to a stop in front of the Shahbandar Hotel. Riker reached for the passenger door. But as he pulled it open, Amena set the emergency brake and opened her own door. She got out of the car and said to Riker, "For appearances sake, it would be better if you drove. It's daytime, and people can see us, and there are many who would think it curious that a woman was driving a man around town. We don't want to draw attention."

Riker walked around the car and got behind the wheel. When Amena had settled in the passenger seat he put the car in gear and eased out of the driveway and onto Al Maghreb Al Arabi.

"Take a left on Ramadan," said Amena. "At Haroun Square, go around the rotary and exit onto Tripoli. This will take us past Tishreen University. Then we'll take Highway 1 past the airport and then on to Jableh."

The morning was cool and clear and, considering it was Monday, traffic was sparse. Riker mentioned this to Amena. "The war has changed everything," she said. "What are people supposed to do? Go to work and just sit there because there's nothing to do—nothing to buy or sell? They just stay home, waiting for things to get better."

"There's something I need to ask you about," said Riker as he drove.

"What is it?"

"When the *mukhabarat* picked me up, they also got my driver. His name is Hussein. We were separated. I assume he was taken to the same place I was, unless there are other places, like the Latakia city jail?"

"There are many places they could have taken him," said Amena. "Some more horrible than others. Is

Hussein Syrian?"

"Yes."

"How did you become connected with him?"

Riker paused. Suddenly he had the sick feeling that perhaps Amena was not what she appeared to be. Perhaps she was part of an elaborate good cop/bad cop plan to get him to talk. Playing the role of a sympathizer, she could gently extract from him every shred of information that the regime needed to proclaim him a spy and condemn him.

He glanced over at her. She was waiting, expectantly, for an answer. Her face bore a faint, quizzical smile.

Riker decided that he had no choice but to trust her.

"My handlers told me that when I came ashore in Latakia, a taxi would be waiting for me in a parking lot. The driver's name would be Hussein. I got off the boat, walked to the parking lot, and there he was, reading the paper behind the wheel. He knew who I was and he drove me to the Shahbandar."

"He's with the CIA?" she asked.

Riker shrugged. "Just like in Syria, the United States has various security services that employ local people in all sorts of capacities. Hussein might not have any formal relationship with an American agency other than being paid to drive Americans around town."

"Do you know his last name?" asked Amena. "Saying his name is Hussein is like going to New York and asking for Steve. You need more."

Riker searched his memory. "Yes—I saw his taxi license, on the dashboard. It had his photograph and his name. His full name is Hussein al-Azmah."

"Okay," she said. "I'll make some inquiries. For all we know, he could be on the payroll of the GSD."

"A double agent?"

"The way things are now, if someone offers you money, you take it today, and tomorrow you figure out whose side you're on."

They passed the airport and, after entering Jableh, they soon found the gates to Beta Syria Pharmaceuticals. As Riker drove closer, an armed man stepped out of the guardhouse.

"Interesting," said Amena as Riker slowed the Mercedes to a stop. "For a supposedly defunct factory, I'm surprised at the level of security. We may be on the right track."

Riker lowered his window. Amena, leaning over the center console, spoke to the guard in Syrian. She gave Riker her identification card, which he passed to the guard. With a scowl on his face, the guard inspected the card. Amena said something else to him in Syrian. After a few seconds the guard handed the card back to Riker. He stepped back and signaled for the gate to be raised.

Riker parked by the front door, and they got out of the car.

"This place is pretty big," remarked Riker as they approached the front door.

"It was once a major producer for the Middle Eastern market," replied Amena. "The civil war has killed Syria's exports. The company struggled and finally closed down last year. Clearly, somebody is working on getting it up and running."

In the cool, quiet lobby they were met by another armed guard. Amena spoke to him, and in turn he spoke into his phone. Then he nodded.

"Mr. Noman will be out in a moment," said the guard.

Presently a door opened and a man entered the lobby. The expression on his face was one of suspicious curiosity.

"I'm Sami Noman, the director of this facility," he said without extending his hand. After a quick glance at Riker he addressed Amena. "Mrs. Qabbani, I understand that you wish to have a tour?"

"Yes," she replied. "The Ministry of Health is taking inventory of facilities used for the manufacturing of medical products. This is in preparation for our expected victory against the criminals who have invaded our country and the subsequent normalization of industry under the leadership of President al-Assad." She gave Noman a thin smile. "I expected to see a shuttered laboratory. It's interesting that it appears to be making a comeback."

"We're exploring certain options," said Noman. He frowned. "To be honest, Mrs. Qabbani, we are very busy here. We cannot possibly take time out of our hectic schedules to indulge every whim of the Ministry of Health, no matter how well intentioned."

"I would think that to continue to enjoy the favor of those at the highest levels of government and at Mount Mezzeh," said Amena, invoking the location of the presidential palace of Bashar al-Assad in Damascus, "You would be willing to spare us a few minutes of your valuable time."

"Very well," said Noman carefully. He nodded at Riker. "And who is this man?"

"He's an American doctor who is in Syria working on a special project," said Amena.

"What kind of project?" asked Noman.

"That's classified," replied Amena. She looked at her watch. "Mr. Noman, we too have a schedule to keep. I would hate to have to come back here again with more people."

"Very well," conceded Noman. "Please follow me."

He led them through the building. They visited a succession of empty offices, a cafeteria, the loading dock, the maintenance department, the boiler room, and even the employee fitness center, which now was nothing more than a big empty space, stripped of all the exercise equipment.

It was while viewing the vacant fitness center that Amena showed her impatience.

"Mr. Noman," she said, "this is all very interesting, but my mission is to inspect the manufacturing facilities, not tour empty rooms. Please take us there at once."

With a sour look Noman led them back to the lobby

and through the set of doors.

They entered the manufacturing space, with its many tables on which rested the test tubes and other equipment. Around the perimeter of the room were the white counters and the big stainless steel refrigerators. There was an electron microscope with its tabletop computer controller.

Noman stood by while Amena and Riker casually strolled around the room, affecting an air of detached indifference. Riker opened several of the refrigerators. They were cold, but generally empty; one contained a box of fresh eggs. He came to the stainless steel door of the containment room. To the outside of the door was affixed a bright red biohazard sign. The door was secured with a big padlock.

"What's in there?" he asked Noman.

The director shrugged. "The previous owners told us that it contained manufacturing byproduct that they were forced to keep onsite during the final months of operations. We haven't opened it yet. I don't have the key."

"I understand," said Riker as he drifted away from the door. He went over to Amena. "I think we've seen enough," he said quietly.

"Very well," she turned with a big smile to Noman. "Thank you very much for your time. The Ministry of Health will be quite pleased with your excellent work here."

"Happy to oblige," said Noman as he gently herded his unwelcome guests to the door.

Noman made sure the Mercedes carrying Riker and Amena had passed through the entrance gate before he went back inside the building.

Once on the highway heading north to Latakia, Riker said to Amena, "I'm sure they're doing something with a viral agent at that factory."

"I got the same impression," she agreed.

"Aside from the obvious red flag of the locked containment room," said Riker, "They've got all the necessary equipment to cultivate a virus. They have an electron microscope, which you need if you want to visually identify one such as smallpox. They have chicken eggs in which to grow it. You take a fertilized chicken egg and make a tiny hole with a small sterile drill. We saw such tools on the tables. Then you inject a bit of the living virus into the chorioallantoic membrane inside the egg. You seal your opening in the shell with gelatin or paraffin and incubate it at thirty-seven degrees for two or three days. Them break it open and harvest the virus, which has multiplied, from the tissues inside the egg."

"You can then flash-freeze the virus for use at a later date," added Amena. "I saw liquid nitrogen freezers in the lab too."

"Okay," said Riker. "It appears as though we've identified the source of the smallpox virus. What we don't know is the immediate purpose, and how Akram Aflaq managed to get himself infected. We need to find out if he had any connection to this operation."

Amena thought for a moment. Then she smiled. "If Sabeen Mahadi is a typical Ba'ath party wife, she should be easy to find. She will be a little butterfly who flutters her way into our net."

11.

Amena dropped Riker off at the hotel. "I have to go to the office for awhile, just for appearances, although of course no one is doing any real work," she said. "I'll call you in a few hours."

After lunch, his phone buzzed.

"Meet me at the Emerald Mall as soon as you can," she said. "It's only a few blocks from your hotel. I'll be waiting in the food court."

Riker caught a cab—alas, not driven by Hussein, whose fate was still unknown—and fifteen minutes later he was ascending the escalator to the main floor of Latakia's most upscale downtown shopping mall. Except for the signs written in both Arabic and English, it looked like any downtown mall in the United States—all glass and chrome, with polished floors leading to storefronts with expansive windows. The most immediately obvious difference between this mall and others of its type in non-wartime cities was that here the big store windows were filled mostly with air. Where in an American store window you'd see four or five mannequins dressed up in the newest looks, along with big blown-up artsy photos, in a typical window at the Emerald Mall you'd see one lonely mannequin wearing an outfit from last season.

Nevertheless, for Latakian women with money—which meant the wives of Ba'ath party members—the Emerald Mall was the last and best place to shop and socialize in comfort, while pretending that just a few hours away their fellow citizens weren't being gassed, barrel-bombed, and machine-gunned by their own government.

The air was cool and lightly perfumed. Riker made his way around the center atrium, past the shuttered Apple store ("CLOSED FOR RENOVATIONS") and the Sunrise Fashion Store with its display of Russian jeans and Chinese tops for women. Here and there fashionably dressed women in twos and threes, some holding shopping bags, with sunglasses parked on top of their sleekly styled heads and with looks of haughty detachment, stood talking or sat on benches. There was very little that was worth buying, and therefore no reason to engage in the aggressive comparison shopping that American women are accustomed to, where you march from store to store, seeking the best bargain. These women were simply killing time until they had to go back to work or to their husbands and get an earful about the deviousness and cruelty of the many enemies of the state.

Just past the Crescent Mode handcrafted silver jewelry store, which offered a sparse selection of thinly hammered bracelets and necklaces, Riker spotted the open expanse of the food court, where an island of plastic tables and chairs was ringed by an international sea of junk food: Star Kabob, Yogen Früz frozen yogurt, Hefy burgers, Al Baik fried chicken, Kudu sandwiches, McDonald's burgers. He scanned the tables and spotted Amena sitting alone in front of the Abu Nawas "broasted" chicken store.

He sat down. "What have you got?" he asked.

Amena put down her coffee cup. "I made some calls to some people I know. One of my sources knows Sabeen Mahadi. She said that every Monday afternoon Sabeen has her nails done at Crystal Nail, which is right over there." Amena nodded in the direction of one of the storefronts. Riker turned to look. It was a small establishment, but you could look through the big window and see the activity inside. Opening her purse, Amena took out her phone and pulled up a photo. She showed the phone to Riker. The screen showed an attractive Arab woman, thirtyish, with wide almond eyes and full lips. She appeared to be posing with a group of other people who had been cropped out of the picture.

"This woman entered Crystal Nail about twenty minutes ago," said Amena. "She should be coming out at any time."

Amena put her phone back into her purse. "I hope you had lunch," she said to Riker, "and that you're not being tortured by having to sit here surrounded by all of this food."

"I think," replied Riker, "That the only torture would be in having to *eat* it. I'm much happier not having any of it. I'll bet I could get ten times my daily sodium allowance with just one French fry or piece of kabob. It's sad that anywhere on the earth, from Kansas to Kazakhstan, you can kill yourself by eating mall food."

"Modern life has its virtues and its hazards," replied Amena.

Riker noticed two men in black slacks and black leather jackets sauntering past the food court. The *mukhabarat* stopped and looked in Riker's direction. He froze, unsure of what to do. The men seemed to discuss between themselves whether to enter the food court. Then one of them turned and went on his way. The other followed.

Riker felt like a swimmer in the ocean who sees two shark fins swim lazily by—and then they inexplicably cruise away without striking.

Suddenly Amena leaned forward, peering in the direction of Crystal Nail. "There she is. Let's go. Let me do the talking."

As they rose from the table Riker saw a slim young woman exit from Crystal Nail. Dressed in cream-colored slacks and a tailored blouse, she walked along the promenade of the mall, stopping occasionally to look at a store window. Within a few seconds Amena had caught up to her. They spoke in Arabic for a moment. Riker overheard Amena say the name Akram. The young woman looked around, with fear in her eyes. Then she said something to Amena, who nodded. The woman walked away.

Amena turned to Riker and said, "That was Sabeen. I told her that I wanted to talk with her about Akram. She thought I was going to have her arrested. After I reassured her, she said that she was afraid to talk here in the mall. I said that I understood completely. She's going to her car. We're going to meet her at Le Meridien, a big hotel about ten minutes north of town."

Riker knew where it was, and he offered to drive Amena's car. She agreed.

At two o'clock they arrived at Le Meridien. The sky was overcast now, and a chill onshore breeze suggested rain. The hotel was once a showplace, as sleek and sumptuous as any in Miami Beach; with its elongated pyramidal shape it looked like a ten-story cruise ship that had been bent in the middle and planted on high ground above the beach. But the war had taken its toll. The poured concrete terraces that stepped down from the hotel to the grassy oceanfront lawn showed cracks and chips. The flagstones of the pathways to the broad beach were faded and interlaced with weeds. The place looked like a luxury car that had been parked in a barn for thirty years—intact, yes, but desperately in need of tender loving care.

Passing the pool, Amena and Riker walked down the concrete steps to the broad palm-dotted lawn that devolved into sand as you got nearer the water. The path led them up a second set of stairs to an elevated patio that overlooked the sparkling blue Mediterranean. This patio surrounded a second swimming pool, bigger than the one nearer the hotel, with rows of reclining lounge chairs shaded by yellow and white-striped umbrellas. Riker saw that the hotel had guests—not many, but enough of them were lounging in the chairs to give one the assurance that the place was not a ghost town.

"She asked us to wait here," said Amena.

Neither Riker nor Amena felt like reclining on one of lounge chairs, but there was a small poolside bar with six stools and no customers. They each took a stool. The bartender asked them what they wanted; they each ordered a soft drink.

They sat and waited. Riker glanced at his phone. It

was two thirty.

"What do you think?" he asked Amena. "Do you think she got cold feet?"

"Cold feet?" repeated Amena. "I don't understand."

Riker smiled. "I mean, do you think she lost her nerve?"

"Oh—I don't know. Let's give her another few minutes."

They waited.

As Riker was considering leaving, they saw a woman cross the sandy lawn and come up the stairs to the patio. When she reached the patio she paused and looked around. To her outfit she had been wearing at the mall she had added a big floppy hat and a pale grey windbreaker. Seeing Amena, she walked over to the bar.

"Who is this?" she asked Amena in Arabic, indicated Riker.

"An American doctor, Martin Riker," replied Amena in English. "He wants to talk to you about Akram."

Sabeen looked around at the scattered guests. "There are too many people here," she said. "Let's walk along the beach." She turned and walked in the direction away from the hotel to the end of the patio, where there was another set of four or five concrete steps. These led directly to the beach, which was nearly deserted.

When they had gotten twenty or thirty yards from the patio, Sabeen stopped. There was no one else around. The only sound was the gentle lapping of waves and the fronds of the palm trees rustling in the gathering wind.

"Why do you think I know anything about Akram Aflaq?" Sabeen asked Amena.

"Because Dr. Riker heard him say your name."

"Where was this?" she demanded.

"In New York, at Mt. Bedford Hospital," said Riker.

"Where is he?"

"Ms. Mahadi, I'm sorry to say that Akram Aflaq has

passed away," said Riker. "He died a few days ago."

Sabeen's mouth tightened and her eyes began to moisten. She turned her head away and looked at the water. After few moments during which none of them spoke, she turned back to Riker. Her eyes were dry but full of sadness. "Did they murder him? Tell me what happened to him."

"Akram died of an infectious disease," said Riker. "By the time I saw him in the hospital, it was much too late. We couldn't save him. By our calculations, he became infected on or about Monday, the second of November, here in Latakia. On Thursday, the fifth, he flew from Damascus to Beirut, and then to Athens. He flew to New York City on Sunday, the fifteenth of November."

"This disease—is it contagious?" asked Sabeen.

"Only after the fever develops, which is at least a week after the initial infection," said Riker. "I think it's highly unlikely that he transmitted the disease to anyone in Latakia—or in Syria, for that matter."

"Does his mother know?"

"Yes, I told her yesterday. Of course she's very distraught."

Sabeen nodded. She looked Riker in the eye. "Tell me exactly what he said when you saw him."

"He said your name—Sabeen," said Riker, choosing to reveal only what he thought she needed to know. "That was all. We tracked down his mother, and when I talked to her yesterday I asked if her son knew anyone named Sabeen. His mother told me that it's an unusual name, at least in Latakia, and that the only woman named Sabeen she knew was the wife of Akram's boss—a man named Bani Mahadi. Dr. Qabbani made a few calls to her colleagues, and we learned that you visit Crystal Nails every Monday at one o'clock. And so here we are now."

"Yes, here we are," replied Sabeen. "Where is Akram's body?"

"Unfortunately," said Riker, "due to the highly infectious nature of the disease, his remains were extremely contagious. His body was cremated in New York. The ashes are being stored at the medical examiner's office. The government will decide how to dispose of them."

"Tell us about your relationship with Akram," Amena gently suggested. "It's very important that we identify the source of this disease."

Sabeen lowered her eyes and thought for a moment. Then she took a deep breath and straightened her back. "Okay," she began. "I come from a small town in the suburbs. After high school I attended Tishreen University. I majored in political science. But my parents divorced and my father stopped paying for my education. I got a part-time job in a restaurant and managed to earn my degree, but finding full-time work was impossible. I was living paycheck to paycheck, with no one to guide me. One night I was in a nightclub, here in Latakia. A man approached me. He was older, and acted like a tough guy. He started talking to me. I had nothing better to do so I indulged him. After a while I said I had to go. He offered to drive me home—and he promised that he would not try any funny business. So I said yes. He drove me home. His car was an expensive Mercedes. I asked him what he did for a living and he said that he worked for the government, in security. He dropped me off just like he promised—he was a gentleman. A few days later he called me on the phone and invited me out on a date. I accepted, and I kept seeing him until a few months later he asked me to marry him. Living in my tiny apartment I was eating instant noodles and had not a penny to my name, and Bani was very sweet, so I said 'yes.' My life changed overnight. He gave me a car and money for clothes, and I had servants in the house. But Bani changed too. The day after we were married, he started treating me like I was a servant too. I became his property. He would take me out and show me off to his colleagues, and when we got home he'd ignore me."

"What sort of people were his colleagues?" asked

Riker.

"I found out that Bani worked for the Ba'ath Party and for the GSD. I had always been taught to fear the GSD, so I didn't ask too many questions. They're tough people. I stay away from them."

"Except for Akram?" said Amena.

Sabeen nodded. "He was in the GSD, but he was a computer technician whose work had nothing to do with arresting people. I first met him when he came to our house for a meeting. Bani wanted me to play the role of the obedient wife, which I did. Akram was charming and funny. Out in the kitchen I talked to him for a few minutes. He said he was 'on the ladder of success.' I thought that was sweet. Unlike Bani, who was always grumbling, Akram really liked his work. He was like a ray of sunshine in my life. We discovered that we both liked the music of Asmahan, the famous Arab Druze singer and actress from Syria who lived in Egypt before the Second World War. Akram was something of an expert in the old Arab popular singers—people who my grandparents would have listened to. We spent hours talking about music and Arab culture."

"And your relationship developed into an affair?" asked Amena.

"Yes," replied Sabeen. "I knew it was wrong and dangerous, but I was terribly lonely. When I was at home Bani either ignored me or criticized me, and I just wanted a kind man who would love me. I enlisted the help of my cousin Ghazal, who understood my situation. She's a widow, and Ghazal allowed Akram and me to meet in her house. It was Ghazal who gave me a message from Akram—he said that he was going on a secret mission and wouldn't be back for a long time."

"Did your husband ever suspect that you were in a relationship with Akram?" asked Riker.

"I don't know," replied Sabeen. "But after I received the message from Ghazal, I noticed a change in my husband. He's always been a bit pompous, but suddenly he was looking at me with a renewed arrogance. He came to my bedroom and forced me to submit to him in the most degrading way. It was like he was saying, "I can do with you what I want." She gave a little shiver. "It's scary. He's a man who is used to getting what he wants."

"Is it possible that your husband threatened Akram?" said Riker.

"Yes, I suppose. He'll threaten anyone who gets in his way."

"Did Ghazal know Akram before you did?"

"Oh yes," replied Sabeen. "She works for the Ba'ath Party, in communications. When I first tentatively mentioned Akram to her, she knew exactly who he was. And of course she knows my husband. Ghazal has been in the party for many years—she knows a lot of people."

The sky was growing darker as the clouds gathered, and the wind off the water was chill.

"Mrs. Mahadi, I want to thank you for agreeing to speak with us today," said Riker. "I'm sorry to have brought sad news. I know it's a difficult time for you."

"If anything else comes to mind, please call me," added Amena.

"Okay, I will," replied Sabeen.

They left Sabeen standing on the beach and walked back to the hotel.

12.

As they drove back to town, Amena said, "I think we need to talk to Sabeen's cousin Ghazal. She's more connected to this case than Sabeen is. She's right in the thick of it."

"Agreed," said Riker. He thought for a moment. "I've had a very disturbing thought," he said. "I'm trying to figure out why Akram Aflaq was infected. It may have been an accident, or it may have been deliberate. If it was done deliberately, either someone like Mahadi was trying to kill Aflaq or Aflaq was a test case for a terrorist smallpox delivery system."

"A smallpox delivery system?"

"There has been talk of an ISIS plan to recruit suicide bombers who have purposefully infected themselves with the Ebola virus. They'd go to a densely populated spot, like a restaurant or nightclub, and blow themselves up. It might be effective because the Ebola virus is spread through direct contact with the blood or body fluids of a person who is sick from Ebola. The virus carried by blood and body fluids can enter another person's body through broken skin or unprotected mucous membranes in, for example, the eyes, nose, or mouth. The bodily fluids and tissues propelled through the air by the exploding terrorist would then, in theory, infect large swaths of innocent civilians with the virus.

"Such an approach would work even better with smallpox. You'd infect the volunteer with the smallpox virus, keep him isolated, and when he developed a fever and the rash, strap a bomb on him and send him out to do his dirty work. While direct contact with smallpox scabs or contaminated clothing or linens can spread the disease, smallpox is most efficiently spread from person to person by aerosolized droplets expelled into the air by the coughing of infected patients. The ability for the smallpox virus to be carried through the air would make it an effective choice for suicide bomber in an enclosed area, like a shopping mall, movie theatre, or cruise ship. Even if bystanders weren't injured by the explosion or didn't come into direct contact with body parts or bodily fluids from the terrorist, they'd still breathe infected air. After the explosion, in their excited condition they'd probably be breathing very deeply, inhaling the airborne virus. And rescue workers who would have no idea that the bomber was infected would breathe the infected air too."

"To use a suicide bomber's own body as a culture for the virus would be an amazingly sinister yet efficient scheme," said Amena.

"Right," said Riker. "There'd be no need for mass production of the virus. You'd only need just enough to infect each bomber. Research suggests that *even one* living virus particle could initiate infection in either the upper respiratory tract or pulmonary region. As an extra advantage, the incubation period for smallpox is at least seven days. Imagine that for seven days the survivors of the attack could be living amongst the general population, with no inkling that each and every one of them was a walking virus bomb."

"Do you think Akram Aflaq was a prototype suicide bomber who, for some reason, left the reservation, went rogue, and wound up in New York?"

"It's possible that he had to hurriedly leave Syria to avoid getting killed by the jealous husband, Bani Mahadi," replied Riker.

"From what we've heard about Aflaq, he doesn't seem to be the type to become a suicide bomber," said Amena. "He's been described as a cheerful guy who, as Sabeen said, saw himself climbing 'the ladder of success.' No one says he was particularly devout."

"In some ways, though, he was typical," said Riker. "The average suicide bomber is an unmarried male between the ages of eighteen and thirty. The average age is twenty-one. They are not poor people, or people who you'd think would have no hope and therefore would be willing to give up their lives. In fact, they're more likely to come from the ranks of middle-class college students. It is said that the main reason for becoming a suicide bomber is a desire to become both a religious and a national sacrifice. It is the ultimate way to give your body and your soul for your country and your religion."

"Yes," agreed Amena. "We also know that suicide bombers rarely act alone. They are recruited and supported by terrorist organizations, which often use religion and religious ceremonies to create a sense of bonding among would-be bombers. In forming their suicide cells, the sponsors—who are often charismatic individuals—consciously manipulate these kinds of communion to form very tight-knit groups willing to die for one another."

"If that's the case, the same process would have undoubtedly been used on Aflaq."

They arrived at the Shahbandar. "Let's keep a low profile from the spies in the hotel," suggested Amena. "You should go inside alone. I'll go back to the office. I've got a call in to Ghazal. Hopefully she'll call back today."

"Sounds good," said Riker as he got out of the car. Amena got into the driver's seat and pulled away from the curb.

Riker went up to his room. He tried to call Hussein; his call went to voicemail. He called a few contacts at the embassy of the Czech Republic in Damascus. They weren't very encouraging; if the GSD had Hussein, there was nothing anyone could do but wait until he was released—dead or alive. He might very well have vanished forever. No one knew.

While driving with Amena was a perfectly pleasant experience, Riker decided he needed to be independently mobile. Two blocks from the hotel was a small Sixt Car Rental lot. Sixt was like the Hertz of the Middle East, and they had managed to keep their office in Latakia open. From the rotund manager with a big walrus moustache Riker rented one of the two cars that were available: a silver Toyota Camry with sixty thousand miles on the odometer.

He drove his new set of wheels to the hotel garage.

Feeling tired and more than a little bit guilty for being the reason why Hussein had been picked up, Riker went to the Yakouta restaurant for dinner. From the limited menu he ordered *dawood basha*—Syrian meatballs in a thin tomato and parsley sauce—and an Al-Shark beer. Then he went up to his room.

At seven thirty, Amena called.

"Ghazal has agreed to see us," she said. "I'll pick you up."

Riker told Amena about his newly found vehicular freedom.

"I'll miss having you as my chauffeur," she said.

Suddenly Riker regretted having mentioned the car to her.

"It might be better if we arrived together at her house," suggested Riker. "It won't hurt the Toyota to stay parked in the hotel garage."

Fifteen minutes later, he was once again behind the wheel of Amena's Mercedes. "Where to, ma'am?" he said.

"We're going to a suburb called Albassa, which is about four miles south of the city center, near the coast. Get on Highway 1 going south, and I'll direct you."

When they crossed the Al-Kabir al-Shamali River, the landscape suddenly changed from urban to farms and orchards. At a coverleaf they left the highway and headed due south. After a mile Amena said, "Turn right here."

A few minutes later they pulled up in front of a charming old villa built of natural stone. Two tall oak trees shaded the red tile roof, and built onto the side of the house was a grape arbor. From the windows came warm golden light. It was the perfect picture of bucolic bliss.

Amena knocked on the wooden door. The door

swung open and they were greeted by a robust woman in a simple print dress. Her graying hair was pulled back and tied with a scarf, and her ruddy face told Riker that she spent a lot of time out in the sun.

After introductions, Ghazal ushered them inside. Riker stepped into a tiled vestibule that led to an attractive open living room with exposed beams and a stone fireplace. Ghazal asked them to make themselves comfortable.

"Would you like something to drink?" said Ghazal. "A glass of wine?"

The question of refreshments having been settled by a bottle of good Shiraz and some crackers and olives, Ghazal sat down on a wicker chair.

"As I mentioned on the phone," said Amena, "we met with Sabeen this afternoon. She told us about her arrangement with you regarding Akram Aflaq. Of course we realize that extreme discretion is necessary. Bani Mahadi is a very tough man, and if he were publicly dishonored the outcome would be terrible for Sabeen."

"Yes, absolutely," nodded Ghazal.

"Have you heard about Akram Aflaq?" asked Riker.

Ghazal shook her head. "Only that he told me he was leaving the country on some sort of secret mission. I haven't heard from him since."

Riker told her the basics of Aflaq's sad fate—he had died of a virulent communicable disease in New York. He confided to her that the disease was smallpox, and that this fact was still very much a secret.

"Smallpox?" said Ghazal. "I thought it had been eradicated."

"Among the general global population, yes," said Riker. "But the Russians and the Americans still hold samples of the virus. Supposedly they are in highly secure facilities, but accidents and nefarious dealings are still very possible."

"It must be a terrible way to die," said Ghazal. "Akram was a nice guy. Very bright. And while I did not approve of the arrangement he had with my cousin, it was difficult to say 'no' because Sabeen was so very miserable and Akram brought a little bit of joy into her life."

"How well did you know Akram?" asked Riker. "Is there any possibility that he volunteered for a suicide mission?"

"Impossible," said Ghazal. "He was full of life. The last time I saw him was at the end of October. He told me that he was getting a raise at work—which was extraordinary, considering no one's getting raises in this wartime economy—and that he was saving his money for a better place for his mother. He wanted to get her out of the city."

"The families of suicide bombers are generally richly compensated," said Riker. "I didn't see any evidence of a financial windfall at his mother's apartment. I think we can conclude that Akram was not recruited to be a suicide bomber whose mission ended too early. There was some other reason he became infected. Ghazal, what about Bani Mahadi? We keep hearing that he's a very tough guy. And—I will share this with you now—the full statement made by Akram as he lay dying was that Mahadi wanted him dead, and it was all because of Sabeen."

Ghazal thought for a moment. "Dr. Riker, have you been to the Beta Syria Pharmaceutical facility in Jableh?"

"Yes—Amena and I went there yesterday morning. We were met by a man named Sami Noman. Amena told him that we needed to inspect the facility on behalf of the Ministry of Health. Noman allowed us inside. We saw clear evidence of an emerging virus-growing operation."

"Smallpox?" asked Ghazal.

"Possibly," replied Riker. "Ghazal, we know that the government of Bashar al-Assad has used chemical weapons against its enemies. We can safely assume that high-level members of the GSD would, at the very least, have knowledge of any program involving biological or chemical weapons. They might even be involved, from a standpoint of security. Have you any knowledge of such a program?"

Ghazal stiffened and her eyes grew hard. She looked at Amena. "I thought we were discussing the marital problems of my cousin Sabeen and how to extricate her from her unfortunate situation, not pry into the confidential operations of the government."

Amena shifted in her chair and leaned forward to speak directly. "Like you, I work for the federal government, and I wish for the destruction of our enemies and a return to peace. While we may have our concerns about the present leadership, I fully appreciate that our fates at the hands of ISIS or the Free Syrian Army will not be pleasant. Forgive me for speaking freely, but we all face a terrible choice: a difficult life with our government or a savage death at the hands of our enemies. This we can agree on, I'm sure. Through no choice of our own, you and I find ourselves in a very delicate and dangerous situation. We have reason to believe that a certain group within our government, with or without the knowledge of our president, is pursuing a program to develop and weaponize the smallpox virus. The evidence is the infection, whether by design or by accident, of Akram Aflaq, as well as the preparations Dr. Riker and I observed at the Beta Syria Pharmaceuticals laboratory. If this is in fact happening, it is an insane and inhuman plan. If smallpox were to be inflicted upon our enemies, there would be no way to control it. And think about this: What would prevent our enemies from sending it right back at us? They could load the diseased flesh of smallpox victims into mortar rounds or rocket heads and shoot it back at us! It will be like medieval armies launching the heads of their foes at each other. It would be a ghastly nightmare. Do any of us believe that the government has enough smallpox vaccine for every Syrian citizen? You can be sure that the president and his inner circle will be well vaccinated, but how about the rest of us? Who will decide who is to be saved from this horrible disease? I ask you, as a patriotic Syrian, to tell us what you know about this terribly misguided project."

Ghazal looked away. Her fingertip lightly tapped the tabletop. Riker and Amena said nothing. Then Ghazal cleared her throat and turned her eyes to them. "All right," she said. "I understand what you're saying. This is a very dangerous situation, both politically and from the standpoint of the extremely hazardous nature of the project. I share your concerns. To weaponize smallpox and to attempt to infect our enemies would be a disaster. Not only is it inhumane but it would come back at us. When you shoot your enemy with a bullet, that same bullet doesn't get fired back at you. But in the case of smallpox, your viral 'bullet' will multiply inside the body of the victim, and from that single bullet you'd have one hundred more sent right back at you. I understand that it may be tempting to use every possible weapon when our survival is at stake, but this is unforgivably stupid."

"I'm happy that we see it the same way," said Amena.

"I agree that we must proceed with infinite caution," said Ghazal. "The people behind this scheme—even, heaven forbid, our own president—will arrest us or kill us in the blink of an eye. We must not reveal ourselves. Now then, as to what I know about this project: In late October, I had given my permission for Sabeen and Akram to use this house for a few hours. There is a spare bedroom upstairs; that's all I need to say about that particular subject. As I recall, they were supposed to meet here at three o'clock in the afternoon. Akram arrived at a few minutes before three. Normally I would wait until they were both here, and then I'd leave the house for an hour or two and do errands. Sometimes I just drove to the park and walked around! All I wanted to do was give them some peace and privacy. Anyway, Sabeen was late. I don't know the reason. Akram and I sat in the kitchen for twenty minutes and chatted. At first we just talked about the weather, but soon we found ourselves talking about our jobs. We worked in different departments of the Ba'ath Party, so we knew each other, but not on a day-to-day basis. Akram was in computer network security, while I'm in communications. I don't know a thing about how computers work—I have my press releases and mailing lists, and that's as far as I get.

"Akram seemed nervous, so I asked him if anything were bothering him. He said that his boss—not his immediate boss, but the guy higher up the ladder—was Sabeen's husband, Bani Mahadi. Of course I knew Mahadi and what kind of person he was, but I didn't know he was Akram's direct superior. That made things more complicated and more dangerous for Akram.

"I asked Akram if Mahadi suspected. He said that he hoped not. This was not the answer I was looking for. I didn't want to hear that Akram 'hoped' Mahadi didn't know. I wanted more certainty. I suggested that he and Sabeen cool off for a while. Akram replied that he wished he could, but he thought he loved her. Again, this was not the answer I wanted to hear. I really wished he had said, 'Yes, you're right, we'll stop seeing each other for a while.' But you know how it is when young people are smitten with each other."

"Could Sabeen have been followed here?" asked Amena.

"Anything is possible," replied Ghazal. "While Sabeen may have been followed by her husband's spies, I never saw them on the street. The reason for their invisibility could be that they were keeping a low profile. I think I'm too high in the Ba'ath Party food chain for Mahadi to attack me directly. Having gotten rid of his wife's lover, perhaps he's satisfied."

"Okay," said Riker. "How about the smallpox project?"

"I've heard a name—Fire Sword," said Ghazal. "Of course, in the GSD cryptic names for secret projects are as common as sparrows. Everyone has their own pet project that they think will curry favor with the president. But Fire Sword is exceptionally hush-hush. Normally I wouldn't put any particular importance on it except that Akram mentioned it during our little talk. He said that Fire Sword would strike a devastating blow against our enemies.

"I said to him, 'What is it, a nuclear bomb?'

"He replied that no, he didn't think so, because it was being developed at Beta Syria Pharmaceuticals. He told me that he was going there soon—to the Beta Syria laboratory, which was being reopened and upgraded."

"Why was he going there?" asked Riker. "Some sort of computer issue?"

"Akram told me that Mahadi wanted him to go there. Yes, Akram assumed it was a computer issue."

"So Mahadi was going to bring Akram to Beta Syria?" asked Riker.

"Yes."

"Do you know when this was supposed to happen?"

"I think in early November."

"This fits with the time line," said Riker. "Medical evidence suggests that Akram Aflaq was infected with the smallpox virus during the first week of November. He then went to Damascus, then to Beirut, then to Athens. On Sunday, the fifteenth of November, he flew to New York. The next day he went to the clinic with symptoms of the infection. This would be the first time he experienced the effects of the disease. On Tuesday the twenty-fourth, the telltale pustules emerged. The disease was quickly diagnosed as smallpox. If Aflaq knew anything about Fire Sword—even just the rudimentary idea that it involved smallpox—he could have concluded that Bani Mahadi had set him up to be infected. Hence his deathbed statement that Mahadi wanted to kill him because of his affair with Sabeen."

Ghazal stood up. "It's getting late and I'm tired—I'm an early riser and I'm usually in bed by now. We can all agree that we have a big problem on our hands. If a group within the GSD is promoting the idea that we can unleash smallpox on our enemies, and if this idea has the blessing of the president, then the outcome will be more terrible than we can imagine. We will have opened a Pandora's box of horrors that will come back to afflict us with the same ferocity that it afflicts our enemies. We need to win this war without destroying Syria herself.

"The people who are promoting this scheme—like Bani Mahadi—are extremely dangerous. They will kill us if they suspect we oppose them. Therefore we must be careful. Until we have proof, we dare not reach out to an international agency like the United Nations. If any accusation were made, the project would be sent deep underground, and we'd disappear."

"Agreed," said Riker. "But we need proof. We need to stop this plan."

13.

The moon was rising over the hills of Tartus as the black Russian ZiL luxury car eased to stop in front of the imposing wrought iron gate. The driver's window powered down and a man's hand emerged to push the red call button.

"Yes?" replied a disembodied voice from the speaker attached to the call button unit.

"Sami Noman, Nizar Mansour, and Dr. Luka Radznev to see Madam Yalstin," said the driver.

"Thank you," said the voice.

From his position in the front passenger seat Dr. Radznev glanced through the windshield at the security camera staring balefully down from atop the massive masonry gatepost.

After a few seconds the gate swung open. The driver guided the big car along the gravel *allée* bordered by mature Lebanon cedars. Ahead was the majestic villa—more of a small château, really—clad in white marble and topped by Roman pediments and massive balustrades. The driver swung the car around the circle, in the middle of which stood an ancient fountain in the form of a nude pouring water from a large amphora. The car stopped under the gleaming white portico. The doors opened and the three men got out. Dr. Radznev turned and said to the driver, "We'll call you when we need you."

As the car glided away with the faint crunch of tires on gravel, the men went to the front door, over which was suspended a multifaceted bronze lantern on a chain. With a glance at the security camera positioned high overhead, Dr. Radznev rang the bell. The door was opened by a butler in a dark business suit.

"Please, gentlemen, come in," said the butler. "Madam Yaltsin is expecting you." He led them across the marble-floored entrance hall to a door, which he opened.

They entered a library, lavishly furnished with French baroque chairs and a long sofa. In the fireplace the logs—big enough to break your foot if you dropped one—burned with a robust crackle. An old-fashioned globe, supported by a polished wood stand, stood in front of one of the many bookcases crammed with leather-clad tomes.

A woman rose to greet them. She was about fifty, taller and more slender than average, with grey-blonde hair perfectly gathered at the back of her head, accenting her long smooth neck. Her blue eyes were wide-set, calm, and direct in their gaze. Her posture suggested training as a dancer; indeed, as a young woman Ilana Yaltsin had been a member of the Mariinsky Ballet, the resident classical ballet company of the Mariinsky Theatre in Saint Petersburg, Russia. Founded in the eighteenth century and originally known as the Imperial Russian Ballet, the purpose of the Mariinsky Ballet was to train young dancers to form the first Russian ballet company.

"Welcome," said Madam Yalstin. "Please make yourselves comfortable. My butler, Amir, will bring us drinks and something to eat."

A man was in the room too, and he rose from one of the ornate French chairs. In contrast to Madam Yaltsin's warm greeting, Henri Kaminsky, who was rarely seen outside of Moscow, eyed the visitors with cool detachment. His sharp grey goatee and trim moustache complemented the rather severe cut and fit of his black suit, which he wore with a thin red silk necktie and white shirt.

"I believe you know Mr. Kaminsky," said Madam Yaltsin to Noman, Mansour, and Dr. Radznev. "He is a trusted advisor of mine and he suggested that I invite you here tonight."

They shook hands.

"I don't believe I've had the pleasure of making your acquaintance," Kaminsky said to Nizar Mansour, a roundish man with rimless eyeglasses. His bald head was circled by grey curls that lightly touched his collar.

"Within the GSD, I'm the assistant director for external projects," replied Mansour smoothly. "I also own Masco, a fuel services company. We supply fuel oil to the Russian Navy vessels that use the port facility here in Tartus. I have other interests as well. But for our purposes, I'm here in an operational capacity for Project Fire Sword."

"Yes, of course," replied Kaminsky with a thin smile.

The Syrians were right to be wary of Kaminsky, whose reputation preceded him. A few years earlier Alexander Kouzminov, a retired agent for Russia's notorious *Sluzhba vneshney razvedki*—the SVR—had written a book called *Biological Espionage: Special Operations of the Soviet and Russian Foreign Intelligence Services in the West*. He supposedly worked in Department 12 within Directorate S, which carried out and directed all special operations in target countries using "illegals"—deep undercover agents. Two months after the book was published—and which Moscow had promptly branded "a pack of lies from beginning to end"—he suddenly contracted a case of MRSA, or, to give it its full name, methicillin-resistant *Staphylococcus aureus*. Most people know it as flesh-eating bacteria, a superbug that resists most antibiotics. Kouzminov was living on an island in Scotland, which ironically sealed his fate—if he had been closer to a hospital he might have survived. By the time they airlifted him to one, it was too late.

British and American intelligence sources pointed to the Kremlin's notorious hatchet man, Henri Kaminsky. He denied any knowledge, but everyone assumed he had been behind it.

The butler entered, pushing a dry bar with bottles of wine, glasses, a silver bowl of caviar on ice, a plate of toast, and small bowls of nuts and dried fruits.

"Please, help yourselves," said Madam Yaltsin. "The caviar is Beluga, from Iran. I think you will find it to be exceptional."

Once the wine had been poured and the caviar sampled—everyone agreed it was of the finest quality—Madam Yaltsin asked for their attention.

"Before we discuss Operation Fire Sword, I'd like you to know something about me, which may give you a better feeling for why I have an interest in this project. I was born in Saint Petersburg. My mother died when I was very young—I have only a few fleeting memories of her. My father, Alexander Dimitrov, sent me to the Smolny School for Girls, a venerable institution which traces its history to a decree issued by Catherine the Great in 1764. The establishment of the school was a significant step in making education available for females in Russia. I received training in dance at the Vaganova Academy of Russian Ballet, and while I never was able to attain the position of principal ballerina—I was perhaps too tall—I enjoyed a brief career onstage with the Mariinsky Ballet. It was around this time that my father, taking advantage of the disintegration of the Soviet Union and the introduction of a market economy, bought controlling interests in several Russian oil companies. He eventually sold them to Rosneft, which is Russia's biggest oil company, for a significant profit. This villa was one of several properties he subsequently acquired. We used to come here during the winter, to enjoy the mild weather. We had a yacht moored in the harbor. We'd go on cruises around the Mediterranean—to the Greek islands, Sicily, and even as far as Barcelona and Gibraltar. We once stayed at the Sunborn Hotel in Gibraltar. Such luxury! We moored the yacht at the hotel dock, enjoyed gourmet meals, toured the island—I could not believe that a little girl from snowy Saint Petersburg could experience such things.

"Ten years ago, my father visited the United States for the first time. He went to Miami, Florida for a business meeting. He was supposed to be there for three days. On the evening of the third day, his business concluded, he went out with some of his colleagues for dinner. He was walking back to his hotel when a man with a gun accosted him. Maybe the man was trying to rob my father—I don't know. The man shot my father on the sidewalk and then ran away. The police never caught him. It was devastating that something like that could happen. Imagine, being shot as you're walking along the sidewalk after dinner! I was incredibly angry—both at the criminal and at the United States. It's like a lawless frontier. My father was only sixty years of age. He left me, his only child and heir, the bulk of his very sizable estate. Suddenly, I was very rich. But all the wealth in the world could not replace him, whom I loved deeply.

"Sadly, he was not the only man in my life to pass away as the result of a cruel and savage act. When I was still a dancer I had met Sergei Yaltsin, a lieutenant in the Russian army. He was the love of my life, and for him I quit the stage and happily became a military wife—although, thanks to my father, Sergei and I could live in better circumstances than the average Russian army family."

Madam Yaltsin paused for a moment with her head lowered. A tear glistened in her eye. She took a tissue from a box and dabbed her cheek.

"Forgive me," she said. "I'll continue. Sergei and I were as happy as two people could be. Naturally, I wanted children. He promised that we'd start a family as soon as he completed his military service and could go into business. I agreed. But it was not meant to be. It was barely a year ago that an event happened we all remember too well: an American F-16 fighter plane from the Turkish Air Force shot down a Russian plane over Syria. In response to this criminal act, Russian helicopters were sent to rescue our brave pilots. Sergei was on board one of the helicopters. I was worried sick about him, but his last phone call to me was that everything was fine and they were confident the mission would be successful. He promised to call as soon as they had returned to the base.

"He never called. I never heard his voice again. A

criminal from the so-called Free Syrian Army shot at Sergei's helicopter with an American TOW missile. Sergei and the other men on the helicopter were killed. The bastards from the FSA even posted a video on YouTube! It was barbaric. Pure animal savagery.

"I am now a widow with no children, and I have no parents. I have only the wealth from my father and the cherished memories of my darling husband. I would give up every penny I own for a chance to have them back again. My heart is hard and seeks the destruction of those who made my life empty and desolate. This is why I have agreed to see you gentlemen tonight and to hear your plans."

She sat down and picked up her glass of wine.

"Thank you," said Dr. Radznev. "Speaking for my Syrian colleagues, I wish to express my deep sympathy for the hardships that you have endured. I hope that our humble plan will assuage, even slightly, some of the pain that you must feel. Now then, to get down to business. As you may know, some of the most potent weapons of war are biological weapons: viral agents that not only kill but cripple and demoralize an enemy population. We believe that smallpox is such a weapon. It has already been used to great effect against an opposing group. For example, in 1763, in North America, the native Indians had laid siege to a British outpost at Fort Pitt, in what is now Pittsburgh. Lord Amherst, the British commander, approved a plan to infect these natives by giving them blankets that had come from the smallpox ward at the fort's hospital. The plan succeeded, and the deadly disease quickly decimated the Indian population, which had never before encountered the virus and thus had no immunity."

"This is very interesting," said Madam Yaltsin, "but I thought smallpox had been eradicated from the earth."

"Not completely," replied Dr. Radznev. "Two national governments—the United States and Russia—have preserved samples of the living virus in secure facilities. The Russians have a supply of smallpox at the Russian State Research Center of Virology and Biotechnology in Novosibirsk, Siberia. It's more commonly called the Vector Institute, or just Vector. I used to work there, and I still have many contacts there. I can procure enough smallpox to cultivate and grow as much as would be needed for a biological campaign of any scale, large or small."

"Thank you," said Madam Yaltsin. "Please tell me more about the research behind the use of the virus as a weapon."

"Our research is ongoing," said Dr. Radznev. "Fortunately, we have an existing knowledge base on which to build. In the twentieth century scientists in the Soviet Union attempted to construct a scenario wherein smallpox was used as the agent in biological warfare. Since such biological weapons had never been used on a large scale, no data was available on the actual danger and expected losses encountered. However, using what was known about smallpox, it was possible to estimate the potential damage. Soviet experts concluded that the effectiveness of smallpox biological weapons would depend on certain characteristics. For example, the virus is very stable when put into an aerosol form, and has the ability to travel for many miles without the loss of virulence."

"Excuse me, doctor," said Madam Yaltsin. "What does it mean to say that the virus is in the form of an aerosol?"

"Scientists define an aerosol as a suspension of tiny particles or droplets in the air," said Dr. Radznev. "Aerosol transmission means person-to-person transmission of pathogens through the air by means of inhalation of infectious particles. Properly aerosolized particles are small enough to be inhaled into the mouth and nose, with some penetrating deeper into the trachea and lungs. Once a person has been infected, aerosols are emitted whenever the infected person coughs, sneezes, talks, or exhales. Pathogens transmitted this way can travel short or long range from the source depending on the size and shape of the particles, the initial velocity—that is, cough versus exhalation—and environmental conditions.

"There are a number of additional factors that our scientists noted in the smallpox virus.

"The smallpox virus is hardy, and in the right environment can survive for days or even for weeks.

"The infectious dose of smallpox is very low. It generally takes anywhere from just one to ten particles to cause infection. When calculating how much you need for a weapon, you could set a target of five particles per intended victim.

"The ordinary length of the incubation period is relatively short, from seven to seventeen days, and the use of smallpox in a weaponized aerosol form will likely shorten this period. The first cases can be expected to appear three or four days after infection.

"The length of time corpses remain infectious can increase the effect. While this is irrelevant under regular circumstances, the event of a massive aerosol attack with high number of casualties, corpses of smallpox fatalities will remain infectious for a long time—days to months, depending primarily on environmental temperature.

"The treatment regimen for smallpox is complex—if it even works at all-- and the duration of the disease is long, requiring efforts of a large number of medical and support personnel for each case.

"All of these characteristics led our experts to believe that there was no biological weapon comparable to smallpox, and it was included on a short list of strategic ones.

"However, times have changed and the Soviet Union no longer exists. In September 1992, Russia signed an agreement with the United States and Great Britain promising to end its bio-weapons program and to convert its facilities for benevolent scientific and medical purposes. A quantity of smallpox was put into storage at the Vector Institute."

"Aside from providing our enemies with infected

blankets," said Madam Yaltsin, "how would it be possible to introduce the virus into the enemy population?"

"A biological attack using smallpox could be conducted in several ways," said Dr. Radznev. "They include contamination of various articles and food; using an intentionally infected terrorist; using mechanical devices to generate an aerosol in the open air or an enclosed space; using explosive devices; or by using 'natural' air movements such as subways or elevator silos to generate an aerosol from dry powders or by evaporation from liquid formulations. Regardless of the release method, the number of people who are infected or are suspected of being infected will be significant. However, the actual number of casualties would be difficult to determine as it would depend on numerous factors including the actual virulence of the strain used, the concentration of the pathogen in the formulation, meteorological conditions, terrain characteristics, the number of people outside versus inside buildings, and so forth.

"Depending on the size of the aerosol attack, the number of casualties would initially vary from a relatively small number to many thousands. As the epidemic progressed, environmental factors would direct its course. Let's not forget that a smallpox biological weapons attack would also be an effective instrument of *terror* that would have ramifications far beyond the actual human casualties. Use of a smallpox biological weapon would result in the disruption of commercial, business, and social activity for a relatively long period of time. It would also create a shortage of medical and auxiliary personnel for trying to stop the epidemic and reduce its consequences; and it would cause panic leading to the disruption of normal life activities and frequent incidents of violence, especially amongst those desiring to be vaccinated against the disease. A bioterrorist attack using smallpox formulations in any form will result in tremendous cost in terms of loss of life and psychological and economic damage to the country in which the attack occurs."

"Thank you," said Madam Yaltsin. "You've made a good case for Operation Fire Sword. Smallpox would indeed be a powerful and terrifying weapon when used against our enemies. Mr. Kaminsky tells me that you need two million dollars to purchase a sufficient quantity of the smallpox virus from your contact within Vector. Is that correct?"

"Yes, that's right," replied Dr. Radznev.

"And I presume you will need additional funds for operating expenses. You have secured the old Beta Syria Pharmaceutical facility in Latakia?"

"Yes," said Nizar Mansour. "Sami Noman is in charge of its daily operations and security."

"And what will be your first target?" she asked.

"That will be determined based on the evolving military situation," said Mansour. "Currently, the heart of the ISIS rebellion is in Raqqa. We may also target the Kurds and insurgents in Aleppo."

Madam Yaltsin rose from her chair and, carrying her wine glass, walked over to the old-fashioned globe. Placing her fingertips on it, she gave it a slow spin. Then she stopped it.

The men sat quietly, watching her.

She turned to them. "Gentlemen, I will provide the funds you need for Operation Fire Sword. But your vision is too narrow. If you want to tinker with ISIS or the Islamic Front or any of the others, be my guest. Do what you think you need to do. But if you want my support and my money, you need to think big. We need to attack our real enemy, the one that has been a thorn in our side for decades, and has been the true source of our national shame and humiliation.

"The primary target of Operation Fire Sword must be the United States of America."

14.

"Are you sure Zafar will meet with us?" said Sami Noman. Over the dark harbor of Latakia the moon was gleaming silver high in the cloudless sky.

"Trust me," replied Nizar Mansour. He gave the younger man a reproaching glance. Noman was so headstrong, so determined, so tough—and yet so full of foolishness. He was like a big playful lion cub who could rip off your face with a swipe of his paw.

They waited by the battered concrete pier. Ever since the insurgency had begun, the ship traffic in Syria's biggest harbor had steadily dwindled. Five years earlier they could not have stood at this place at midnight because the burly longshoremen would have yelled at them to get out of the way. The powerful cranes would have been busy lifting palettes of cargo—food, clothing, electronics, luxury goods—from the oceangoing freighters that gradually rose higher in the water as their holds were emptied. The pier would have been crowded with forklifts and trucks, and the big steel shipping containers would have been stacked high like children's building blocks. Now only a few ships a week docked here, and an increasing number of them were Russian. To Noman and Mansour, it seemed as though Russia was Syria's only remaining friend, ready to stand behind the government in its fight against the rebels who had claimed much of the country to the east, away from the coast.

This feeling had been confirmed by the promise by Madam Yaltsin, made at the secret meeting at her villa a few hours earlier, to fund Operation Fire Sword. But with her pledge of cash support came a breathtaking condition: Regardless of the Middle Eastern opponents chosen for a smallpox attack, the United States must be the primary target.

It was a daunting but tantalizing proposition. To

spread smallpox in America! What greater wave of terror could there be? And with an ocean separating North America from the Middle East, the task of keeping the disease out of Syria—which they knew would be a big problem should the virus be unleashed against their local enemies—took on a better perspective.

Mansour's phone buzzed. He looked at it. "A text from Zafar," he said. "He's waiting for us."

The two men turned away from the glittering Mediterranean and walked two blocks along Gamal Abdel Nasser Street before talking a left into Al Mutanabbi Street. The buildings—apartments, shops, offices—were lit less brightly than they used to be. Here in Latakia, life managed to continue but on a vastly reduced level, as residents tried to pretend that the war would soon be over and their president would continue his reign in peace. The shops were open only if they had electricity, the shelves were often empty, and the restaurants served only boring local foods— nothing imported.

They came to an alley and turned into it. Among the other doorways, they went to one that was painted green. It had no number, but a bell. Mansour pulled the handle. From within they heard the sound of footsteps and the door opened. A young man with hard eyes peered at them.

"We're here to see Zafar," said Mansour. "I just received his text."

"Okay," said the young man. When he stepped back Mansour saw that on his hip was a pistol in a holster. Mansour and Noman entered a small vestibule. The man closed the door and then led them up a flight of stairs. They came to a landing. The man knocked and opened the door.

Mansour and Noman found themselves in a parlor comfortably furnished with two sofas, antique chairs, low tables in the Arab style, and more than one *narghile*. The air smelled of tobacco and spices. On the wall were ornately framed portraits of President

Bashar al-Assad and his father Hafez al-Assad.

The portraits were more than mere decoration—they spoke of a personal relationship. It was said that Zafar had become close to Bashar al-Assad when the future president of Syria was a cadet at the Homs Military Academy. Bashar, a practicing ophthalmologist, had been sent there by his father to be groomed as his successor after the sudden death of Bashar's brother Bassel in a car accident. Like the Assads, Zafar was an Alawite. He had been a spiritual leader at the academy, not unlike a base chaplain in the military. The Zafar and Bashar al-Assad had become close, but when Bashar al-Assad became president by an unopposed referendum in 2000, Zafar chose to maintain what he called a "life of asceticism." Despite this professed attitude of spirituality, many Ba'ath Party members assumed Zafar held a position of high authority within the feared GSD, and he had the power to approve the most secret and clandestine operations.

The young man with the pistol bade Mansour and Noman sit down before he disappeared behind another door. After a few minutes the door opened and another man entered. He was dressed like a cleric and wore a grey beard. From behind wire-rimmed glasses his sharp black eyes glittered. Extending his hands he greeted Mansour and Noman as they rose. "Sit down, sit down," he said warmly. "Please have some coffee."

A woman wearing a black *abaya* but no veil entered with a pot and several cups on a silver tray, which she placed on the table.

"Kalila will serve you," said Zafar in his fatherly voice. "Milk? Sugar?"

A few minutes later, having quietly and efficiently taken care of the coffee service, Kalila withdrew.

"Before we begin," said Zafar, "We have a matter to discuss. It seems as though our comrade Akram Aflaq has vanished. He was last seen about three weeks ago. His own mother doesn't know where he is. She appears to be genuinely distraught—after all, her son was her sole means of support. Do either of you know anything about this?"

Mansour and Noman shook their heads.

"Is it possible that he has defected to one of our many enemies? The Americans? The French? The Israelis?"

"Absolutely not," replied Mansour. "Akram is very loyal. He would never betray us. Perhaps he has been killed by the Americans and his body disposed of somewhere."

Zafar's scholarly eyebrows tightened in a frown. "That seems an unlikely event, even for the CIA," he said. "They would try to recruit him and use his knowledge to work their way up the ladder. Unlike the three of us, who hold more senior positions, Akram is a low-level employee of the General Security Directorate. He's on the edges of our project. He knows very little about our operations." After a moment his face relaxed. "We can only hope that over time the answer will come to us. Now then, let's discuss the matter at hand: Project Fire Sword. Have you made a connection with the Russians?"

Mansour nodded. "Our contact within the *Sluzhba vneshney razvedki* has introduced us to Dr. Luka Radznev, a Russian virologist who worked at the State Research Center of Virology and Biotechnology in Novosibirsk. He is acting as our liaison with the center, which they call the Vector Institute, or just Vector. He is getting us what we need."

"And the cost?" asked Zafar.

"Our friend at the SVR—who is highly placed within Directorate S—has arranged for a wealthy Russian named Ilana Yalstin to underwrite the operation," said Noman.

"This friend is Henri Kaminsky?" asked Zafar.

Mansour nodded. "We met him earlier this evening at the villa of Madam Yaltsin."

As he sipped his coffee, Mansour pondered the nature of their new benefactor, Kaminsky. Getting into bed with the SVR was like getting into bed with a thousand-pound bear. While the bear could keep you warm, it could also eat you. It was well known that the SVR was expert at eliminating its enemies by devious and painful means. He thought of Igor the Assassin, the legendary SVR and former KGB officer who allegedly killed defector Alexander Litvinenko with radioactive polonium. Supposedly the official suspect of the murder, Andrei Lugovoi, had only distracted the attention of Litvinenko while Igor the Assassin—whose name has never been uncovered—placed the polonium into the cup of tea served to Litvinenko. A few hours later, Igor the Assassin was seen at an airport in London, boarding a plane bound for Moscow.

But these were desperate times, and with Syria under vicious attack on many fronts, the nation needed a spectacular countermeasure—something that would set the West back on its heels and prove to the world that nobody could intimidate the GSD.

"We are very gratified that Madam Yaltsin has agreed to fully fund Operation Fire Sword," said Mansour. "She has made one condition: that the primary target is the United States."

Zafar gave a thin smile. "I can understand why. Her family has suffered greatly at the hands of the United States. And frankly, I agree with her. The Americans sit over there, across the ocean, smug and complacent. For decades they have been meddling in the affairs of sovereign nations, fomenting 'regime change' (as they term it), and acting like we are nothing but camel-riding puppets with our strings held by Washington. Others have tried big terror events—the takedown of the World Trade Centers was a praiseworthy victory—but when you destroy a building, the Americans just build another one. A disease can keep attacking your enemy over and over again. Smallpox is particularly hideous, and it can sap the resources of even the wealthiest society. Therefore, while my reasons are not as personal as hers, I fully support Madam Yaltsin's assessment."

Mansour swallowed hard. What had begun as a

nasty trick to play on the Kurds and the Free Syrian Army was rapidly mushrooming into a major clandestine attack on the world's wealthiest and most powerful nation. Zafar's commitment would transform the idea of an assault on America from a passing fantasy to stark reality.

"Thank you," said Mansour. "We are of one mind."

"Very well," said Zafar. "The pieces of the project are coming together. Now then, please tell me your conception of its execution."

Placing his cup on the silver tray, Noman explained that the smallpox virus had several attributes that made it appropriate for a biological attack. The virus could be grown in tissue culture, was very stable at room temperature, and could be spread by contact. It could stay infectious for years in scabs that fell off infected people. It could be spread by aerosols. Because of the hideous physical appearance of the masses of red pustules on the face and hands of victims, outbreaks of smallpox produced widespread fear. While prophylactic vaccination was effective, in the United States compulsory vaccination before entering elementary school was abandoned in 1976; hence almost everyone except senior citizens has never had a smallpox vaccination and they're thus susceptible. And even in those older ones, immunity has probably declined to almost nothing. The mortality rate of infected, unvaccinated people was between thirty and seventy percent, depending on strain of the virus.

"Are you in possession of samples of the virus now?" asked Zafar.

"We are not, but a colleague within the GSD has obtained a small sample from the Russians," replied Mansour.

"Who is this colleague?" asked Zafar.

"Bani Mahadi," replied Mansour. "He's a highly placed Ba'ath party official who works for the GSD. He demanded a sample in return for his blessing of the project."

Zafar's eyes flashed. With barely restrained anger he said, "From now on, no Damascus politicians and no party cronies are to be involved! Gentlemen, we need absolute discipline! We're working with dangerous materials. This virus is not something to show off at a cocktail party. If any more Damascus blowhards try to pressure you, tell me about them. I have my own set of contacts at Mount Mezzeh and I'll have the right people set them straight. Our president would not want this operation to fail because of the stupidity of low-level functionaries."

At the mention of the president, Mansour swallowed hard again. This really was serious.

Zafar settled back in his chair and sipped his coffee. Putting down the cup he reached over to a nearby *narghile* and, after packing a bit of tobacco into the bowl at the top, he picked up the mouthpiece at the end of its long woven tube. After lighting the tobacco, he puffed on the mouthpiece. Smoke gurgled softly in the water-filled glass bowl of the pipe. "Gentlemen, feel free," he said with a wave at two other slender *narghiles*. From his pocket Mansour took out a mouthpiece and some tobacco while Noman continued with the presentation.

While Zafar and Mansour puffed, Noman explained that in their preliminary calculations—hurriedly prepared just after their meeting with Kaminsky and Madam Yaltsin—spreading the disease quickly in the United States required populations who would carry the disease and yet be at a distance from the health service providers who could quell it. The first tranche of targets could be groups of vulnerable individuals at what Noman called "fault lines" in American society. By this he meant groups that fulfilled three criteria:

One, where the main middle-class / upper-class white "conventional" majority was not well represented.

Two, where there was significant societal and police prejudice and hostility against the members.

Three, where within these communities many members "laid low" and kept a low profile to the "outside world of the mainstream," yet they had many interactions, languages and jargon, and behaviors with other members of their distinct group.

Hence, while any infected person would have multiple friends and family contacts to whom they could spread the disease, they would resist or hide from government workers trying to trace contacts of infected people.

Noman had concluded there were three such population groups he would recommend for targets of dissemination:

One—Hispanics who had illegally immigrated from Mexico and Central America and who had settled into what Noman called quasi-"barrios," particularly in Texas and Los Angeles.

Two—African-American slums in New York City, Philadelphia, Baltimore, and Chicago.

Three—Gay men, via bars and nightclubs in New York City, Washington, D.C. and San Francisco.

The American Centers for Disease Control and Prevention had recently estimated that the number of gay men who ought to be taking the prophylactic antiviral drug Truvada was one in four. But despite publicity to doctors and the gay community, few actually were. This indicated that they were at risk for HIV infection, or indeed might already have a silent one. This would further decrease any slim resistance they might have had to smallpox.

Mansour added that for all three of the target groups, additional spreading might be possible through sexual transmission. Ebola and Zika viruses have been found in the semen of infected patients. And two case reports had shown the *vaccinia* virus used for inoculation had been transmitted to sex partners, so probably its dangerous cousin, smallpox's *variola* virus, could also be spread that additional way.

Zafar closed his eyes for a moment and appeared to be lost in thought. Then he looked at Noman. "Has smallpox been studied in AIDS patients?" he asked.

Noman shook his head. "While the disease itself has not been studied in men with HIV or actual AIDS, there are reports that even the mild *vaccinia* virus used for vaccination can quickly sicken men who have HIV because their immune systems are significantly suppressed. No doubt the effects of the full-strength *variola* virus would be much worse. But since most AIDS cases have occurred after smallpox had been eradicated, there's no data. There have been a couple of case reports of the deleterious effects of the vaccination in HIV cases."

"Gentlemen," said Zafar, "While I'm impressed by your deep knowledge of the subject, and I have every confidence in your capabilities, the primary question in my mind is this: How do we get the virus into the United States and properly dispersed? Despite its many failings, the United States has an effective counter-terrorism capability. Anyone from Syria will have extreme difficulty in carrying out such an operation. The Americans have evolved since the attacks on the World Trade Centers. Today, such a plan would be impossible to carry out. The Americans are too vigilant." He paused for a moment to puff on his *narghile*. "It goes without saying that the most likely way to get the virus into the United States would be in the living host body of a volunteer. Someone willing to martyr themselves for the cause of Syrian freedom."

"With all due respect," said Mansour, "While it's one thing to ask someone to die instantly as a suicide bomber, it's another thing to ask a volunteer to die a slow and horrible death from a painful disease, or to be permanently disfigured."

"And we need to spread the virus quickly, over a large population," added Noman. "Even several volunteer martyrs would be quickly isolated and neutralized by American health authorities."

"Quite right," nodded Zafar. "What we need is a way to get a sufficient quantity of the virus into the

United States and then quickly and widely dispersed. This cannot happen without someone on the 'inside,' so to speak. An American who is willing to help us. Someone who shares our belief that the United States is out of control and needs to be brought to its knees."

"I may know of such a person," said Mansour.

"Who?" asked Zafar.

"There is an American doctor in Latakia who was picked up by the GSD a few days ago, and then suddenly released," said Mansour. "I have heard that the reason he was released was because he is working undercover on behalf of the government to identify if our enemies are developing biological weapons to use against the Syrian people. If he's sympathetic to our cause, he may be willing to help us."

Zafar puffed thoughtfully. "This is extremely risky," he said at length. "If we're wrong about him, our entire operation will be in jeopardy."

"We need to feel him out very carefully," said Mansour.

"And if we suspect he's not sympathetic, we'll kill him quickly," added Noman.

"Yes—kill him quickly," agreed Zafar. "Thank you, gentlemen. We have much to think about. Please give me some time to consider the plan. We cannot afford to fail, and every detail of this complex operation must be perfect. I'll get in touch with you within a few days. Have a good evening. My man will escort you out."

With those words, after setting aside his *narghile* mouthpiece Zafar rose and vanished through the same door through which he had entered.

15.

On Tuesday morning, Riker went to breakfast at Al Teras, on the hotel balcony. The sky was overcast and traffic on the Al Maghreb Al Arabi was desultory. The coffee shop was nearly deserted, with only a pair of businessmen—Russians, probably—seated some distance away at another table.

As he was sitting and sipping his coffee, a man approached him. The man was plumpish and smooth-skinned, wore rimless eyeglasses, and his head was bald save for the delicate grey curls that draped onto his collar. He looked like a college professor, except that his eyes were notably cold.

"Excuse me—Dr. Riker?" the man said.

Riker looked up from his newspaper. "Yes—that's me."

The man smiled. "Please forgive me for the intrusion. My name is Nizar Mansour. I'm a local businessman—I own a company in Tartus called Masco. We do transshipping of petroleum products. I also have interests here in Latakia. May I have a moment of your time?"

"Yes, of course," replied Riker as he folded his paper. "Please sit down. Would you like some coffee?"

"Thank you, but no. It irritates my stomach. Allow me to explain why I've come to you. Through some friends in the government, I understand that you have an interest in the safety and well being of the people of Syria. For that, all Syrians are very grateful."

What the hell? thought Riker. Then he remembered what Amena had told him about how she had gotten him released—by asserting that Riker was in fact sympathetic to the Syrian regime and was researching the possible use of biological weapons by Syria's many local enemies.

"You seem to know something about me," replied

Riker blandly. "I'm afraid you have the advantage."

Mansour shrugged. "I'm sure you appreciate the climate in which we're living. The stakes are very high. We're surrounded on all sides by enemies who would destroy us. The survival of the nation of Syria is on the line. Under such conditions, when it seems as though a friend has appeared among us, it's an event that deserves a response. But I haven't come here out of blind faith. I must confess that I've done a bit of snooping on the internet. You've written some very positive articles." He took out his phone and scrolled through some files. "Ah—here's one. The title is, 'In a region of chaos, Bashar al-Assad is Syria's best hope.' You argue very forcefully that the United States must stop its policy of regime change, accept the democratically elected government of Syria, and work with the government to restore health and human services to the embattled people of Syria."

"Yes, that is what I believe," replied Riker.

"That must make you unpopular at home," smiled Mansour.

"Sometimes you have to stand up for what you believe. And—despite its many faults—in America you can say what you like and they can't arrest you."

"Of course," said Mansour, with his mouth showing a faint curl of a smile.

"Do you represent the government of President al-Assad?" asked Riker boldly.

"In Syria today, you have two choices: loyalty to the government or alliance with the terrorists. There is nothing in the middle. There is no path of nonalignment. Here, within the borders of Syria, such as they are, there is life and hope. Outside of our borders, where our enemies are massing, there is only death. Dr. Riker, I'd like to talk to you in greater depth about the situation here in Syria. But not here. This hotel is too public. I'd like to show you a place where you can get a fuller understanding of the Syrian culture and where we can talk more freely."

Riker's blood went cold. This strange man had

presented himself to Riker, had known who he was, and was now suggesting they go somewhere even more off the beaten path than a half-deserted hotel in downtown Latakia.

What could the man possibly want?

Riker considered that this was simply a ruse to get him to a place where the *mukhabarat* could arrest him again and throw him back in jail. But the GSD was all-powerful. If they wanted him, they'd just send a goon squad to the balcony and haul his ass away. There would be no niceties because none were necessary, and in fact it was a good thing for ordinary Syrians to once in a while see a foreigner dragged off to prison.

No, this wasn't a ploy to get Riker into custody. The GSD didn't have to play footsie with its enemies. And perhaps—just perhaps—Angela Powell's idea to seed the internet with phony articles signed by Martin Riker was becoming the key to his survival.

"Where do you want to go?" asked Riker.

"I want to show you the National Museum of Latakia. It's not far from here, on Sharia Jamal Abdel Nasser and Al Quds Street."

"I know where it is. It's a bit too far to walk. Do you want to meet me there?"

"If that makes you comfortable, that would be fine," replied Mansour. "The museum opens in half an hour. It will give you time to finish your breakfast and freshen up."

With those words Mansour rose, gave Riker a smile and a nod, and walked off the balcony and into the hotel.

Riker sat for a moment. "Well, I'll be damned," he said to himself. "I've fallen down the rabbit hole."

His first impulse was to contact Amena. He reached for his phone and then stopped.

No, they might be watching me. Better to wait until I learn more.

At the appointed time of ten o'clock, Riker, having parked his rented Toyota on Al Quds Street, went to the entrance of the museum, a handsome two-story rectilinear structure built in the Moorish Mediterranean style. The street level was constructed of big stone blocks pierced by five burly Romanesque arches; each arch sheltered a classical statue or a sculptural fragment on a pedestal. The second level featured delicately formed Italianate arches supported by thin columns; behind these, tall louvered doors punctuated the walls of the shaded walkway.

After paying the admission fee to the old lady who was manning the front desk, Riker entered the dim foyer. Mansour was waiting for him. There were no other people in sight. The coat rack held only a few lonely wire hangers.

"Thank you for coming," said Mansour. "This museum, while rather modest, is a gem that celebrates Syrian history and culture. It formerly housed the residence of the governor of the Alawite state, and before that it was a sixteenth-century Ottoman *khan* or *caravansary*. This means that it was a public inn with a spacious courtyard, inside which trade caravans could remain overnight. The khan historically served not only as an inn, but also contained private residences. This particular building was known as Khan al-Dukhan, meaning "The Khan of Smoke," as it served the tobacco trade. As you'll see, the exhibits include inscribed tablets from Ugarit—an ancient port city, the ruins of which are located very near here at what is now called Ras Shamra—jewelry, ceramics, pottery, coins, figurines, and early Arab and Crusader-era chain-mail suits and swords."

They paused next to a case containing a nearly life-sized, beautifully carved bust of a young man wearing a conical headpiece. Riker looked at the yellowed typewritten label.

Ivory head of a Prince. Royal Palace at Ugarit, Ras-Shamra. Phoenician, 13th century.

"It's exquisite," said Riker. "While the face is idealized, it clearly suggests the force of personality. The faint smile, the steady gaze, the slightly jutting chin—here's a young fellow who's got a bit of an attitude, wouldn't you say?"

"Yes," said Mansour. "You can feel the humanity, even after eight centuries."

They moved on. The museum was devoid of visitors and the footsteps of Riker and Mansour echoed in the hollow galleries.

"I understand," said Mansour as they stood in front of an ancient bronze statuette of Ba'al, a pre-Christian deity of the Canaanites, "that you have an interest in, and knowledge of, biological warfare."

"Yes, I do," replied Riker. *Now the game's afoot!*

"I also understand that you are engaged in ascertaining the degree to which the enemies of Syria have used, or may use, such weapons against the Syrian people."

To give his strange interlocutor what he wanted, Riker quickly searched his mind. Over the past several years he had seen many reports....

"There have been some disturbing indications," he said. "A *Strategic Defence and Security Review* published by the British government reported that ISIS terrorists are trying to buy chemical and biological weapons to inflict a new wave of terror on the world. They also want to get hold of 'dirty bombs' that spread radioactive waste.

"In France, Prime Minister Manuel Valls has said that his nation could face the risk of chemical or bacterial warfare in its fight against Islamist militants.

"In the United States, the Pentagon has said that ISIS likely used mustard gas against Kurdish fighters in Iraq. It's unclear if the gas was leftover from Saddam Hussein stockpiles or if they were somehow obtained from Syria.

"Terrorist groups in the Middle East have used crude weapons including chlorine, rat poison, and cyanide.

"Perhaps most alarmingly, ISIS and others may also be thinking of using Ebola as a low-tech weapon of bio-terror. Such groups could simply use human carriers to intentionally infect themselves in West

Africa, and then disseminate the deadly virus via the world's air transportation system. The individual 'viral suicide bomber' exposed to the Ebola virus would be the carrier. The idea is then once they had intentionally infected themselves, they would try to interact with as many people in their target city or country of choice. The operational challenge is that if ISIS or another terrorist actor were to use human Ebola carriers, the possibility of identifying those infected as they enter and leave the country would be very high. And in a country like the United States, the virus wouldn't spread exponentially simply because the nation's advanced health care systems would be equipped to identify, isolate, and stop the virus."

"Yes," nodded Mansour. "The idea of using a human carrier—a 'viral suicide bomber,' as you say— would seem to be an inefficient and cumbersome strategy."

They paused before another exhibit in a glass case—a stone bas-relief showing an Assyrian king fighting with lion. Judging from the solid stance of the king, the lion was destined to be the loser in the contest.

"Dr. Riker," said Mansour, "Based on what I have read on the internet and what we have discussed today, would it be accurate to say that you support the government of Syria and the presidency of Bashar al-Assad?"

Now I have to lie, thought Riker. *A really big lie. Let's see where it goes.*

"Absolutely," said Riker.

"But is it not the case that the American government opposes our government? That your president has called for our president to resign? That you want regime change in our country?"

Riker turned to Mansour and looked him in the eye. The words came like an actor reading from a script. "For too long the United States has acted as an imperial power. Ever since 1953, when the Americans meddled in Iran and, in cahoots with the British, engineered the overthrow of democratically elected Prime Minister Mohammad Mosaddegh in favor of Shah Mohammad Reza Pahlavi, Washington has fomented instability and oppression in the Middle East. It sickens me. That's why I came here. I could not stand by any longer while the United States and its allies once again tried to impose their will on the sovereign nations of the Middle East, and in particular Syria."

"I'm pleased to hear you say that," said Mansour slowly. "But what can we do? Compared to the United States, Syria is a small country. We have few friends in the United Nations. We cannot exert economic pressure against the United States—even in peacetime, our national economy is no bigger than your state of New Hampshire. We have no military capability to strike back across three thousand miles of ocean. Aside from our friendship with Russia, it seems as though we are destined, as you say in America, to get sand kicked in our face, over and over again."

The thought flickered through Riker's mind that Mansour wanted Riker himself to offer something—a course of action against the United States. He decided to probe a little deeper.

"You seem to be suggesting," he said to Mansour, "that Syria embark upon some sort of action against not only your local enemies—the various terror groups who seek to enslave the Syrian people—but against the United States as well. Is this what the government wants?"

Mansour put his hand on the top of the glass case, as if to feel its polished hardness. He appeared to be lost in thought. Then he turned to Riker. "What we are hoping for is a way to send a message to the politicians in Washington. The message would be, 'Leave us alone—or suffer the consequences.' It needs to be a powerful message. It needs to be long lasting, not just something like a bomb whose debris you can clean up in a few days, or a plane crash that kills a handful of people. We're looking for an agent that will work its way into the population and cause significant disruption."

"It sounds to me," replied Riker, "that you're looking for a biological weapon."

"What do you think?" said Mansour. "What better way could there be for a small nation like Syria to gain leverage? We cannot fight America with conventional weapons. We need to think outside the box, as you Americans say. We need to choose our battlefield." Mansour paused, still with his hand on the glass case. He pointed to the bas-relief of the king and the lion. "Two thousand years ago, this was reality. We were the proud and the mighty. But kingdoms rise and fall. Today the United States is on top. It won't last forever. History comes around in a circle. All we seek is to be the agent of history, in our own small way."

He wants me to suggest a smallpox attack, thought Riker. *Okay, I will.*

"I must make a confession to you," said Riker. "It's not by accident that I came here, to Latakia. A few days ago a man appeared in New York. He was infected with smallpox. He died. His name was Akram Aflaq, and he was a resident of Latakia."

Riker searched Mansour's face for a response. The Syrian's expression did not change.

"Public health officials in the United States dismissed this event as a fluke," continued Riker. "I, however, saw it as a sign. I saw it as the first tiny wavelet of a tsunami. I concluded that Akram Aflaq had contracted smallpox because either the government or one of the terrorist groups is trying to develop smallpox as a weapon. For some reason, after he was infected Aflaq came to the United States— either as a test case or for some other reason. When he left Syria he wasn't showing any symptoms. He may not have known that he had the disease. I don't know. But I decided that this tantalizing scrap of evidence needed to be investigated. If a terror group was developing the program, it had to be ruthlessly crushed. But if the legitimate government of Syria was developing the program, I would be willing to provide my support."

There, thought Riker. *I've said it. May God have mercy on me!*

Mansour did not reply.

"Mr. Mansour," said Riker, "Which is it? A terrorist group or the government?"

Mansour tapped the glass case with his fingertip. Tap, tap, tap.

"This afternoon," he said, "I would like you to meet some people. Okay?"

"All right," replied Riker. "Where and when?"

"Go back to your hotel. Wait there. I'll call you."

With those words Mansour turned and walked out of the gallery. Riker heard the echo of his footsteps grow increasingly faint until there was nothing but silence.

16.

An hour later, Nizar Mansour pulled the bell next to the green door in the alley off Al Mutanabbi Street. The man with the sidearm ushered him upstairs. Bani Mahadi and Sami Noman were already waiting. Kalila served them coffee and sweets.

Presently Zafar entered and sat down in the upholstered chair that was always reserved for him.

"You have some news for us," said Zafar to Mansour.

Mansour recounted the story of his meeting with Martin Riker. When he had finished, the group waited for Zafar to make a comment. Rather than making a statement, he asked, "Well, gentlemen, what do *you* think?"

"I think it's madness to trust this man Riker," said Mahadi. "What do we really know about him? He shows up in our city, snoops around, and gets himself arrested. Then an official from the Ministry of Health—of all places!—tells us that Riker is working on our behalf. He's set free. We go online and find some articles that he's written in which he expresses support for our president. Now, today, he says that he wants to help with Operation Fire Sword."

"I never used the name," corrected Mansour.

"Okay, okay," nodded Mahadi. "But nevertheless, we know next to nothing about him. His appearance in Latakia could very well be part of an American plot to infiltrate our most sensitive operations. What better cover could there be than to pretend to be a disaffected American who is ready to turn against his own country? Are we so desperate that we will grasp at any straw?"

"Thank you, Bani," said Zafar. "I hear what you're saying."

"I disagree with our colleague," said Noman, nodding towards Mahadi. "I've read what Riker has written and I've considered all the alternatives. As we recall, when we left this room yesterday we agreed that if he made a false move, we'd simply kill him. This can be done without warning at any stage in his involvement. We have very little to lose by seeing what he can do for us."

"But we do have much to lose!" said Mahadi. "He could pass information to the CIA as soon as he gets it. If we show him something, an hour later the knowledge could be on someone's desk in Washington. I think it was foolish for our colleague Nizar to tell this man Riker as much as he did, or even to meet with him."

As Mahadi spoke, Zafar began to pack tobacco into the little bowl of the *narghile* next to his chair. Having done this, he took a mouthpiece from his pocket. After sliding the mouthpiece onto the tube of the *narghile*, he lit the tobacco. As he smoked, the water gurgled like a baby.

"My friend Bani," said Mansour with a shark smile, "I'm not sure that you're the one who should be making these judgments. We have already had one extremely serious breach of security, and it was not by me. Dr. Riker told me that he was in New York when Akram Aflaq arrived there. A few days later Akram was *dead*. According to Dr. Riker, he died of *smallpox*. It is the death of Akram that led Dr. Riker to us. He said that—thankfully—doctors in New York have dismissed Akram's disease as a fluke occurrence. No action has been taken to track down the source and no general alarm raised. In that regard we are extremely lucky. But the fact remains that Akram was exposed to the smallpox virus. It had to have happened at Beta Syria. He was sent into the containment room. And then, for some reason, he went to America. It's quite a mystery, isn't it, Bani?"

Mahadi threw up his hands. "I don't know what you're getting at, but you're on the wrong track."

Putting his hands down, he then pointed at Mansour. "Be careful. Don't make wild accusations that you cannot substantiate."

"You asked the Russians for a sample of the virus, didn't you?" pressed Mansour. "Why? And what made Akram suddenly put three thousand miles between himself and Latakia? It was no secret spy mission—at least not one that anyone in the GSD knew about or approved."

"Gentlemen," interrupted Zafar. "Let's not point fingers. We're all on the same page. What's done is done. All that matters is that we move ahead with one purpose and one spirit. Now then—it's my judgment that we should proceed with the recruitment of Dr. Riker. We will remain vigilant. Get as much information out of him as we can. Then we can terminate him. Fair enough? Once he becomes a liability, we'll remove him. Agreed?"

"Yes," said each of the three men.

"Nizar, you may contact Riker as soon as this meeting is over," said Zafar. "Now then, as to the operational questions that we discussed at our previous meeting. I want to thank Nizar and Sami for sharing your ideas. But in your presentation you described a possible *target population*, not the *delivery system*. What we need to determine is how we can disperse the virus to as large a *number* of people as possible. And, to be honest, it's a matter of not just the *quantity* of the victims but their *quality*. Rather than focusing on those who are marginal, we want to infect as many *important* people as possible—leaders in government, business, healthcare, and finance."

"On this subject we've done some thinking and completed some research," said Noman. "We have a variety of proposals."

"Please—go ahead," said Zafar.

"We're looking for a way to spread the virus widely and quickly," said Noman. "Initially, we considered using the nation's package delivery system—UPS and FedEx. Each has a major hub, a nightly exchange port.

The one used by FedEx is their World Hub in Memphis, Tennessee. This huge facility can process over two million packages every night. For UPS, it's Worldport in Louisville, Kentucky, which can process nearly half a million packages every hour. Each weekday night, within the space of just six hours, millions of packages from all over the United States pass through these centers to be sorted and then flown out to final recipients in all major American cities. We believe that an aerosol spray device mounted over a conveyor line could contaminate many packages, which would then be handled by loaders, drivers, and finally recipients. However, we've noted that relatively few of these boxes go to businesses; most go to homes. Would they be touched enough during opening to spread the relatively few virus particles on the one side of each package? This is a question.

"We have also considered Amazon, which reportedly ships three million packages a day. Our research revealed that they are sent out from nearly fifty different distribution centers in the United States, so there is not one single building where a sprayer could be located to contaminate all packages shipped in a single night.

"The idea of using a package delivery service brings up an additional question—the matter of the *quality* of the victims, as you, Zafar, mentioned a moment ago. Targeting Amazon, UPS, or FedEx would actually *miss* the most powerful people, because they don't open their own packages. They have other people who do this for them."

"True enough," said Zafar. "Deliveries to government offices are closely screened. I assume it's the same for wealthy Wall Street people. They are keenly aware of dangerous packages, and take steps to protect themselves from them. We would also have the problem of attaching some sort of device that would spray an infected solution onto the packages as they went past it on the conveyor belt. Such a device would be noticed instantly by the workers at the facility. I don't see how this approach could work." He puffed on his *narghile*. "What's next?"

"We are considering a sporting event. For example, a typical American professional football game is attended by over sixty thousand spectators. The biggest venue is the Los Angeles Memorial Coliseum, which holds over ninety thousand people. It's open air, with no roof. If we could load the virus into a bomb that would disperse a toxic liquid over the stadium, we could infect many thousands at one time."

"Interesting," said Zafar. "Please continue."

"A suicide bomber might be able to get through the security screening at a stadium if the explosives and the viral agent were strapped to his body. If a martyr blew himself up and dispersed the virus into the crowd, the disease would emerge seven to ten days later."

"Anyone who was near the blast would be under intense medical supervision," said Zafar. "The disease might be detected sooner. Plus, we'd have the challenge of recruiting and training a volunteer, and then getting them into position. We don't have years to execute this plan. We need to move more quickly than that."

"Rather than trying to spray people or objects directly," said Noman, "we've also considered taking a more subtle approach. What if we could infect a common item that people handle on a daily basis? Perhaps we should consider one of the most ubiquitous things that in any society is passed from person to person—paper money. If we were to infect a few thousand dollar bills, within days these little messengers of death could spread the contagion throughout a wide population."

"How do we get the virus to stick to the paper?" asked Mahadi.

"We put the virus in the ink," replied Noman. "This could be done at the Bureau of Engraving and Printing, on 14th Street in Washington, D.C. Bundles of new bills that locally distributed to banks and other financial services companies could spread the virus. Eventually, the source of the virus would be traced to the ink used to print dollar bills, and if people refused to touch paper money it would wreak havoc on the American economy."

"I think that from the point of view of operations, this would be difficult," said Zafar. "I cannot imagine how we would be able to penetrate the security surrounding the printing plant itself and its supply of ink. The printing inks used for currency are tightly controlled and continuously inspected. In addition, there's a time lag between when a bill is printed and when it is actually handled by someone. A virus can't last forever. We can't have a virus on a piece of currency that will be sitting in a bank vault."

At that moment Kalila entered with a tray of cakes and fruit, which she passed among the men. Zafar thanked her and she withdrew.

"Okay," said Zafar. "Let's put those ideas aside for the moment. Here's another way to approach the problem. In major centers of power—for example, New York City and Washington, D.C.—many people in authority still read the daily newspaper. A newspaper is grasped in the hands of the reader, typically at breakfast, or on the subway, or in the office. Because of this close personal contact with a potential victim, a newspaper can provide a highly efficient mode of delivery of a virus. There is a historical precedent for this. In my research I have found a British Royal Commission report that was published just before the Second World War. The report describes an outbreak of smallpox in a London hospital. Investigators concluded that that an infected patient loaned his neighbor in the next bed the newspaper he had been reading. The person receiving the newspaper then became infected. The smallpox particles had attached to the pages and were picked up by the hands of the paper's recipient."

"Spread the virus by the *New York Times* and the *Washington Post!*" said Mansour.

"Yes," said Zafar. "Newspapers, while perhaps read by a greater concentration of upper-class people, reach every stratum of society. This will spread the disease to the lower classes as well, and make identifying the source more difficult. It will also ensure that the first symptoms of the disease will appear widely and suddenly, without warning, between seven and seventeen days after exposure—or the 'date of the attack,' as we will call it. By infecting thousands of newspapers on a given day, we will cause a massive outbreak of a virulent and contagious disease against which the vast majority of victims have no immunization.

"When health investigators respond, there will be no obvious causal agent. This is because newspapers are disposable. Most people get rid of their newspapers within a few days of reading them. They throw them away or recycle them. Therefore, by the time the smallpox epidemic—and it will be an epidemic—is identified, our delivery devices—the newspapers—will have vanished!"

"It's a brilliant plan," said Noman.

"But how do we get the smallpox particles on thousands of newspapers at one time?" asked Mansour.

"Ah—that is the next question we must answer," said Zahar. "Let us ponder it. For now, I instruct Nizar to arrange another meeting with Dr. Riker. Bring him into our confidence. Then watch him carefully. If he makes one false step, do not hesitate to kill him. We will dump his body in territory controlled by the terrorists. They can take the blame—or credit, if they choose—for killing an American. Gentlemen, good day."

With those words Zafar stood up and left the room.

17.

As Martin Riker walked out of the National Museum of Latakia he took out his phone and punched Amena's number. She picked up.

"Hi, it's Martin," he said. "Let's meet for lunch."

She begged off, saying that she was busy with some meetings.

Assuming her phone was tapped, he said, "No, I think we *really ought* to have lunch today."

"Okay," she replied. "The usual place. I'll be there in fifteen minutes."

Riker was already seated in a back booth at Antika when she entered and joined him.

"Things are happening?" she asked.

"Yes—big things," replied Riker. They paused while the waiter took their orders—a bowl of lentil soup for Amena and chicken kababs for Riker, plus a bottle of cheap red table wine.

When they were alone, Riker continued. He told Amena of the sudden appearance of Nizar Mansour and their meeting at the museum that morning.

"Did he specifically acknowledge the existence of the smallpox program?" she asked.

"No," replied Riker. "He wants me to meet him again. It will be sometime today. Do you know anything about him? He told me he was a businessman with a company called Masco in Tartus, and he has interests here in Latakia. He drove an expensive Mercedes. Very well dressed, too—his suit looked custom made."

"Yes, Nizar has done very well for himself," replied Amena. "I've known him off and on since we were in high school. He's made a lot of money with Masco; currently he has the contract to provide fuel oil to the Russian naval vessels that layover in Tartus. He also owns a couple of businesses here in Latkia, including the Blue Horizon hotel, which before the war was known as the place where the regional Miss Syria contest was held every year in the big ballroom there. Of course the hotel is now a ghost town, but like everyone else he's waiting for the regime to defeat the terrorists and for things to get back to normal."

"And if the regime doesn't win?"

"Then those of us who are still alive will be on a boat to Greece," she said. "As for Nizar, he also happens to be highly placed within the GSD. That's his day job, so to speak. His other interests—Masco and the hotel—are really just investments that are run by managers. It's all part of the crony capitalist system that helps keep Bashar al-Assad in power. It's a very quiet but very corrupt system. Of course every country has corruption, but in Syria it went to the next level in the year 2000, when the president presented a series of economic reforms that allowed entrepreneurs without government connections to open their own businesses. Sounds like a good idea, right? But there was a catch. If you didn't pay a bribe to the right person, the government would make life miserable for you and your business. They could tax you, force you to sell, or revoke your permission to change the sewage or electric lines. Everyone who's connected to the president has their hand out. For example, there's a guy named Rami Makhlouf, who is a cousin of the president. They say he's the richest man in Syria. His nickname is 'Mr. Ten Percent,' because he knows how to get a cut of any business deal made in Syria. He controls our nation's largest phone company, as well as much of our banking system, real estate, department stores, and more. They say he's a major financial backer of the al-Mayadeen television network, set up to rival Qatar's better-known al-Jazeera."

"I've heard of Makhlouf," said Riker. "He's been called 'Assad's bagman,' and he's been on the sanctions lists of both the United States and the European Union."

"That's the way it is around here," shrugged Amena. "Nizar is plugged into the crony system. He's financially very comfortable. And I think that within the GSD he would have the power and influence to be privy to a covert program. Perhaps he even holds a position of real authority. It's hard to say because the GSD is extremely opaque. You could say, 'Oh, so-and-so is with the GSD,' but unless you were on the inside you wouldn't know whether that person was a low-level analyst or a guy with real power."

"I assume that if the GSD wanted me dead—"

Amena snapped her fingers. "Like that. You'd be gone."

"Which means that Mansour is serious. He must really believe that I want to help."

"Yes. Right now, he's probably reporting to his bosses. The decision will be made whether to bring you into their confidence. Just remember—they will kill you the moment it becomes better for them that you aren't around."

"Like the male black widow spider—after he mates with the female, he's got about one second to get his ass off her web. Otherwise he's dead."

"Exactly."

Riker's phone rang. He answered it. "Okay," he said. Then he hung up.

"Speaking of black widow spiders, that was Mansour," he said. "In half an hour a car is coming to the hotel to pick me up."

Amena raised her glass. "Good luck, my friend."

At the appointed time Riker, who was sitting in the lobby of the Shahbandar, saw a black Russian ZiL luxury car pull under the portico that shaded the entrance. He got up and, under the watchful eye of Shakira, who was manning the front desk, went out through the revolving door. The back door of the car opened. Riker got in and closed the door behind him.

Seated next to him in the back seat was a man he had never met. Mansour occupied the front passenger seat. The driver was a guy who looked like he worked in security—from what Riker could see of his face, he was lean and tough, with a military haircut. He did not turn around, but kept his eyes forward.

Mansour swiveled in his seat. "Good afternoon, Dr. Riker," he said. "Thank you for joining us. I'd like to introduce you to a fellow medical professional—Dr. Luka Radznev. You might say that Dr. Radznev is our expert on the supply side of the equation, while we hope that you can be of assistance on the delivery side."

Riker was stunned. It was true! The Russians were supplying the smallpox virus, probably from Vector. Riker was walking into an international conspiracy.

Mustering up as much personal warmth as he could, Riker turned to Dr. Radznev and extended his hand. "Pleased to meet you," he said.

"Likewise," said Dr. Radznev coolly.

They shook hands.

"Where are we going?" asked Riker as the big car glided away from the hotel.

"There is someone who wants to meet you," replied Mansour. "This person has, shall we say, the power of approval over key aspects of our program."

Riker, who had by now learned the basic topography of the city, watched the landmarks roll past—bustling Haroun Square, the odd A-shaped stone marker in the center of Al Ziraa Square, the campus of Tishreen University. The car was headed south, out of town. Following the new Highway M1 they passed the farms along the coast, went through the town of Jableh, and, after about an hour's drive, they crossed the winding Al Hsain River. Here the driver left M1 and took the old Route 2, which hugged the coast and brought them into the port city of Tartus.

The car turned toward the harbor. There, tied up to a pier, was a big motor yacht.

The car stopped. Mansour and Dr. Radznev opened their doors. Riker followed suit. The three stood on the wharf. Riker was impressed by the craft that lay quietly before them. He estimated that it was one hundred and fifty feet in length, and it looked antique, as if it had been built in the nineteen-twenties for a Vanderbilt or Rockefeller. The hull was black and sleek, with a jaunty bowsprit jutting from the prow, while a single funnel thrust upwards in the center of the uppermost cabin, which was painted cream with natural teak trim. This boat was not the crude phallic ego symbol of a man, but the refined expression of taste that a woman might prefer.

As if anticipating Riker's thoughts, Mansour turned and said, "A lady owns this vessel. Her name is Madam Ilana Yaltsin."

"Royalty?" asked Riker.

"No," smiled Mansour. "She calls herself Madam, and everyone goes along with her. It's a charming affectation."

They ascended the short gangplank and stepped onto the deck of white oak. It was now, when he could see the vessel close up, that Riker realized it was no antique. Every surface and every fitting looked contemporary.

"When was this yacht built?" he asked Mansour.

"About ten years ago," he replied. "Amazing, isn't it? It's the best of both worlds—modern technology and classic styling."

A man in a black business suit approached them.

"Before we go inside, we have a small formality," said Mansour. "I'm sure you understand."

The man in the black suit expertly patted down Riker. Satisfied, he nodded to the steward, resplendent in his uniform of a crisp blue nautical jacket over white pants. The steward ushered Riker, Mansour, and Dr. Radznev into the main salon, comfortably furnished with a Persian carpet, armchairs upholstered in cream leather, and a gleaming mahogany table. Between the curtained windows, ornate wall sconces with faceted crystal panes gave the cabin a distinctly Edwardian vibe.

The steward offered them drinks. Riker accepted a cup of tea.

From deep within the hull came a sudden rumble. A moment later Riker saw a deckhand cast off the lines, and the bow of the yacht swung away from the pier. In a few minutes the ship had passed the breakwater of the port and was cruising in the open ocean.

The door to the salon opened and a woman entered. Without ceremony she walked over to Riker. Reflexively he stood up.

"Dr. Riker," she said as she extended her hand. "I'm Madam Ilana Yaltsin. It is a pleasure to meet you. I hope you are comfortable?"

"Yes, very, thank you," replied Riker as he took her hand. Her grip was firm and confident, and without affectation.

"Good," she said. "Some people get—how should I say—*queasy* when they're on a boat."

"No, I'm fine," he replied.

A steward entered and spoke to Madam Yaltsin in Russian. She replied, also in Russian, and the man excused himself.

Madam Yaltsin sat down in one of the creamy leather armchairs.

"Mr. Mansour, you are responsible for introducing Dr. Riker to us?" she asked.

"Yes, I suppose," he said with a nervous glance at Dr. Radznev. "But we have discussed his involvement at the highest levels. Zafar himself has approved."

"Ah—of course," said Madam Yaltsin.

Riker had seen the name of Zafar in briefing books. He didn't know much about him—not many Americans did. All the intelligence community knew was that Zafar was a "spiritual advisor" to President al-Assad. Clearly, the guy was influential.

"Dr. Riker," she asked, "Why have you chosen to come to Syria?" Her eyes were hard, like two glittering sapphires.

He repeated to her what he had said to Mansour at the museum—that as an American he was appalled at his country's history of meddling in the affairs of sovereign nations, and there needed to be a dramatic correction. The politicians and generals in Washington needed to understand that having a big army and a big air force do not make you immune from other forms of power. In nature there existed weapons that are as destructive as any atomic bomb, and which are freely available to anyone who has the boldness of character to employ them.

"Do you have family in the United States?" she asked.

"Yes. I live in Naples, Florida. I moved there with my wife, who passed away a year ago. She had pancreatic cancer. It progressed very rapidly and there was little we could do. We had been married for twenty-nine years. My sister lives nearby, and my daughter and her husband live a few hours north, in Tampa. We also have two sons—one in Chicago and one in Baltimore."

"Please accept my condolences on your wife's passing," she said. "Children are a blessing; unfortunately, my late husband and I were not granted any. Dr. Riker, if there were some sort of biological attack against the United States, wouldn't you be concerned about the safety of your family?"

"Yes, of course," he said. "But my sister and children are not the only people we need to be concerned about. In America there are Russian diplomats and other workers, and even many Syrians who are loyal to President al-Assad. If they are at risk, they need to be immunized in advance. We don't want any Russians to get the disease, do we?"

Madam Yaltsin smiled with her teeth. "No, of course not. Speaking of immunization, why do you think that the United States could not simply start vaccinating on a mass scale?"

"If we are talking about smallpox—which I assume we are—you can be vaccinated against the disease, but to be truly effective it must be done within three days of exposure. Four to seven days after exposure, vaccination will offer only some protection from disease or perhaps modify the severity of disease.

"The problem is that the smallpox infection shows *no symptoms* for the first seven to seventeen days after exposure! Therefore, when the first rashes, blisters, and pustules are noticed, it's *too late* to vaccinate the victim. Those individuals are very infectious at that point. When they go to their doctor or a hospital emergency room, the medical personnel who are in contact with them—and who will probably not recognize the disease as smallpox—are unvaccinated and thus liable to come down with infection themselves, unless they somehow get vaccination within three days. Because of the fact that people believe smallpox has been eradicated and most healthcare workers have never seen it, the national response will be delayed, giving the disease time to spread."

"Is anyone in the United States currently vaccinated?" asked Madam Yaltsin.

"My best information," replied Riker, "suggests that among the over three hundred million people living in the United States, only members of the military are currently vaccinated, as well as those few lab workers at the Centers for Disease Control and Prevention in Atlanta who work in the highly secure lab where smallpox is stored.

"The stored smallpox vaccine is locked away in a secure facility—I'm not sure where—and would have to be retrieved and batches divided and sent to each area showing an outbreak. But remember, during the first few days nobody would know for sure the origins of the disease or how it was being spread.

"You may ask, who would really be safe enough to perform all the emergency vaccinations? Nobody. To lessen or prevent the smallpox infection they acquired by touching the victims, or breathing in aerosol virus from the victims, these would-be vaccinators would have had to be vaccinated within three days of being exposed themselves. Is it realistic that this very early-stage responsive vaccination could be planned and implemented within three days? I doubt it. Thus, massive paralysis of the population and facilities would occur as people *feared* getting infected. Remember—the fear of infection will be just as powerful a weapon as the disease itself. The organism under attack—the United States—will overreact, as it always does. Politicians will demand that the borders be closed, that airline travel be stopped, that foreigners be arrested. It will create mass chaos."

"I agree," said Madam Yaltsin. "Americans are a fearful people and they panic very easily. Their response will be just as destructive to their country as the disease." She paused to look out of the window next to her armchair. The Mediterranean Sea was rolling past the yacht, and the coast of Syria appeared as a long low smudge on the horizon.

Suddenly Madam Yalstin got up and went to a small gilded table, on which was a purse. Taking the purse in her hand, she turned to the group.

"Why don't we all go outside for some fresh air? This way, please." She turned and walked through a door towards the stern of the vessel.

The three men followed.

Outside, the winter air was chilly and grey clouds hung low. With his hands jammed in his pockets Riker stood by the cabin door, wondering why they were standing on the deck. There seemed to be no point to it.

Madam Yaltsin came over to Riker. "Please," she said. "Come with me to the back of the boat. By the railing."

With some misgivings Riker obliged. He went and stood next to the flagpole, on which the Russian flag flapped in the breeze. The sea was calm, and the churning wake from the big yacht's twin screws stretched out behind the ship.

Madam Yaltsin reached into her purse and pulled out a pistol. She pointed it at Riker's head. "Dr. Riker, please get up on the railing. You may hold onto the flagpole."

"Excuse me?" he replied. "You want me to—"

"Stand up on the railing," she repeated, keeping the gun trained on him. "Believe me, I know how to use this. Now do it, or take a bullet."

18.

With his right hand grasping the flagpole, Riker stepped up onto the railing. Twenty feet below him the sea frothed as the ship hurtled forward. With his left arm outstretched, he balanced precariously. One moment of lapsed concentration and he would plunge into the ocean.

Madam Yaltsin stood with the gun aimed at his back. Mansour and Dr. Radznev watched in silence.

"Dr. Riker," she said, "Turn around. Face me."

He did so.

"Tell me that you renounce the United States of America and its criminal government."

Riker took his eyes from the black hole of the gun barrel and focused on the distant horizon. Somewhere over the edge, far away, lay America, and his home. Jeanne, Nancy, Tim, and Addison. His granddaughter. His friends and colleagues. All of whom could die if the sinister plot were allowed to succeed.

He was the only person who could stop it.

"Yes," he said.

"Yes, *what*?" said Madam Yaltsin.

"Yes—I renounce the United States of America and its criminal government." The words choked like stones in his throat, but he forced them out.

"And you pledge allegiance to the people of Syria and their noble destiny of glory?"

"Yes, I pledge allegiance to the people of Syria and their noble destiny of glory."

With gun in hand, Madam Yaltsin stood for a moment on the gently rocking deck. Riker, holding on to the flagpole, kept his gaze on the place where sea met sky.

Madam Yaltsin opened her purse and placed the pistol inside.

"Very well," she said to Riker. "Please step down

onto the deck."

Riker did as she said. Madam Yaltsin turned and walked back into the salon. The three men followed.

Once they were seated, Madam Yaltsin called the steward. "Bring some vodka, on ice," she said in Russian. As the waves slid by outside the windows, the group sat in silence. Presently the steward returned with a silver tray, which he put on the table. From a bottle of Putinka vodka—yes, it's actually named in honor of Vladimir Putin, and it is said that if you drink five shots of Putinka very quickly, you can hear the sound of tanks rumbling into the Crimea—he poured four shots into small glasses. Holding the tray, he presented each with their serving.

Riker took his. The glass was ice-cold. Madam Yaltsin raised hers and said, "To the success of Operation Fire Sword."

"To Fire Sword," they said as they downed the shots.

"Now then," said Madam Yaltsin as the steward collected the glasses, "Dr. Riker, while we are pleased that you have joined our enterprise, one thing surprises me."

"And what is that?" he asked.

"You have not named your price."

"My price?"

"Are we to believe that you are turning your back on your country out of the goodness of your heart? That you expect nothing other than the gratitude of the Syrian people, which will probably never be offered in public? There is no such thing as someone who acts for purely altruistic reasons. Everybody has their price. During and after the calamity ahead, you will need to provide for yourself. You will need to move somewhere safe—perhaps to Russia? Come now, Dr. Riker, let's not pussyfoot around. How much do you want?"

Riker knew he had to come up with an answer. But what was realistic? What was the current price for becoming a traitor?

"Five million," he said.

"Dollars?"

"Yes."

"That's a little steep," said Madam Yaltsin. "Mr. Mansour, please show Dr. Riker the video."

Mansour held up his phone and pressed "play." Riker saw himself standing on the stern of the yacht, holding onto the Syrian flag. He heard himself saying that he renounced the United States.

"Now let's be more reasonable," said Madam Yaltsin. "Two million dollars—payable *after* the success of Fire Sword—and the use of one of my *dachas* by the Black Sea. I'm sure that you'll quickly find employment—am I right, Dr. Radznev?"

"I'm sure that any number of Russian institutions will find Dr. Riker's skills to be very useful," he replied.

"Good," said Madam Yaltsin. "Then it's settled."

Glancing out the window, Riker saw that the yacht had entered the harbor. On deck, the crew had the lines ready. Within a few minutes the vessel was tied up at the pier.

"Dr. Riker, thank you for joining us today," said Madam Yaltsin. "The car will take you back to your hotel. Please wait there for further instructions."

Dr. Radznev, Mansour, and Riker went out onto the deck and then across the short gangway. They got into the car. On the ride back to Latakia, Riker tried to engage his new colleagues in small talk, but they were unwilling.

More mind games, thought Riker. *Now that I've passed the initiation, they want to remind me who's in charge.*

By the time Riker entered the lobby of the Shahbandar it was early evening. From behind the counter, Shakira gave him a cool smile. Riker went up to his room.

During the trip to Tartus he had kept his phone shut off. He powered it up. There was a text. It was from Hussein.

"I'm out," it said. "Still alive! Call me."

Riker punched the number. He heard the familiar

voice. "They let me go this afternoon," he said. "Knocked me around a bit but I'm still in one piece. What are you up to?"

"Do you still have your taxi?" asked Riker.

"Sure! Do you want to go somewhere?"

"Just for a ride—maybe get some dinner."

"Okay. I'll be at the hotel in ten minutes."

Riker went down to the lobby, gave Shakira a polite nod, and walked through the revolving doors just in time to see Hussein's taxi pull into the hotel driveway.

"Good to see you," said Riker. "Are you hungry?"

"Yes—I know a good place near the university," he said as he put the taxi in gear and rolled out onto the street. "The best authentic Lebanese and Syrian food."

"Sounds good. So—what did they do to you?"

"They held me in Sedaboud Prison for forty-eight hours—the same place they took you. I was interrogated twice. They wanted to know why I was driving you around, and why I tried to evade them when they were following us. I insisted that I thought you were just a tourist, and that I wasn't trying to evade them; you just wanted to see the sights, so we drove around a lot. But I was getting nowhere with them—it seemed like they really wanted to give me hell. But they allowed me to call my family, which suggested to me that maybe it wasn't about making me disappear. Then they let me go. I walked out of there and my brother Fahd was waiting for me. He told me he had paid a so-called 'fine' of fifty thousand Syrian pounds."

"That's over two hundred dollars," said Riker. "A hefty bribe, no?"

"I thank Allah that Fahd had the money. I'll pay him back little by little. It's just the way it is around here. Anytime a security guy wants to make more money, he just arrests somebody and makes their family pay to get him back."

"Tonight, my friend, we are going to be as visible as possible," said Riker.

"Oh, really? Why?"

Riker held himself in check. He glanced at Hussein and his open, friendly face.

How much do I know about Hussein? he thought. Before Riker had arrived in Latakia, Hussein had been hired by someone in the State Department. But what did that really mean? In this crazy city where everyone was paranoid about being on the wrong side and everyone hedged their bets, who was to say that Hussein was trustworthy?

Riker knew that he was being watched. Mansour and the others would want to know if he tried to contact anyone and pass along information about the project—Operation Fire Sword, as Madam Yaltsin had called it. Riker knew the general concept of the plan, but he didn't know the proposed delivery method or the timing. It was too soon to blow the whistle. He needed more information.

Could Hussein be his new Syrian handler, charged with keeping an eye on him?

Riker wished he could be certain it was otherwise. But he couldn't.

"It's nothing," said Riker. "All I mean is that I don't want to cross the GSD again, and neither do you. I'm just visiting Latakia to check on a possible case of smallpox. So far, I've seen nothing. It looks like a wild goose chase."

"Okay," shrugged Hussein.

Riker turned around and glanced behind them. "Yep, they're back there," he said to Hussein.

The driver looked in his rear view mirror. "You're right. You seem to be a very popular guy with the GSD. Okay—let's change our plans. We're going to a restaurant that's frequented by government officials. It's near City Hall. We can go in there and talk about how grateful we are to live in Syria today."

A few minutes later Hussein parked his taxi in front of the Naranj. As they walked in the door, the place looked busier than any other restaurant Riker had visited in Latakia. The clientele looked well heeled—the men wore business suits and the women showed off fashions that, if they weren't exactly the latest styles from Paris runways, were hardly rustic. They found a table in the rear, near the door to the kitchen.

A few minutes after they sat down, two *mukabarat* entered the restaurant. A few of the patrons glanced at them, but their presence aroused no particular anxiety. The two guys found seats at the bar.

The waiter came to take Riker and Hussein's order. Before they could begin, Riker's phone rang. With an irritated look—no one likes a guy who talks on his cell phone in a nice restaurant—he answered it.

"Dr. Riker," said the voice of Mansour. "If I'm not mistaken, our instructions to you were quite clear. We asked you to remain in your hotel until we contacted you. And now we see that you are at the Naranj with your taxi driver friend. Dr. Riker, it's very important that we maintain a clear working relationship. We cannot be in the position of having to chase you to find out where you are."

"And yet you have found me—and very easily," replied Riker. "Unfortunately, the dining room at the Shahbandar is extremely limited. Tiresome, really. Eating there night after night will not be an option. Furthermore, I can see that we are under the watchful eyes of two very capable men. So, clearly, keeping track of me is not so difficult. When and if you need me to be at a certain place at a certain time, rest assured that I'll be there."

"In fact," said Mansour, "you have an appointment tonight. At eight thirty—which is in about an hour—a car will pick you up at your hotel. Please plan accordingly. Thank you."

He hung up.

19.

At eight thirty the black Russian ZiL pulled up in front of the Shahbandar. Riker got in the back seat. He was the only passenger.

"How're you doing, my friend?" he said to the driver—the same tough-looking guy who had been behind the wheel earlier the same day.

The driver ignored him.

Riker sat back as the car made its way north, along the Cote d'Azur Road. Passing the Blue Beach, they came to Ras ibn Hani, the small cape jutting into the Mediterranean Sea. An important archaeological site with the coast's best natural harbor, it had been occupied almost continuously from the late Bronze Age and the rise of the ancient people of Ugarit. From its low white cliffs it was known as the White Harbor, and was the spot where during the Mesopotamian campaigns of 114–117 CE, the Roman Emperor Trajan landed to join his troops in Syria in his bitter wars against the Parthian empire.

The car came to a stop outside a villa. In the moonlight Riker could see that the structure, which appeared to be centuries old, was perched on a rugged bluff with the sea on three sides. The old casement windows showed warm light from within.

As he walked to the door he noted four cars parked in front of the old garage. With a shock of recognition he saw that one of them was Amena's Mercedes.

Riker stepped onto the stone porch and, before he had a chance to knock, the iron-strapped wooden door opened.

"Dr. Riker, welcome," said Mansour. "Please—come with me."

Riker followed Mansour into a large and comfortable living room furnished with a rustic oak table, leather-upholstered armchairs, and several *narghiles*, all illuminated by a circular chandelier of delicate wrought iron.

"Of course, you know Sami Noman and Amena Qabbani," said Mansour. "May I also introduce Bani Mahadi." A fleshy, sour-looking man rose from his seat and offered his blunt hand, which Riker shook.

So this is the guy who killed Akram Aflaq, thought Riker as he smiled.

A servant offered Riker tea, which he accepted.

Riker glanced at Amena. She was looking straight ahead, holding the handle of her teacup with one hand while supporting the saucer with the other.

A man entered the room, not by the way that Riker had come but through a door that led to some other part of the house. With his somber gray *thawb*, grey beard, and wire-rimmed glasses, he looked like a Muslim cleric. When he entered, the others stood up.

"Welcome," the man said in a warm fatherly voice. He approached Riker. "Ah—Dr. Riker. My name is Zafar." He extended his hand, which Riker took. Zafar's grip was firm and confident. "I've been told that you are interested in assisting us in our project." His black eyes shone like dark diamonds.

"Yes," replied Riker.

"Even though it will mean the deaths of many of your countrymen?"

"Sometimes the greater good must be served."

"Yes, of course. Very well, let's get started. I hope you will be comfortable—I bought this place a few months ago from the estate of the previous owner, who unfortunately had died in prison. I haven't had much of an opportunity to fix it up." Zafar took a seat in one of the leather armchairs. At his elbow was a tall bronze and glass *narghile*. Taking out a pouch of tobacco, he packed a bit of it into the bowl before putting his mouthpiece on the flexible tube. "Smoking," he said with a sigh. "Not a healthy habit, but it gives me great pleasure." He lit the tobacco and inhaled. The cloudy water bubbled.

"When we met last time," began Mansour, "You,

dear Zafar, had proposed the idea that the smallpox virus be introduced into the target population through the use of newspapers. Following this thought, I've done some research. Here's a list of the biggest papers in the United States, by circulation."

Mansour provided these figures:

1. The Wall Street Journal—2.3 million readers, nationwide.

2. The New York Times—1.8 million nationwide and in the greater New York City area.

3. USA Today—1.6 million, nationwide.

4. The Los Angeles Times—600,000 in the Los Angeles area.

5. The Daily News—500,000 in New York City.

6. The New York Post—500,000 in New York City.

7. The Washington Post—470,000, nationwide and the Washington, D.C. area.

8. The Chicago Sun-Times—470,000 in the Chicago area.

9. The Denver Post—400,000 in the area of Denver, Colorado.

10. The Chicago Tribune—400,000 in the Chicago area.

"What exactly does the term 'circulation' mean?" asked Mahadi. "Is it copies sold, or the number of readers?"

"Circulation is one of the principal factors used to set advertising rates," replied Mansour. "A newspaper's circulation is the number of copies it *distributes* on an average day. Circulation is not always the same as copies sold—often called *paid* circulation—since for various reasons some copies are given away free of charge. What really matters, though, are a paper's *total readership* figures, which are higher than circulation figures, because of the assumption that a typical newspaper is read by more than one person."

"Indeed," said Noman, "At our house, the newspaper that I buy is read by four or five people during the course of the day."

"Do we know how many of these readers are digital, as opposed to receiving the print edition?" asked Zafar.

"No, we don't," replied Mansour. "Obviously, for our purposes that could be a significant difference, but at this time we can't get those figures."

"Dr. Riker, what do you think about the effectiveness of a newspaper as a delivery vehicle for smallpox?" asked Zafar.

Riker felt his stomach tighten. This was the first time that he was being asked not to merely *learn about* a deadly plot but to actually *contribute* to it. But what should he say? Should he try to lead the plotters astray, and give them false information? It would be the better moral choice, but if the group suspected they were being deceived, they'd kill him and continue with their plans. Should he give them truthful information? Perhaps—but then the stakes would only get higher.

He had no choice but to tell the truth.

"I've lived and worked in New York," he said. 'It's a big city—the population is now over eight million people. And while there are huge areas of poverty, like there is in any major city, people from all walks of life quite literally rub shoulders. New York City has over two hundred miles of subway lines and, on the streets, is served by thirteen thousand taxicabs and fourteen thousand Uber cars. All day long, people are getting in and out of these vehicles—subway cars, taxis, hired cars, executive cars. Many thousands of these travelers will be carrying the newspaper—the *New York Times*, the *Daily News*, the *Post*, *USA Today*, the *Wall Street Journal*. They will handle the paper themselves, and then leave it on the seat of the subway, in the taxicab, or on the lunch counter. Someone else will pick it up. Or, they'll leave it at home for their family to read, or share an article with a colleague.

"Even if someone has only glanced at the headlines, they've still come into *direct contact* with the paper. Then they'll touch their hand to their nose or face and inhale. Into their respiratory system will come the usual bits of dust, dirt, and rag or pulp from the newspaper. Along with these everyday pollutants they will also inhale the smallpox virus. Typically, it takes only takes five or ten particles of the smallpox virus to achieve infection. Sometimes, theoretically, just one. Therefore, if a mechanism can be found to attach particles of the smallpox virus to a daily newspaper that has wide circulation, it would be an effective distribution system."

"Thank you, Dr. Riker," said Zafar. "Amena—you're from the public health sector. What do you think?"

She cleared her throat. As she began speaking, Riker watched her expression closely. He soon realized that she appeared to be as skilled an actor as he hoped *he* had been.

"I think that infected newspapers would produce chaos," she said. "Imagine if the morning edition of a newspaper were treated with the virus. In the course of a day—probably as long as the virus would be expected to survive—thousands of readers would become infected. But they would not know it! For those who became infected, the virus would have entered the incubation period. The average length of incubation—during which there are no symptoms and the victim is not contagious—is twelve days. It can be as short as seven days. At the end of the incubation period, the first symptoms would appear. As people began going to their doctors and showing up in emergency rooms with a fever and a rash, it would take several hours for the public health system to correctly diagnose the disease. By this time, the initial batch of victims would be contagious, and they would be spreading the disease among health care workers.

"There is no known *treatment* for smallpox. Once you have a full-blown case, you can only do the best you can and hope you survive. As you know, the various vaccines are probably effective, but they must be given within three days of the initial infection, at a time when the patient isn't even showing any symptoms.

"After the identification of the disease, the political response would be extreme. The country would virtually shut down. There would be a frantic effort to immunize citizens. Political fights would break out over who was getting the vaccine. Of course, rich people, and people who were well connected with the government, would be vaccinated first. This would create massive social tensions, with the political leaders of the lower classes screaming that their people were being left out in the cold to suffer while rich folks got immunized. The United States would be revealed to the world for what it really is: not a democracy but an oligarchy ruled by the richest one percent."

"Thank you," said Zafar. "Your perspective is very important. What about vaccines, Dr. Riker? Can you tell us about the state of smallpox vaccinations in the United States, and what we might expect should we launch the attack?"

"Currently," said Riker, "very few people in the United States are vaccinated against smallpox, and certainly not your average citizen of New York or any other major city. In 1972, after the disease was eradicated in the United States, routine smallpox vaccination among the American public stopped. Four years later, the recommendation for routine vaccination of health-care workers was also discontinued. In 1982, the only active licensed producer of vaccinia vaccine in the United States discontinued production for general use, and in 1983, distribution to the civilian population was discontinued. For several years all military personnel continued to be routinely vaccinated, and the US government provided the vaccine only to a few hundred scientists and medical professionals working with smallpox and similar viruses in a research setting. According to the CDC—where I used to work—only selected groups of military personnel are currently vaccinated against smallpox."

"But how about stockpiles of vaccines?" asked Mansour.

"After the attacks of September 11, 2001 and the anthrax scare that followed," replied Riker, "the US government took increased actions to improve its level of preparedness against biological attack. One of many such measures—designed specifically to prepare for an intentional release of the smallpox virus—included updating and releasing a smallpox response plan.

"In September 2002, the CDC released to health officials in all the states a contingency plan to quickly inoculate all Americans if the need should arise. Today, the US government claims it has enough vaccine to vaccinate every person in the United States in the event of a smallpox emergency. However, some experts have recommended what they call 'controlled vaccination.' This means that in the event of a smallpox outbreak, only people having close contact with infected persons would receive the vaccine. In this, I agree with Amena that such an approach may in fact trigger class warfare.

"For completeness, let me add that back in 2003, about thirty-eight thousand people who could be considered first responders were vaccinated. But this was nationwide; how many of those would be available in a particular American city on a given date today is anybody's guess. And the criterion for choosing those subjects was that they *might be* designated to investigate initial smallpox cases.' So who knows who would actually be designated if this planned crisis erupts? And if there were hundreds, or thousands, of cases, all at once, the challenge would be compounded."

"Are people vaccinated before 1972 immune to the disease?" asked Mahadi.

"Not necessarily," replied Riker. "In the United States, the level of immunity among those vaccinated before 1972 is uncertain; therefore, these persons are assumed to be susceptible. Most estimates suggest that the vaccine gives full protection for only three to five years. This means older Americans who got immunized when they were kids have, at best, partial immunity. The same, maybe, for those inoculated back in 2003."

Riker paused to take stock of the room. He noticed that Mahadi seemed to be glowering at him, while Zafar puffed on his narghile. Amena had put her teacup and saucer on a small table. Noman was sitting with his chin in his hand, as if he were pondering the deepest aspects of the problem.

"Dr. Riker, tell us about the existing vaccines," said Zafar, who alone among the men seemed to be keenly interested in the crucial details of the proposed operation.

"Unlike many other vaccines, which contain a dead virus of the type you're inoculating against," said Riker, "the smallpox vaccine contains the living vaccinia virus, a "pox"-type virus related to smallpox. For that reason, the vaccination site must be cared for carefully to prevent the virus from spreading. Also, while the vaccine can have side effects, it does not contain the smallpox virus and cannot give someone smallpox. Smallpox vaccination provides a high level of immunity for three to five years and decreasing immunity thereafter. If a person is vaccinated again later, immunity lasts even longer. Historically, the vaccine has been effective in preventing smallpox infection in ninety-five percent of those vaccinated. But as I said, this resistance declines over time.

"Currently, three vaccines exist. Where they are and how—during a panic—they could actually reach people at risk are big questions."

Riker paused and thought to himself: *And God help us if the first cases were spotted the day before a blizzard hit Washington and New York, paralyzing everything.*

"Yes, Dr. Riker?" said Zafar.

"In a pinch," continued Riker, "drugs might save a few. Cidofovir and brincidofovir are antivirals that could be used. Both have proven activity against poxviruses in *in vitro* and animal studies, but their effectiveness against smallpox is undetermined. Maybe also a drug called tecovirimat ST-246. It's currently in the U.S.'s Strategic National Stockpile for emergency use. But drugs are really impractical for a big outbreak."

Riker glanced over at Mahadi. He appeared bored, and was fiddling with his phone.

"Dr. Riker, I'm pleased that you are so well versed in these important technical matters," said Zafar in a voice that was deliberately loud enough, thought Riker, to get Mahadi's attention. Indeed, like a kid in the back of a high school math class, Mahadi looked up and pretended to be alert before discreetly putting away his phone.

"I agree," said Amena. "Thank you, Dr. Riker. It's necessary to not only correctly formulate our attack but to accurately judge the defenses of our target. While the United States may have the latent capacity to respond to a smallpox assault, the element of surprise will give us a tremendous advantage. Mobilizing a response will take time, and meanwhile the disease will be spreading throughout the population."

Zafar nodded, validating what Amena had said. As he nodded, Mahadi, Mansour, and Noman also nodded, as if their chins were connected to Zafar's with strings.

Riker turned to Zafar. "May I ask a question?"

"Certainly," said Zafar as he leaned over to repack the bowl of the *narghile*, which had gone out.

"This may not be any of my business, because it's a political issue, but there is the matter of credit for the attack."

"Credit?" asked Mansour.

"Yes," said Riker. "The moment the size and severity of the smallpox outbreak becomes apparent, the response from the American press and its politicians will be to proclaim it a terrorist attack. They proclaim every crime committed by a Muslim to be a so-called terrorist attack, but this time they'll be right—it will have been a deliberate assault. Now then, since we are planning this with the express purpose of asserting Syrian hegemony, for our effort to have the desired effect we need to take credit for it. If we do not, the Americans will invent the opponent of their choice, and it will probably be ISIS. Despite the fact that there will be no evidence that it even has the capability to launch an attack like Fire Sword, the Americans, needing to do *something*, will massively retaliate against them. There will be bombings and perhaps even 'boots on the ground,' as they say. In such a scenario, what will Russia do? What will President al-Assad do? If, on the other hand, the Syrian government takes responsibility for the attack, that will put us in direct confrontation with the United States. Again, what would Russia do?"

Zafar, who had been listening while he fussed with his *narghile*, put down his mouthpiece and stood up. He walked to a window, which was closed due to the chill evening air. He stood in front of the window, peering out at the dark sea. Then he turned.

"The political question is a delicate one," he said. "You are correct, Dr. Riker, that we are undertaking this action to help balance the scales of history, so to speak, and restore to Syria some of her former glory. This represents a good reason to take credit for the operation. And as long as we enjoy close relations with Russia, the Americans will be reluctant to attack us directly. They don't want war with Russia.

"On the other hand, focusing the wrath of the Americans on ISIS would have significant advantages. Many American politicians say that the United States must first get rid of them before they come after us. This will provide the U.S. a good excuse to do exactly that. This will give us more time to strengthen the legitimate government of President Bashar al-Assad. Then, with Syria strong and stable, they may decide to accept reality and cease their persistent interference in our affairs."

Zafar glanced at his watch. "It's getting late. I want to thank you for coming tonight. We have much to consider, and we need to make some more decisions, both political and operational. I'll be in touch. Meanwhile, Sami, are you making progress at Beta Syria? Do you need Dr. Riker to add his expertise?"

"We're in the process of setting up the laboratory," said Noman, "but we haven't yet received the quantity of smallpox that we need to grow. To get the smallpox viruses, Dr. Radznev has returned to Russia, to Vector. Madam Yaltsin has promised to underwrite our expenses, including buying the viruses from Dr. Radznev. As soon as Dr. Radznev delivers the smallpox that we need, we should be able to begin production. There may be a few technical issues that Dr. Riker can assist us with."

"Very well," said Zafar. "Good evening." He walked out the door through which he had entered the room.

20.

The group stood up to leave. Mahadi gave Riker a sour look before walking to the door with Mansour and Noman.

Instead of leaving with the others, Amena approached him.

"How did you get here?" she asked. "Did you drive?"

"No," he replied. "A car picked me up."

"Oh," she smiled. "That was Mansour's doing. He wants to remind you that you're an outsider. He's not ready to have you drive yourself to these meetings. He'd rather keep you dependent on the inner circle. Listen—why don't we let the driver go on his way? I'll give you a ride back to town."

"Sounds good to me," said Riker.

They went outside. The night was clear and cold. As they paused on the porch, the Russian ZiL that had delivered Riker pulled out of its parking spot near the garage and swung around to pick him up. Instead, Riker stood where he was while Amena went to the driver's window. After she spoke to him, the driver put the car in gear and eased it out of the driveway.

Amena reached into her purse and tossed Riker the keys. "I rather enjoy having you drive me," she said with a laugh. "It makes me feel important."

"Anything to please the lady," he replied as he clicked open the doors. "Where to, madam?"

"You're supposed to be a doctor investigating a possible case of smallpox, right?" she said after they had fastened their seat belts.

"That's my story."

"Then I think you'd better get an idea of the possible places where a communicable disease could be most easily spread, especially by inhalation. I should think that a night club or a disco would be on the top of your list."

"Are there such things in Latakia today?" he asked incredulously.

"Martin, you still have a lot to learn about life during wartime." She pointed at the road ahead. "We're almost at the rotary where we pick up the Cote d'Azur Road. You'll want to head south, towards downtown."

"Yes, ma'am," said Riker, tipping an imaginary chauffeur's hat.

"Where was I? Oh yes. Around here—and I suppose it's true anywhere people are at war—people who aren't actually fighting cling to every bit of normalcy they can. They go to movies, the kids play soccer, the girls try to buy nice clothes, the boys show off their cars. They try to have fun and keep some romance in their lives, even though the fighting is only a few hours away, and should the Syrian army lose, their lives would become a living hell."

"It's the same the whole world over," said Riker. "After the attacks of September 11, the American president urged everyone to go about their usual business—to go to the mall or to a movie. The message was, 'If we change how we live our lives, the terrorists will have won.' Of course, some things changed drastically, like airport security. But people understood the point. You try to maintain some semblance of regularity and familiarity in your life."

Cote d'Azur Road merged with Sports City Road, and Riker continued south past the Fishing and Tourism Marina. "Turn here, and go towards Hassan Azhari Square," said Amena. "Let's see...there's a little street off to the right. Yes, there it is—Al Alfamia Street."

Riker followed her directions. They had entered a seedy industrial part of town, and the street was dark. In the middle of the block Riker saw a small, lighted sign that read "Tornado."

"That's it," said Amena. "It's in a converted garage. Everybody goes here because the club is open until two in the morning and the DJ plays the newest hits, which he downloads from the internet."

Riker parked at the end of the block, which was as close to the club as he could get. As he and Amena walked down the broken sidewalk, Riker noticed the mix of cars parked on the street—the usual crummy Toyotas and Fiats, but here and there he saw an expensive BMW, and even one big black Cadillac Escalade.

Riker pulled open the battered steel door. After a burly man collected the cover charge of five hundred Syrian pounds each—a little over two bucks—Riker and Amena ascended the long curving concrete ramp that Riker guessed was once part of the garage. He could hear the boom of the music as it reverberated towards them.

At the top of the ramp they passed through an open door into the club itself. The space was big and dark, with its high ceiling painted black and punctuated by colored lights clustered like glowing flowers. A long bar ran along one wall. The mirror behind it reflected the scattered bottles perched on the glass shelves. Riker peered closer at the bottles on the shelves. Half of them were empty placeholders.

The DJ booth occupied most of another wall, and the rest of the space near the walls was filled by a random assortment of metal chairs and small cocktail tables. The center of the room, on the dance floor, was dominated by what Riker could only describe as a free-form sculpture of junk—a twisting tower of bolted-together artifacts that included an electric guitar, a store mannequin (naked), a plastic pink flamingo, a wooden dollhouse, and several plastic fish.

Taking his arm, Amena pointed to the sculpture. "That's the tornado," she said. To be heard, she had to practically shout into Riker's ear.

The nightclub was interesting and even fun—Riker had been to dozens of such places all over the world, and always enjoyed them—but what was much more exciting was Amena's sudden physical closeness. When she put her hand on his arm, it was, he realized, the first time she had touched him outside of the formality of shaking hands. By speaking so closely to his ear, he could feel her breath on the side of his neck. It had been many years since he had experienced such contact with a woman who was not his wife. The sensation was novel and invigorating.

Amena led the way to the bar. Riker could not help but notice, and enjoy, the way her hair shone under the flashing lights and the gentle sway of her hips as she walked.

She leaned against the stainless steel counter top and Riker joined her. In the mirror he could see her face, animated by the pulse of the music and the energy of the mostly younger crowd. The bartender—a young man with tattooed arms, green Bob Marley t-shirt, and black baseball cap—came over.

"What do you want?" asked Riker, putting his mouth near Amena's ear with its little silver daisy earring.

"Just a beer," she said, this time cupping her hand beside her mouth when she spoke and grazing her fingers alongside his hair.

Riker ordered two Al-Sharks. He turned to face the crowd.

"It's pretty busy here," he said. Perhaps because the DJ was playing a new track by Rihanna, the dance floor was elbow-to-elbow. "Can you imagine if someone who was contagious with smallpox came in here? A couple of good sneezes or a coughing fit, and you'd have enough virus in the air to infect everyone here."

Amena turned to him. Moving her body close enough so that Riker could feel her pressing against him, she said, "Okay—we've done our scientific research for the evening. Let's have no more shop talk. Agreed?"

"Sure, sure," replied Riker. As he said this he placed his hand lightly on her shoulder. It was the first time he had ever put his hand on any part of her body.

Under her cotton dress, her shoulder felt toned and firm.

She looked at him and smiled. Her teeth were perfect and white, and her eyes were clear.

It was at this moment that Riker, who had not entertained such thoughts in years, suddenly realized that he wanted Amena to be with him that night.

Under the flashing lights, consumed by their private thoughts, neither Riker nor Amena saw the young man in the leather jacket and blue jeans who had taken a position at the edge of the dance floor and was seemingly watching the dancers. Glancing in their direction, he lifted up his phone and snapped a series of photos of Riker and Amena as they stood close to each other at the bar. The young man then punched a few buttons on his phone, and then, satisfied that the images had been emailed to their destination, slipped the phone back into his pocket.

The DJ played a slow song, and for a few minutes it was no longer necessary to shout to be heard. Riker said to Amena, "Please forgive me for being so nosey, but I could not help but notice that you're not wearing a wedding ring. Are you—you know—attached?"

She shook her head. "Divorced. I've been single for two years. And to answer your next question, I have no children. I'm a perfectly happy single woman."

Suddenly the music changed to a throbbing EDM beat. "Would you like to dance?" shouted Riker.

Placing her beer bottle on the bar, Amena smiled and nodded. They moved out onto the dance floor. Riker felt strange and awkward—not because he was dancing with a new woman who was not his wife, but because there was a *war* going on, *dammit*, and both of them had just come from a meeting where they had discussed a plan to use ghastly biological weapons to kill and sicken many thousands of innocent Americans. Of course the plan would never be carried out—not if Riker could help it.

Unless his supposed co-conspirators killed him first.

He looked at Amena. Along with the others on the dance floor, she looked carefree, as if it were a normal Tuesday night in New York or Paris or Tokyo. An electric shock of doubt flashed through his mind. He had thought of it before, and dismissed it—could *she* be his GSD handler? Is that why she was suddenly included in the planning session? And now—had she been assigned to *seduce* him?

As they danced, the young man in the blue jeans and leather jacket again took out his phone and snapped photos.

21.

At the end of the song, without thinking about it, Riker extended his hand, which Amena took in hers. "Well, that was fun," he said as they turned toward the bar, still hand in hand.

"Yes," she agreed. "That was fun."

Riker glanced around the crowded club. "We can't really talk here, can we?"

She smiled. "There are many things we can't do here."

"What do you want to do?"

"Why don't we go back to my place?" she said. "The drinks there are much better, I assure you. And I'm sure you're sick of being at the Shahbandar."

"Yeah—at the hotel I feel as though I'm living in a fishbowl. I'm sure they track my every move, and while I'm gone they search through my stuff. This afternoon I returned to my room and found that my toothbrush had been put into the glass with its bristles down, inside the glass. I *never* put my toothbrush in the glass with its bristles down—they are always facing up."

"Fewer germs that way," said Amena.

"Yes, and it drains better too," said Riker.

"They must have thought you had a secret spy toothbrush."

"Don't laugh," said Riker. "You can go to Amazon.com and buy an electric toothbrush that comes equipped with a pinhole digital movie camera. You can film all the naughty activities in your bathroom and watch them on your television."

"That's the very last thing I want to do," said Amena. "I can assure you that there are no toothbrush cameras in my house."

Riker took the last swallow of his beer. "Am I driving, or are you?"

"Like I said before, I rather like being driven

around by a handsome man." Her face turned pensive. "It makes me feel *normal*. Like someone living in a place where there isn't endless war and misery."

"If I can make you feel normal, I'd be happy to oblige," said Riker. "Shall we go?"

Pushing through the crowd of people and the pulsing lights and spine-jolting sound, they made their way to the exit and the long concrete ramp. As they left, the man in the blue jeans and leather jacket made a phone call. After speaking for a moment he nodded before putting away his phone.

Riker and Amena walked to her car. The night air was cool and the moonlight diluted the shadows that easily overpowered the occasional working streetlight. Riker, who had kept the keyless entry fob to the Mercedes in his pocket, unlocked the doors. He opened the passenger door for Amena.

"Normal life," he said with a smile as she slid onto the seat. He closed the door and went to the driver's side. When he had buckled his seat belt, he started the engine.

Before he could put the car into gear Amena leaned over and put her hand on his cheek. Gently turning his face towards hers, she kissed him hard on the lips. Her mouth was warm and soft.

She lowered her hand and pulled away. "I'm sorry," she said. "You must think that I'm some sort of desperate woman."

"No, not at all," replied Riker as he discreetly wiped the lipstick from his lips. "Listen—we'll just have a nice time hanging out. No pressure, okay? Whatever you want is fine with me."

"Okay," she smiled. "To get to my house, we're going to take Highway 1 north to a suburb called Baksa. It's a ten minute drive."

As Riker pulled away from the curb, a black Range Rover idling at the end of the block switched on its lights. At a distance it followed the Mercedes out of the industrial district to the highway that led north. After a distance of four miles, the Range Rover tailed the

Mercedes as it turned east toward Baksa, and, after passing farms and olive groves, entered a short road that led towards the lake. Here the Range Rover stopped and turned around. The driver knew exactly where the Mercedes was going.

Riker pulled up in front of a modernistic house that looked like it had been built in the nineteen-sixties— low and sleek, with a single massive chimney. At the side was a small scrubby lawn, and beyond the lawn Riker saw the reflection of moonlight on a lake.

"Nice little spot you have here," said Riker as he stepped out of the car.

"We'll go in the back door," said Amena as she led the way around the house. "I bought this house because of the lake—it's nothing much, really; you can barely drive a boat on it. But it's peaceful and you have a sense of being away from the city." After pausing for a moment to enjoy the quiet solitude of the lake, they retreated to the patio, on which were a few tubular lawn chairs and an awning. "When it's cool in the evening it's nice to sit out here." She produced a key and opened the back door. When she flicked on the lights Riker saw that he was in a tidy kitchen, which, except for the wall hangings in Arabic, could have been a kitchen anywhere in the United States.

"What would you like to drink?" said Amena.

"Whatever you're having will be fine," said Riker.

"I have a bottle of pretty good Château Bargylus," she said. "I've had it since before the war. I take it out on special occasions." She opened a cabinet door and took out the bottle. From another cabinet she got two wine glasses.

"Bargylus—it's from Latakia, isn't it?" asked Riker.

"Yes. The estate is east of here, in the coastal mountain range further inland. Two millennia ago, the Romans used the same slopes of what used to be called Mount Bargylus—now Jabal Ansariya—for their own wineries, as did the Greeks and Phoenicians. Sandro Saadé, a Syrian-Lebanese guy, runs the wine estate along with his brother Karim. Every once in a while a mortar shell will come crashing into the vineyards. I'm sure it's the world's most difficult and dangerous place to produce wine. Somehow, they carry on, and they've even won international awards."

"Cheers," said Riker as he raised his glass. "To normalcy."

"Yes, normalcy," said Amena. "Something that you don't appreciate until it's gone."

They went into the living room and sat, side by side, on the sofa. Amena kicked off her shoes and tucked her legs underneath her.

"It feels good to be here," said Riker. He ventured to put his hand on her calf. He was pleased when she did not pull away, and more pleased when she put her hand on top of his—not to pin it in place, but to encourage further contact.

"What's going to happen?" she said.

"You mean with the terrible plot to infect people in America?"

"Yes."

"We have to stop it," said Riker.

"Without getting ourselves killed," she said.

"Yes—without getting ourselves killed."

"Will they really carry out their plan?" she asked. "It just seems so fantastic. So nightmarish."

"I think the Russians are whispering in their ear," replied Riker. "The Russians are saying, 'Yes, you can do it; we'll pay for it; it will strike a blow against the evil American empire.' The Syrians are so desperate they'll try anything."

Amena put her wine glass on the small end table. "Okay," she said. "Enough dreary talk. I want to relax." Snuggling closer, she kissed Riker on the lips.

"Hmmm, you taste like red wine," he said.

"There's a lot more where that came from," she whispered. She stood up and, taking Riker by the hand, led him into the bedroom.

Together they fell into Amena's big comfortable bed.

At dawn, Riker awoke. The sky outside the

bedroom window was pale pink. Next to him, Amena was still asleep. He kissed her forehead. She sleepily smiled and reached up to stroke his face.

"I need to shave," he said with a smile.

"Mmmm, I like it the way it is," she murmured. Her eyes opened. "What time is it?"

"Almost eight o'clock."

She sat up in bed. Riker kissed her bare shoulder.

"I'd better get up," she said as she stretched her arms. "I have a meeting at work at nine thirty."

"Okay—we can't have you arrive late," said Riker. He swung his legs onto the floor and stood up. It felt good to have been in bed with a woman again, and to be naked in front of her in the morning. He felt like a *man* again. And he was sure that Amena felt like a woman.

Amena got out of bed and put on a sheer dressing gown. Riker wanted to tear it off her and throw her back onto the sheets, but he held his impulses in check. He was sure there would be other nights and other mornings.

Suddenly there came a loud knock on the front door—forceful enough to shake the walls of the house.

"Get into the bathroom," said Riker to Amena. "Get dressed." He hurriedly put on his pants and a shirt.

The knock was repeated. Then came the sound of someone trying to break through the door.

"I'm coming!" shouted Riker. Zipping up his pants, he hurried to the vestibule. He could see the door panels flexing under the strain of being battered.

"I'm opening the door!" he called. The pounding stopped. As Riker pulled open the door, four *mukhabarat* muscled their way inside. One was carrying an automatic weapon. Without saying a word they roughly grabbed Riker by the arms, handcuffed his hands behind his back, and hustled him to a waiting ZiL. He resisted and turned around. "Amena!" he called.

He glimpsed her, still dressed in her sheer gown, being led from the house in handcuffs. Then he was shoved into the back seat of the black car. His head was held down by one of the *mukhabarat* as the car lurched forward. After a hood was pulled over his head, he was made to sit upright.

With his arms held tightly, the car traveled for what seemed like fifteen or twenty minutes. No one said a word. Then the car stopped. The doors opened and Riker was roughly hauled from the car. With strong hands holding each arm he was marched for a short distance. A voice said, "Go up the stairs." He was guided up a flight of stairs and through a doorway. A familiar smell came into his nostrils—the odor of mold and rust. After going up another flight of stairs he was taken down a straight hallway.

He knew where he was—Sedaboud Prison. The same place he had been taken just a few days earlier.

They stopped. A door was opened—the familiar metallic sound. Riker was marched through the door. His hood and handcuffs were removed. The *mukhabarat* slammed the door and he was alone.

He was being held in a cell similar to the one in which he had been confined just three days earlier—this one was dirtier, and the bed frame was painted white, but otherwise it was the same size and shape. In the corner of the cell sat the familiar bucket, and in the metal door was the slot for meals. He went to the window. It was the same view of the brick wall.

Riker sat on the edge of the lumpy mattress. What a fool he had been! No doubt he and Amena had been followed home from the nightclub. How elementary it was, and how stupid he had been for allowing the agents to tail the Mercedes straight to Amena's house. When he and Amena were making love in her bed, were the *mukhabarat* lurking outside? Could he and Amena have been photographed through the window, or tape-recorded? Were his and Amena's most intimate moments now being gleefully shared among the crude thugs in Assad's secret police?

He sat and waited.

22.

At noon, Zafar greeted the visitors who had hurriedly assembled in living room of the apartment on Al Mutanabbi Street. Without disguising his weariness, he took his customary seat.

"Gentlemen," he said, "I understand that we have some sort of crisis?"

"Absolutely," replied Bani Mahadi. "This morning I ordered the arrest of the American, Martin Riker, as well as Amena Qabbani. Last night, after our meeting, they went to a nightclub. Then they drove in her car to her house in Baksa. He spent the night there, no doubt in a sexual dalliance. Agents of the GSD went to the house this morning and arrested them. Both were taken to Sedaboud Prison."

"What are the charges?" asked Zafar.

"Conspiring against the government, of course," replied Mahadi. "I have never trusted this man Riker. I believe he is a double agent. I do not believe he's willing to help orchestrate an attack against his own country in which his own friends and colleagues might become victims. And clearly he and the woman are in collusion."

"I admit that their behavior was unseemly," said Sami Noman. "But I'm not convinced that it's anything more than two people doing what people do."

"How about you, Nizar?" asked Zafar.

"I think we need to stick to our game plan," said Mansour. "Riker has knowledge that we need. He has come forward and offered to help us. His motivation seems to be the same as other American citizens who turn away from their country—people who go and join ISIS, or who bomb government buildings, or who reveal state secrets and flee to Russia, like that kid Edward Snowden did. I don't care who he has sex with.

Our plan is to use him to the fullest extent possible and then kill him. It's too early to eliminate him. There are too many operational holes in our program that I'm not sure we can fill. We still need how to figure out how to get the virus to the United States and dispersed among the population."

Zafar nodded thoughtfully. He took a moment to pack some tobacco into his *narghile* and light it. After taking a few puffs to get it started he held the mouthpiece in his hand. "Before we resolve the matter of Dr. Riker, I'd like to discuss an aspect of Operation Fire Sword that needs to be solidified. Sami, the other day you mentioned putting the virus in the ink that was used for printing currency. Could this approach be used with newspapers? Would it be possible to add the virus to the ink used to print *The New York Times* or *The Wall Street Journal*?"

"Yes, I think it would be possible," replied Noman. He pulled out his phone and did a quick search. "To take one example, *The New York Times* utilizes about two dozen printing facilities in the United States. They are located in every region of the country, from Seattle, Washington to southern Florida. The one in New York City is located in Queens, on the Van Wyck Expressway, half a mile from LaGuardia Airport. It's called the College Point facility. It has three hundred and fifty employees. Every weeknight it prints three hundred thousand newspapers. The job has to be completed by three thirty in the morning so that the trucks can be loaded. The newspapers are sent to destinations as far away as the New York state capital in Albany; New Haven, Connecticut; and Trenton, New Jersey.

"The large amounts of newsprint used comes in the form of huge rolls that weigh over a ton apiece.

"The pages of the are printed from plates. In the plate room, a laser etches a digital file onto a piece of oxidized aluminum, which is then washed in a sugar-based chemical, like a roll of film being developed. The finished plates are locked onto the press, and then inked.

"Having been printed, each page is simultaneously folded in half by another machine and sliced apart, to be sent along the miles of conveyor belts to where the papers are baled and put onto pallets. The goal of the assembling machine is to get each paper out the door without being touched by a human hand. The facility can manufacture up to eighty thousand complete newspapers per hour."

"That's interesting," interjected Zafar. "I like the fact that we won't be intentionally infecting anyone at the pressing plant. When the outbreak begins, if there are relatively few victims at the newspaper itself, health authorities will be slower to trace the virus back to the source."

"Let's see...." continued Noman as he peered at his phone. "The Sunday edition of the paper can be very large. Its average weight is four pounds. Sometimes it can be really huge. One of those 'big papers' was published on September 14, 1987. It weighed twelve pounds and consisted of 1,612 pages. It made the *Guinness Book of World Records*."

"What about the ink used?" asked Zafar.

"*The New York Times* prints in black and four colors," said Noman. "As for the ink itself, there are dozens of formulations. The basic components include an ink oil, which is either petroleum based or soy based; pigments to color the ink and make it opaque; resins and film formers (which bind the ink together into a film and to the substrate that protects the pigment from rubbing off); and additives, such as waxes, slip agents, and in some inks, a catalyst to assist in drying. Due to the absorbency of newsprint, newspaper inks can contain a high vegetable oil content. To my best knowledge, for its colored inks *The New York Times* uses soy, while for the black ink it uses mineral oil ink."

"If we could put the virus into a colored ink, would the presence of soy make any difference to its longevity?" asked Mansour.

"I'm not sure," replied Noman. "That's the kind of question for which we need Dr. Radznev's expertise. But he has returned to Russia to pick up the virus. He is coming back with it through the Russian naval station at Tartus."

"How about Riker?" said Mansour. "He should be a part of this discussion."

Zafar puffed his *narghile*. A cloud of smoke curled up from his mouth. "Yes—we need to resolve the question of Riker. After all, he's the reason we're here today. This is my viewpoint. While his expertise is not absolutely essential to the project, if we didn't have him we'd be facing much bigger challenges and we'd be forced to spend more time and resources on the American side of the plan. He is useful to us now, and once he is no longer useful we can dispose of him. On this we are in agreement. As for his relationship with Amena Qabbani, this does not concern me. However, if he has affection for her, then it may useful for us to keep her in prison for a while longer."

"Do you mean as a guarantee of his continued cooperation?" asked Mansour.

"Let's just say that we can tell Riker she'll be his reward for a job well done," said Zafar. "A little sugar plum at the end of the day."

"She has powerful friends on Mount Mezzeh," said Mansour. "I don't know how long she can be kept in prison without proof of a crime. Sleeping with an American doctor who is helping us with Project Fire Sword is a flimsy offense. The longer we keep her there, the more pressure will fall upon us—and particularly on Bani—to explain ourselves. Do we really need that kind of conflict?"

Zafar puffed thoughtfully. "Circumstances are telling us to push ahead quickly with Fire Sword. The longer we spend in development, the more risk there is of discovery and compromise. I'm going to pay a visit to Dr. Riker and tell him what he needs to do."

At that moment Mansour's phone buzzed. He glanced at it, and then smiled.

"Gentlemen," he said, "I have received confirmation that Dr. Radznev has arrived in Tartus with the container of smallpox virus. He's on his way to Beta Syria now. He'll be there in an hour. When we pay him the balance of one million dollars—which Madam Yaltsin has entrusted to me—we'll turn over the virus to Sami and begin the process of cultivation."

Zafar rose. "I'm going to get Riker and bring him to Beta Syria. We'll be there in time to meet Dr. Radznev. For the time being, Amena Qabbani will stay in prison. I will ensure that she is not mistreated."

Twenty minutes later, Zafar walked into the office of the superintendent of Sedaboud Prison. It was not often that Zafar visited the prison, and Colonel Razzin hoped that this highly placed spiritual leader wasn't there to interfere with the daily business of the facility.

"It is an unexpected pleasure to see you," said the colonel cordially but with reserve. "How may I help you?"

"Thank you for admitting me without prior notice," replied Zafar. "I've come to discuss two of your prisoners—the American, Martin Riker, and Amena Qabbani."

"Yes—they arrived together this morning."

"I need to take Riker with me. It is a matter of national security."

Colonel Razzin regarded Zafar coolly. "I suppose that could be arranged."

"As for the woman, she needs to stay here for a few days," said Zafar. He leaned towards the colonel and spoke precisely: "She is not to be mistreated. She needs to come out of here in good condition. All right?"

Colonel Razzin shrugged. "As you wish." He picked up the phone and ordered Riker to be brought to his office.

A few minutes later Riker appeared at the door. He was unshaven and his clothing was disheveled. On his feet were a pair of plastic sandals given to him by a guard.

"Dr. Riker, we have business to attend to," said Zafar. "Let's go to my car."

Riker and Zafar went down the stairs and got in the back of the idling ZiL. "First we'll go to the Shahbandar," Zafar told the driver. "Then to Beta Syria."

As the car pulled away from the prison entrance, Riker turned to Zafar. "What the hell was that all about?" he said. "I thought we were on the same team."

"The climate we live in is volatile," said Zafar. "Unfortunately, these things happen."

"What about Amena? Where is she?"

"Miss Qabbani is being held at the prison," replied Zafar. "She faces serious charges."

"Charges? For what?"

"That has not been determined yet. However, you can influence her case."

"Me? How?"

"I'm quite sure that if your assistance to Project Fire Storm is sincere and substantial, her situation will be looked upon much more favorably."

Riker glowered. "So you're holding her hostage."

"I wouldn't call it that. As I said, your contribution to our effort will be a significant mitigating factor."

"What if I just say, 'Screw you, I'll tell you nothing until she's released'?"

Zafar smiled. "Then I'll tell the driver to turn this car around, and you will disappear forever into the Syrian prison system. My friend, don't take it so hard. It's just business."

They arrived at the hotel. Riker hurried up to his room to shower and change clothes. He returned to the car to find Zafar in the back seat, reading a copy of the *Al Ba'ath* newspaper.

"I'm sure it feels good to get cleaned up," said Zafar as he folded the paper. The car eased onto Al Maghreb Al Arabi. "You're probably wondering what's going on. We have settled on a strategy of attack: we're going to contaminate an issue of *The New York Times*—and possibly *The Wall Street Journal* and the *Washington Post*—with the virus. We believe we can do this by putting the virus into barrels of printing ink."

Zafar's words struck Riker like a thunderbolt.

The plan was brilliant.

Newspaper ink dries by evaporation and through absorption into the paper. There would be no chemical or heat disruption to the cozy, inky environment into which the smallpox virus would be introduced. The virus would survive in the ink medium for several days while the newspaper was handled by multiple readers and transported across a wide region by taxicabs, subways, and even commercial airliners.

Just one edition of a major newspaper could be the vehicle for infecting thousands—even millions—of people with a disease that had been the scourge of humanity for centuries.

23.

For the first time, Riker knew the method of the attack and the intended victims. He did not know the timetable.

"What do you think of our plan, Dr. Riker?" said Zafar as the car sped towards Beta Syria.

"I think it's audacious and could very possibly work," replied Riker. "We face two significant challenges: how to get the virus into the United States and how to get it into one or more barrels of ink. What's your schedule? Is there a target date set?"

Zafar smiled with his mouth while his eyes stayed hard. "No, the date has not been set. It may be weeks or it may be months. There are many pieces that need to fall into place."

The car arrived at Beta Syria. Zafar and Riker went inside. They found Mansour, Noman, and Mahadi waiting in the former office of the director, which Noman had taken over.

A few minutes later Mansour's phone rang. He picked it up and listened. Then he hung up. "Dr. Radznev has arrived."

The group went to the central vestibule of the office. The Russian was standing next to the armed guard. He was carrying a nondescript metal attaché case. "Gentlemen," he said, "I have what you need."

They went into the office. Dr. Radznev put the deadly case on floor next to where he was standing. "Before we go any further," he said, "When I was here last Sunday, I vaccinated Noman, Mansour, and Mahadi. That was four days ago. Today we need to vaccinate Zafar, Dr. Riker, and anyone else who could possibly come into contact with the virus."

"I have the vaccines that you brought," said Noman, handing Dr. Radznev a plastic box.

"Good," replied Dr. Radznev. In a few moments he

had given Riker and Zafar the distinctive double prick on the arm.

"Let's go into the lab," said Noman.

"I'll stay here in the office," said Mansour. His hand was on a black airline carry-on suitcase that sat on the floor next to his chair.

With Dr. Radznev carrying the attaché case he had brought, they entered the lab. Dr. Radznev put the case on a table next to an electron microscope.

Noman then led the group into the changing room.

"We have obtained the necessary biohazard suits," said Noman. "We need to each put one on. Even though we've all been inoculated, it's imperative that we wear the suits so that we don't inadvertently carry away a virus particle on our clothing or skin."

"Nor do we want to inhale a particle and then expel it—by coughing, for instance—minutes or even hours later," added Dr. Radznev.

"Let me look at one of these suits," said Riker. He inspected one of the blue plastic full-body suits, which had manufacturer's markings in Russian. "It's a standard chemical protection suit designed for biosafety level three," he said. "It's got taped seams, an attached hood, attached sock boots and outer boot flaps, elastic wrists, a standard PVC face shield, and exhaust vents. I see that it's got an expanded back to accommodate a self-contained breathing apparatus." He turned to Noman and Dr. Radznev. "It's not a bad suit, but without positive air pressure inside the suit, it's not enough protection."

"I think you're being an alarmist," said Dr. Radznev. "These should be fine."

"With all due respect," replied Riker, "in the United States, working with a contagious virus like smallpox requires biosafety level four—the highest there is. As I'm sure you know, this level is required for work with dangerous agents that pose a high individual risk of aerosol-transmitted laboratory infections, and with agents that cause severe to fatal disease in humans for which vaccines or other treatments are not available.

This includes the Ebola virus and smallpox. When dealing with biological hazards at this level the use of a positive pressure personnel suit with a segregated air supply is considered mandatory. Positive air pressure ensures that if you rip or punch a hole in your suit, the airflow is always going out of the suit so that no airborne particles can enter."

"I'm well aware of the American standards," replied Dr. Radznev tersely.

"To reassure Dr. Riker," said Noman, "we are currently engaged in upgrading our safety systems. Positive air pressure will be delivered to the suits through an overhead system of tubes. In our suit room we will have multiple showers and other safety precautions designed to destroy all traces of the biohazard."

"Listen—do you want the virus or not?" Dr. Radznev said to Noman. "I can take it back to Russia."

"We're going to inspect a sample, just as we have planned," said Noman. "Let's not waste any more time."

The three men donned their cumbersome suits before making their way to the lab and the table on which rested the attaché case. Dr. Radznev opened the case to reveal, nestled within a foam cushion, twenty small vials.

"We have transported the virus in a liquid sorbitol solution," said Dr. Radznev. "I invite you to choose any of the vials to examine."

With his gloved hand Noman picked up one of the vials. He carefully unscrewed the top and inserted a slender pipette into the vial. Then, with a tiny drop of the liquid on the end of the pipette, he handed the vial to Dr. Radznev, who replaced the top.

Noman dragged the pipette across a tiny copper disc before dropping the pipette into a biowaste canister. He then placed the disc into the liquid nitrogen freezer. When the sample was frozen he slipped it into the vacuum chamber of the electron microscope. He then sat down at the table with its control keyboard and twin display screens.

After a few seconds of adjusting the controls and searching the image of the specimen, Noman said, "Ah—there it is. Dr. Riker, please have a look. Give me your opinion."

Riker stepped closer to the screen.

If he were not seeing it with his own eyes he might not have believed it. Before him was the characteristic lozenge shape of the virus's outer envelope, cloaked in the tiny pellet-like surface tubules, and on the inside the dumbbell-shaped core membrane with its internal DNA genome. Too small to be seen with a conventional light microscope, here was one of the greatest killers and scourges of humanity, an implacable foe that had been defeated only a few decades earlier. It was ancient, prehistoric, and without consciousness or the ability to make a choice, but yet had survived even after being eradicated in the general population. Ironically, the virus had its human caretakers in both Russia and America to thank for its narrow escape—it was they who had saved it from extinction.

"It's smallpox," said Riker as he stepped away from the screen.

"Okay," said Noman. "Let's go back to the office."

After putting the attaché case, the disc, and the bio-waste container into the biohazard cold storage room, the men changed out of their hazmat suits and went to the office.

"The product is good," Noman said to Mansour.

Mansour placed the carry-on suitcase on the desk and opened it. "Ten thousand Benjamins, as they say in America." Indeed, the case held ten shrink-wrapped bundles of hundred-dollar bills. Dr. Radznev glanced at them before closing the suitcase.

"You don't want to look at them?" asked Mansour.

"Should I?" smiled Dr. Radznev. "You're not suggesting that Madam Yalstin would be deceptive, would you?"

"No, absolutely not," replied Mansour.

Dr. Radznev picked up the suitcase. "My friends, it has been a pleasure doing business with you. I look forward to witnessing the unfolding of Operation Fire Sword. You will, of course, provide both Henri Kaminsky and me with the precise timetable of the attack. We will relay that information to the necessary people. This is a powerful weapon and it's imperative that none of our people are put at risk."

"Yes, of course," replied Mansour.

Dr. Radznev glanced at his phone. "My car is here. Good day, gentlemen." He turned and walked out the door.

Zafar took a seat at the head of the compact conference table. From inside his robe he produced a package of Turkish cigarettes. "I hope you don't mind," he said as he lit one.

"No, not at all," said Noman as he retrieved a heavy glass ashtray from a shelf and placed it in front of Zafar.

"Now then," said Zafar, "We have some operational decisions to make. First, however, you will be pleased to know that we have identified a man who works at the College Point printing plant operated by *The New York Times*. He has access to the drums of ink and knows how the ink is loaded onto the presses. He's willing to sabotage the ink."

"Sabotage?" asked Riker. "Does this man know what we're asking him to do?"

"Of course not," said Zafar. "He's under the assumption that he'll be adding some sort of adulterant that will damage the presses. For this we are paying him handsomely."

"But it's imperative that he know that he's handling a deadly virus," said Riker.

"He will know that the substance is toxic," said Mansour. "Obviously we cannot tell him that it's a deadly virus. He would never agree to handle it."

"But he could die," insisted Riker.

Zafar smiled. "As you said to me when we first met, sometimes the greater good must be served. Yes?"

"Yes," replied Riker with a nod. "The greater good."

"We're looking for others who will either serve as a backup at *The New York Times* or provide the same service at *The Washington Post* or *The Wall Street Journal*," said Zafar. "We may attempt to strike at all three newspapers or attack only one. That decision will be made later. Now then, let's discuss our work here at Beta Syria. Dr. Riker, tell us about propagating the virus."

"You already have the basic equipment that you need for successful cultivation," said Riker. "You begin with an egg, seven to twelve days after fertilization. It is placed in front of a light source to locate a non-veined area of the allantoic cavity just below the air sac. In the old days they called this 'candling' the egg, because the light source was a candle. This area is marked with a pencil. Using a jeweler's scribe, the technician makes a small nick in the shell at this position. Next, after disinfecting the surface with iodine, a small hole is drilled there at the top of the egg. If this is not done, when the virus is injected, the pressure in the air sac will simply force out the inoculum.

"For the actual inoculation, he technician should use a tuberculin syringe—a one-milliliter syringe fitted with a half-inch, twenty-seven-gauge needle. Don't use a bigger insulin syringe. The needle passes through the hole in the shell and the chorioallantoic membrane. The virus is placed in the allantoic cavity, which is filled with allantoic fluid.

"When this has been done, the two holes in the shell are sealed with melted paraffin. The eggs are then placed in a holding chamber at thirty-seven degrees. During the incubation period, the virus replicates in the cells that make up the chorioallantoic membrane. As new virus particles are produced by budding, they are released into the allantoic fluid.

"After forty-eight hours, the virus is harvested. The top of the eggshell—the part covering the air sac—is removed. There's a special tool that can do this. It's placed over the egg and makes a clean crack around the top of the egg. The flap of shell is then removed with tweezers. Using a pipette, the technician then pierces the shell membrane and chorioallantoic membrane, and removes the allantoic fluid—about ten milliliters per egg. That fluid is full of the virus."

Zafar ground out his cigarette into the ashtray. Riker was happy that the damn thing was dead; it had been decades since he had attended a meeting inside a medical facility where anybody smoked. In his community, smoking had nearly gone the way of smallpox. He had forgotten that the world was big place and over a billion people still had the habit—most of them being in Eastern Europe and China, according to a World Health Organization report he had read. Interestingly, the United States and Syria had smoking rates that were about the same. You never know what seemingly unrelated people are going to have in common.

"Therefore," said Mansour, "because of the short amount of time needed to reproduce the virus—only two days per batch of fertilized eggs—our capacity to cultivate is limited only by our equipment and the number of technicians we can assign to the project."

"That's right," said Riker.

"This evening, I intend to put ten technicians to work," said Noman. "Within one week we'll be ready to strike."

Riker's blood went cold. One week! What madness was he witnessing—and participating in? The time line was short. The clock was ticking. The lives of thousands—perhaps millions—of people were at stake.

His mind flashed to his sister Jeanne. She subscribed to *The New York Times*. She especially liked the Sunday edition with its huge arts section. So did his colleagues Dr. James Gilmore at the CDC in Atlanta and Dr. Nancy Winthrop at Mt. Bedford Hospital in New York. They read the paper in the break room and left it for others to peruse. Hell, practically every professional person he knew either read *The New York Times* or claimed to hate its liberal bias and instead read *The Wall Street Journal.* A few truly open-minded friends read both of them. The plan being hatched by Zafar and Mansour and the others was truly diabolical and, in its own way, perhaps even more shocking and evil than the attacks of September 11, 2001. This plan was quieter, stealthier, and more horrifyingly self-sustaining. How many months—years! —would it take the healthcare system of the United States, and perhaps those of other nations, to conquer the disease and eradicate it from the earth for a second time? What would be the cost in money, resources, and human lives?

To Riker, his mission was clear: Derail the plot. Save thousands of lives. Restore some small amount of sanity to the world.

And—if possible—get Amena out of prison and to safety.

As if he were reading Riker's mind, Zafar said, "Dr. Riker, do you have doubts? Is there anything you want to share with us?"

Riker took a deep breath. He quickly responded, "No. I'm good. The plan is excellent."

"Very well," said Zafar coolly. "Let's move on to the next problem. How can we transport the virus to the United States? Dr. Riker?"

Riker's mind reeled. For a split second he considered proposing a mechanism that he knew would be faulty and would result in the destruction of the virus in transit. But was this question simply a test of his dedication to the cause? These people weren't stupid. He remembered his first visit to Beta Syria just two days earlier. He had seen all the equipment necessary to begin cultivating a virus. Noman had done his homework. No, to try to fool these people could be a fatal mistake.

"Dr. Riker?" repeated Zafar.

"I'm sorry—I was thinking," said Riker. "Here's how you can ship the virus to the United States, or anywhere, for that matter. You create a liquid concentrate consisting of the virus particles suspended in a solution of fifty percent glycerol and fifty percent distilled water. Meanwhile, you obtain from a hardware store several re-freezable plastic canisters or blocks of the type that you can place in your picnic chest to keep food cold. The freezer packs are about the size of a paperback book.

"Using a syringe, you carefully withdraw the fluid from within one of the freezer packs and replace it with the smallpox-glycerol liquid. You then flash freeze the pack at minus eighty degrees Celsius. You have the necessary equipment to do that here at Beta Syria.

"The weaponized freezer pack is then placed in a Styrofoam air-express shipping container holding a quantity of caviar or other food product, and shipped to your contact in the United States. The weaponized pack would be one of six or ten such artificial ice blocks surrounding the caviar tins to keep them cool. The operator receives the shipping chest and takes out the weaponized freezer pack for use. He or she thaws it to make the concentrated liquid they will divide into subunits for each of the target printing plants or several ink barrels in one plant."

"How many freezer packs do we need?" asked Mansour.

"Let's say the smallpox liquid contains a concentration of a million virus particles per milliliter," said Riker. "Let's also say the total volume of a freezer pack of smallpox-infused liquid is five hundred milliliters, which is roughly the size of a unit of blood or a pint of milk. That means you have five hundred million smallpox particles in one freezer pack. If you put this liquid into a fifty-gallon gallon drum of ink, you've introduced five hundred million particles of smallpox into fifty gallons of liquid. You've now diluted your smallpox liquid by a factor of eight times fifty, or four hundred. Therefore, your new solution—the barrel of ink—has 1.25 million particles of smallpox per pint of liquid ink.

"A pint is a little bit less than four hundred seventy-three milliliters. The figures I've seen suggest that this amount of black ink can print the text of roughly two thousand newspaper broadsheets. If *The New York Times* consists of an average of fifty pages, a pint of black ink will print the text of forty complete copies of the newspaper. Of course you also have the other colors—magenta, cyan, and yellow. These are used in smaller quantities. But if we use the figures for black ink, we might expect that each individual copy of those forty newspapers could have thirty thousand smallpox particles embedded in its ink.

"Of course, if you want additional deadly pages, you just contaminate more barrels of ink in the same way."

"And it takes only five or ten particles to produce an infection?" asked Zafar.

"Possibly only *one*," replied Riker. "In any case, it's difficult to imagine that a newspaper which is printed with contaminated ink would not release enough virus particles to end up in the respiratory tract of the person who was reading it and turning the pages."

"And the effect could be compounded in a subway car," added Mansour. "In such a crowded and confined space, especially during rush hour, one would expect that many people who did not read the newspaper could also become infected, thereby making it more difficult for authorities to trace the disease back to its source."

"Very good," said Zafar. "I think we have concluded our business here today. Sami, you're ready to begin cultivation this evening?"

"Yes," replied Noman. "We have our technicians coming at eight o'clock tonight."

"Good," said Zafar. "Dr. Riker, I want you to be here to lend your expertise."

"All right," replied Riker.

"Let's go," said Zafar. "Dr. Riker, you may ride with me. My driver will take you to your hotel."

24.

At sunset, Riker sat in the dismal Yakouta restaurant at the Shabandar, eating what was purported to be *sayadieh*—normally a tasty dish with spiced fish and caramelized onion, garlic, ginger, and other spices. His nose told him that the fish—probably a sea bass—was not exactly "fresh off the boat," as the menu advertised. "Fresh off the truck" was probably more accurate. At least the bottle of Al-Shark was cold and refreshing.

He glanced at his watch. Seven thirty. A half hour until production of the smallpox virus was to begin at Beta Syria.

A man in a grey business suit approached him. "Martin Riker?" asked the man. His voice was cordial and non-threatening.

"Yes, that's me."

"My name is Ghassan Faris. I'm the lawyer for Amena Qabbani. May I sit down?"

"Yes, please do," said Riker.

"I hope I'm not interrupting," said Faris. Like his voice, his face was smooth, and his eyes, sheltered by carefully groomed eyebrows, regarded Riker with interest.

"No, not at all," said Riker. "Can I get you anything? A beer?"

Faris smiled. "No thank you. I won't be long. Actually, I'm here to deliver a message." He looked around at the nearly empty dining room. A waiter was loitering by the kitchen door, out of earshot.

"A message?" asked Riker.

Faris leaned closer. "Amena is going to be released tonight."

"That's good news!" said Riker.

The lawyer gave a little shrug. "Of course it is. But there's more to the story. Amena told me something that a guard had told her."

"What was that?"

"This afternoon, before I was told she'd be released, she was pestering the guards—demanding to set free, asking for her lawyer, and saying all the usual things that prisoners always say, at least until the guards start to beat them to make them shut up. One of the guards came to her cell door and taunted her. He said, 'You whore, I'll bet you want to run to your American boyfriend. Is that what you want to do? Let the doctor get back into your pants? Well, tough shit. By the time you get out, he'll be—' and the guy drew his finger across his throat. Then he laughed and walked away."

"And you were told she'd be released tonight?"

"Yes."

Riker nodded. "Okay. Thanks very much. If you can talk to her in the next few hours, tell her to go straight to her house after she's been released."

"All right," said Faris. He stood up. "Good luck." He turned and walked out of the restaurant.

A moment later the waiter approached Riker's table. "Sir—there's a car outside for you."

Riker thanked the waiter, but instead of going directly to the car he hurried to the elevator and went up to his room. He took the cash he had hidden behind the bureau but left his luggage and clothes undisturbed. He then went down to the lobby, walked past the attentive gaze of Shakira, and pushed through the revolving doors. The black ZiL was waiting. Riker got into the back seat and closed the door. The familiar nameless and nonspeaking driver guided the car onto Al Maghreb Al Arabi. They drove past Tishreen University to the old Highway 1, skirted the Martyr Basil al-Assad International Airport, and soon entered the town of Jableh.

At eight o'clock, the guards—there were now four of them, armed—allowed Riker to pass through the glass and chrome front door of Beta Syria.

In the lobby were two more armed guards. They told him that Noman wanted him to report directly to the suiting room. Riker went there and donned his blue plastic biosafety suit, taped on his gloves and boots, and put on the hood and face shield. Thus protected—inadequately, thought Riker, due to the lack of positive air hookup—he went through the airlock into the main room of the lab.

Before him he saw a space that had been transformed. Only a few hours earlier the room had been like any other semi-abandoned pharmaceutical laboratory, with bare tables and a sense of randomness to the arrangement of the equipment. Now he saw carefully organized work stations—a dozen of them— each with a hazmat-suited technician, cartons of eggs, syringes, liquid nitrogen freezers, and most importantly of all, one of the little vials of smallpox virus that Dr. Radznev had delivered in the metal attaché case and for which the Fire Sword unit had paid two million dollars.

"Good evening, Dr. Riker," said Noman, his voice muffled by the face mask and shield.

"Is the work going well?" asked Riker.

"Yes, but we have several serious issues," said Noman. "Some of the syringes are breaking the eggs. We're wasting time and resources. Here—I'll show you." He went over to a technician, anonymous in his blue plastic suit and hood. He asked the technician for one of his syringes, which he then handed to Riker.

After quickly examining it, Riker said, "The needle is too thick. It's a twenty or twenty-one gauge, which is almost twice the diameter of a twenty-seven gauge. I assume you know that needle diameter goes opposite of the gauge, right? A twenty-seven-gauge needle is less than half a millimeter in diameter, whereas a twenty-gauge is almost a full millimeter in diameter. This needle will crack the egg's shell. Make sure your guys are using thin, short needles."

Riker went to another technician. He watched for a moment before turning to Noman. "Does this man speak English?"

Noman shook his head.

"Tell him, then, that he's injecting too much of the smallpox broth. He only needs a tiny amount. One drop contains more than enough virus to produce vigorous growth."

Riker walked around the room, coaching the technicians on how to efficiently produce their little incubators of death and misery. Eventually he turned to Noman. "I think we've got a good assembly line here," he said.

"Okay," said Noman.

Riker knew what was next. Operation Fire Sword had been launched. The wheels were in motion. The machine was working. All that was left was to harvest and package the virus particles—a straightforward task—and smuggle them into the United States. Then the recruit—whoever he or she was—only had to dump the deadly broth into a barrel of printer's ink at *The New York Times*. The calamity would unfold on its own, with no human hand needed to guide it. The microscopic virus would do the work of a thousand suicide bombers.

Riker also knew that his time had run out. He was no longer useful to the Fire Sword unit. He had become expendable.

He took one last walk around the lab. Noman seemed to be watching him the way a prison guard eyes a condemned man. Riker paused by a table. On the table were several cartons. They were open. Inside were freezer packs and tins of caviar. He glanced at the labels. They read, "Adana Four Star Black Caviar— Product of Turkey."

Riker casually strolled away from the table and made his way to the suiting room. As he was changing out of his blue biosafety suit one of the armed guards entered the room and stood silently. When Riker was finished the guard said in English, "Your car is here." He motioned for Riker to walk in front of him through the door and into the lobby. Another guard was there, holding an automatic weapon. Together they escorted Riker through the doors and out of the building. The black ZiL was waiting with the engine running. One opened the back door. Riker had no choice but to get in. The guard closed the door.

Behind the wheel was the usual nontalkative, unnamed driver. But sitting next to him in the passenger seat was another man whom Riker had never seen before. He was thin and oily, with protruding ears, like a rat.

So that's what a GSD killer looks like.

The car accelerated into the night. Riker saw they were taking Highway 1 north, as would be expected.

At what point would the car take a turn off the highway and head down a lonely side road? It could happen at any minute.

They passed the airport and entered the suburb of Al-Sanobar. Riker sat calculating his chances if he had to act. They passed through Al Hannadi on the outskirts of Latakia. The two men in the front seat had said not a word.

As the car approached the bridge over the Al-Kabir al-Shamali River, Riker saw the man with the rat's ears reach into his inside jacket pocket. The car slowed down and the driver took an exit.

They're going to shoot me by the river.

Riker lunged forward, reached his arm around the driver and pulled hard on the steering wheel. The car lurched over the curb and plunged down the embankment toward the dark water. It slammed into a concrete culvert, flipped on its side, and rolled over on its roof. Riker saw the head of the rat-eared man slam into the window of the passenger door.

In the upside-down car, the driver struggled with his seat belt. Riker unlocked his and grabbed the inside door handle. The door resisted before he shouldered it open. As he tumbled into the underbrush, the smell of gasoline came into his nostrils. Riker got to his feet and saw orange flames flickering from the engine. Inside the car, the driver was frantically trying to free himself. The rat-eared man wasn't moving.

Riker backed away from the smoldering car. The driver's face turned toward him. His eyes were beseeching.

I'm a doctor, thought Riker. *I can't stand by while someone dies, even if that person is trying to kill me.*

At that moment the car exploded in a fireball.

25.

The explosion knocked Riker onto his back. An intense flash lit up the sky and a heat wave poured over him as if he had opened an immense oven door. With his face shielded by his hands, he hugged the earth. Burning fragments of metal and plastic fell from the sky.

A moment later, the only sound was the crackle of flames from the car. Riker raised his head. In the twisted passenger compartment he saw two ghastly charred bodies. For them all hope was gone.

Riker stood and took stock of his surroundings. He was on the woody embankment of the south side of the river. His hotel was three miles to the northwest. Should he risk walking there, he could cross the river and follow the railroad tracks to the Latakia Railway Station, which was about a mile from the Shabandar. There he could get his rented Toyota out of the garage and make his escape.

But escape to where?

He realized the only way he could get out of Syria was the way he had gotten in—by a fast boat. And what about Amena? The moment the GSD found out that he was alive, she'd be in danger.

Riker needed help. Who should he call? If he chose the wrong person, it could mean death.

The first order of business was to get away from the car. In this remote area by the river, it was possible that no one had seen the crash and the fire. But eventually the place would be swarming with police.

Riker followed the shore of the river in a westerly direction, towards the sea. This side of the river was agrarian, with olive groves and wheat fields. Across the dark water shone the scattered lights of the few warehouses and factories that were still operating in the wartime economy. After walking half a mile Riker came to an old boathouse, with a concrete ramp going down into the muddy current. In the moonlight Riker could see that the structure was in disrepair, with broken windows and junk piled outside. He stepped onto the uneven wooden porch and paused. No sound came from within and no light. He grasped the dented brass doorknob and turned. The door creaked open. The air inside was musty. In the gloom he saw an old rowboat, a pile of metal folding chairs, a stack of battered cardboard boxes, and a wooden worktable. Something—a rat or a mouse—scurried away into the shadows.

Riker pulled a chair off the pile, brushed it off, and sat down. He took out his phone. The bright glow from its face was reassuring.

He punched Amena's number. The call went to voicemail. He did not leave a message.

He then called Hussein.

"Yes?" said the familiar voice.

"It's Riker."

"What's going on?"

Riker quickly sketched his situation. "I need to get out of Syria."

"That will be difficult," replied Hussein. "The GSD is going to be looking for you. You'll have to stay in hiding until arrangements can be made. I can come get you—but we need to figure out where I'm going to take you."

"I've got an idea," said Riker. "I'll call you back in five minutes." Riker hung up and without hesitation pressed another number. He knew he was taking a huge risk, but he had no choice.

On the other end of the line, the phone rang.

"Hello?" said a woman's voice in Arabic.

"Is this Ghazal?" said Riker in English.

"Yes—Dr. Riker? Is that you?"

"Yes, it is. Please forgive me for the intrusion. I have an important question to ask you. May I speak very frankly?"

"Yes, of course."

Riker took a beep breath. It was time to roll the

dice. "The GSD wants me. I'm hiding from them. I need to get out of Syria, but it will take time to make the arrangements. Would you be willing to help me?"

There was a moment of silence. In his mind's eye Riker could see Ghazal calculating the reward she could get for turning the American over to the GSD. His finger moved to end the call.

"Yes, I can help you," she said. "What do you want me to do?"

With relief mixed with wary apprehension, Riker said, "Would you be willing to hide me in your house?"

There was another pause. Then, "You say the GSD is after you? What did you do?"

"I know too much about Fire Sword. It's a plot to attack the United States with biological weapons."

"Attack the United States? Are you serious? I assumed that Fire Sword was to be directed against the enemies of Syria here in the Levant, not in America."

"The initial target is New York City," said Riker. "They want to introduce smallpox on a massive scale. Start an epidemic in the United States."

"This is much worse than I thought. Much more foolhardy. Okay—can you get yourself here?"

"I think so," replied Riker. "I'll call you back."

After hanging up, Riker called Hussein, who agreed to pick him up and drive him to Ghazal's.

For a while, Riker waited in the darkness of the boathouse. Then he went outside. The night air was chilly. He walked across the scrubby yard to a small grove of trees. Picking his way through the brush that covered a low hill, he positioned himself behind two stout trunks. He had a clear view of the driveway, the yard, and the door of the old boathouse.

Soon, Riker saw a pair of headlights probe the darkness at the edge of the old estate. With its tires crunching on the gravel, a car came slowly down the driveway. Riker recognized it as Hussein's taxi. The yellow "available" bubble on the roof was dark.

Hussein stopped his taxi by the door of the boathouse. After a moment he opened his door and got out. The interior light illuminated the inside of the passenger compartment. Riker could see that Hussein had come alone.

Riker stepped out of the underbrush. "Hussein!" he called.

Hussein turned and smiled. "You got yourself in a real fix, didn't you?" he asked.

"Yeah, well, the plan is getting serious," replied Riker. "Let's get out of here before they discover the wrecked car with its two fried GSD agents."

Riker hunkered down on the floor of the back seat of the taxi. Hussein turned the car around and drove back along the gravel driveway. "We can take the back roads to Albassa," said Hussein. "Ghazal lives only about two miles from here."

Five minutes later the taxi pulled up in front of Ghazal's villa, with its two big oak trees sheltering the red tile roof.

Riker knocked on the wooden door. Ghazal answered it, and Riker and Hussein stepped into the tiled vestibule. After closing the door behind them, she ushered them into the living room with its exposed beams and reassuring stone fireplace.

"So the plan is really happening," said Ghazal.

"Yes," replied Riker. "The lab at Beta Syria has begun full production of the smallpox virus. The initial target is *The New York Times*. They intend to ship a quantity of smallpox particles to New York, where an undercover operative will dump it into the ink used to print the newspaper. The initial exposure will infect thousands of people who handle the newspaper. They in turn will infect thousands of others, and the disease will spread like wildfire before health authorities have identified it."

"This is a sickening and monumentally stupid plan," said Ghazal. "What has happened to us, and to our country? Syria used to be a marvelous place of culture and refinement. Now we are barbarians. We remember all too well the fleeting hope of the Damascus Spring. Dr. Riker, you were not here then, but for us it was a brief moment of real promise. It started after the death of President Hafiz al-Assad in June 2000 and continued for about a year, when it was crushed by the government. We saw the blossoming—like flowers—of the *muntadayāt*, which translates to English as 'salons' or 'forums.' Groups of free people met in private houses and discussed political matters and wider social questions. People from every group participated—the Syrian opposition, intellectuals, members of the Syrian Communist Party, and even reform-minded Ba'ath Party members. Prominent intellectuals signed the 'Manifesto of the 99,' demanding the right to form political parties and civil organizations, the cancellation of the state of emergency, abolition of martial law and special courts, the release of all political prisoners, and the return without fear of prosecution of political exiles. The salons debated many political and social questions, from the position of women to the nature of education methods.

"In November 2000, the government of Bashar al-Assad released of hundreds of political prisoners and closed the notorious of Mezze prison. The effects of the Damascus Spring were felt across the Arab world, and many of us were optimistic that real change was coming. It was exhilarating!

"In the autumn of 2001, it all came crashing down. The government returned to its repressive methods with imprisonments and the forced closure of the salons. The Damascus Spring withered and died.

"Now we have civil war, and only a few hours away barbaric terrorists seek to destroy us. Into this toxic brew, Operation Fire Sword adds a new international horror that will certainly result in the destruction of Syria at the hands of the Americans. Such monumental stupidity! We must do everything in our power to ensure it never happens."

"I need to get back to the United States before the plot is launched," said Riker.

"Isn't there someone you can call to give them a

warning?" asked Ghazal.

Riker shook his head. "They would never believe me. The plot would seem too incredible. I have to go to Washington and pound on doors. I need to see people face to face and explain to them what's going to happen if they don't recognize the threat."

"What if we organize an action here, in Syria?" said Ghazal. "Can we destroy the Beta Syria factory?"

"We'd need an air strike by American F-18 Hornets," said Riker. "That's not going to happen without absolute proof that the American government can take to the United Nations."

"What kind of proof?" asked Ghazal.

"A video showing the technicians cultivating the smallpox virus," replied Riker. "Or one of the conspirators—Zafar, Mahadi, Mansour, or Noman—talking on tape."

"I can do that," said Ghazal boldly.

"No—it's too risky," said Riker.

"Dr. Riker, we are very close to not having a nation any more," said Ghazal. "And now, instead of rational thinking at the highest levels of government, we have extremists cooking up insane schemes that will bring ruin upon us all. It would be criminal of me to stand by and not try to stop them. You are a wanted man; you cannot go back to Beta Syria. And Amena—once they release her from prison—cannot not go back there. I have the necessary connections to get inside. I know Bani Mahadi. He is a boastful and vain man. If I tell him that we need to shoot some video to document the stunning death blow that we are striking against the Great Satan—video that will be released only after Fire Sword has been triumphant—then he will not only give his consent, he'll throw open the doors."

"I cannot imagine a man like Zafar would agree to something like that," said Riker. "He is neither vain nor boastful."

"Then I'll have to get in and get out quickly, won't I?" said Ghazal. With those words she rose and addressed both Riker and Hussein. "It's getting late, and I'm sure you are tired and hungry. I have some *kibbeh* pie I can heat up, with some yogurt and salad."

"Thank you, but I must be going," said Hussein. He turned to Riker. "Please do not hesitate to call upon me when you need me."

"Thanks, Hussein," said Riker. "You'll be hearing from me."

After Hussein had left, Riker followed Ghazal into her kitchen. She took a covered baking dish from the refrigerator and put it into the oven. "That will take fifteen or twenty minutes to heat up," she said. "Meanwhile, we can enjoy a glass of wine." She went to the cupboard, returned with a bottle of Chianti, and poured two glasses.

"Dr. Riker, do you have family at home?" she asked.

"My wife passed away last year," he said. "I have two sons and a daughter. One grandchild."

"I'm very sorry about the loss of your wife," said Ghazal. "My husband died two years ago in the war. He was in the army. So I suppose we have something unfortunate in common."

At that moment a flash of headlights briefly illuminated the kitchen window.

Ghazal put down her wine glass. "Someone's coming," she said. "Give me your glass—quickly!"

Riker handed her his glass, which she hurriedly placed inside a kitchen cabinet. "Now come this way!" She led him into the big pantry where there was a door, which she opened. Riker saw a set of stairs leading down. "Go into the basement," said Ghazal. "Behind the furnace you'll find a door. It leads to the back yard. Wait there. If anyone comes down into the basement, sneak outside."

Riker did as she told him. At the bottom of the stairs he found himself standing on a rough concrete floor in a room cluttered with old furniture and junk. He had to stoop to avoid hitting his head on the joists that supported the kitchen floor above him. In the gloom he saw a door. He went to it and entered a second room that he deduced was underneath the back part of the house. Here there was more junk and musty boxes, and also a cast-iron oil-burning furnace with a tangle of pipes hooked up to it. Going behind the furnace, he saw a door. Opening it, he was met by a wave of cool air. In front of him was a set of old stone steps that led to another door—the way to the outside.

Here, in the dark, he waited.

26.

As Ghazal closed the door to the basement, she heard pounding on the front door. She went to it and opened it.

Standing on her front porch was a Latakia police officer. Behind him stood a man in a black leather jacket and black slacks—a *mukhabarat*.

"Yes, gentlemen, may I help you?" she asked.

"I'm Officer Shamadi," the cop said with a shallow smile. "May we come in?"

"Certainly," replied Ghazal with the same phony politeness.

She led the two men into the living room. "May I get you some tea or coffee?"

"No thank you," said the cop.

"What seems to be the problem?" asked Ghazal.

"We're investigating an auto accident that happened by the river about an hour ago," said the cop. The *mukhabarat* stood and glowered.

"I hope no one was hurt," replied Ghazal.

"Actually, the reason we're here is because we have reason to believe that a very dangerous criminal may have escaped from the car as a result of the accident," said Officer Shamadi. "He's an American." He showed Ghazal a photo of Martin Riker. It looked like a mug shot that would have been taken when he had been arrested and brought to prison. "Do you know him?"

"Why should I?" replied Ghazal. "I'm not in the habit of associating with American criminals."

"Has anyone come here tonight?" asked the *mukhabarat*.

Ghazal paused. If the secret police had been watching her house during the past hour, they would have seen Hussein's taxi arrive and then depart. If she asserted that *nobody* had come to her house that night, the police might accuse her of lying and tear the house apart.

"Only the taxi that I called," she replied.

Officer Shamadi frowned. "You called a taxi? You went somewhere?"

"No. I changed my mind. I was going to visit a friend, but decided to stay home. So I sent the taxi away."

"Don't you own a car?" asked the *mukhabarat*.

"Yes, but it needs servicing. I didn't want to drive it tonight."

The cop sniffed the air. "Cooking something?"

"Just heating up some leftover *kibbeh* pie."

The cop and the *mukhabarat* drifted into the kitchen. They carefully scrutinized the countertops, the dishes in the drainer, the table with its four matching chairs.

"We need to look around," said the *mukhabarat*.

"What for?" replied Ghazal.

"To ensure the escapee is not hiding here," replied the cop.

"Are you searching every house in town, or just the homes of loyal Ba'ath Party members and employees?"

Officer Shamadi glanced at the *mukhabarat*, as if to say, *this is your problem*.

"This man is very dangerous," said the *mukhabarat*. "He may have threatened you. We need to verify that he's not here. We'll start upstairs. Please show us the way."

As Ghazal went to the entrance hall of the house and up the stairs to the second floor, she said, "I want you to know that I've been working as a communications manager for the Party for nearly ten years. I find this intrusion to be highly insulting."

"We're very sorry for the inconvenience," said the cop as the *mukhabarat* rudely opened closet doors, peered into the bathroom, and looked under the bed.

"Okay," said the *mukhabarat*. "Take us to the basement."

Ghazal dutifully led the men down the stairs and into the kitchen pantry, where she opened the door to the cellar. "Be my guest," she said as she flicked on the light. The bare bulb cast a weak glow as the men descended the creaky steps.

The men scanned the room, with its moldering junk and old furniture. The *mukhabarat* made his way into the furnace room. After poking at the dusty boxes, he circled around the furnace.

"Where does this door go?" he asked Ghazal.

"To the outside," she replied.

He pulled it open. He then went up the stone steps to the outside door. He pushed it, but it didn't open. He pushed harder. It still didn't open. "What's wrong with this door?" he said.

Ghazal shrugged. "Nothing is wrong with it; it just doesn't open. I was having trouble with rats. That door has been shut for years."

"Okay," said the *mukhabarat* as he dusted off his pants. He looked at the cop. "Let's go."

They went back up to the kitchen, and then to the front door. Officer Shamadi turned to Ghazal. "If you notice anyone unusual, let us know," he said. "This man is very dangerous."

"Of course," replied Ghazal. She closed the door behind them, and watched through the window as their car pulled out of the driveway.

When their lights had disappeared she went outside. The night was still, and the moonlight created long shadows across the small front courtyard. She walked around to the back of the house. The old wooden door to the basement had been jammed closed with a piece of pipe. Without speaking, Ghazal stood next to the door.

As she expected, after a moment Riker emerged from the shadows of the trees behind the house.

"That was a close call," he said.

"Maybe it's better that they came so quickly," she shrugged. "Now they can cross me off their list. Usually a Latakia city cop would hesitate before entering the house of a Party member. But the *mukhabarat* are in charge of this investigation. You can be assured that someone will pay a price for letting you escape."

"Aside from the two guys who got burned to death?"

"In this climate, suspicion and blame are the default positions that everyone takes. Now let's go inside and get you something to eat."

After dinner—for which Riker was particularly grateful because Ghazal's homemade *kibbeh* pie was a welcome relief from the slop they served at the Shabandar—they retired to the living room. While it felt good to sit by the fire and relax, there was business to do. Riker pulled out his phone and dialed Amena's number.

After three rings, his heart leapt when he heard her say, "Hello?"

"It's Martin. Are you at home?"

"Yes. They released me a few hours ago. My phone battery was dead, so I had to charge it. Are you all right?"

Riker told her about his visit to Beta Syria, the attempt to kill him, and finding sanctuary in Ghazal's home. "My next job is to get out of Syria alive," he said. "I'm a wanted man. We are all under suspicion. At this moment, I'm sure the *mukhabarat* are watching your house. They may knock on your door and demand to come inside and search it."

"Okay, thanks for the warning," she said. "Listen—I have an idea. I know a guy who's got a fishing boat. He's a loyal Syrian who, like Ghazal and myself, is appalled at what our country has become. I'll contact him. He may be willing to take you to Lebanon. From there you can get back to the United States."

Riker's conversation with Amena reassured him and also made him apprehensive. Assuming he could get out of Syria alive, there was the question of Amena and her future. He found himself imagining what it would be like if she came home with him. Would she be willing to give up her life in Syria? Would the United States government admit her into the country as a political refugee? And if she came to America, would she like it? Perhaps she'd be happy in Naples—the climate was similar to Latakia, and the Gulf of Mexico was a reasonable substitute for the Mediterranean Sea. It was equally possible that she'd be miserable, although Riker would make every effort to make her feel valued and appreciated.

There was no doubt that having Amena with him would transform his life.

27.

Riker awoke at dawn. He was in the spare bedroom—the same room where Sabeen and Akram Aflaq had enjoyed their moments together. Outside his window, the sky was a rosy pink. Riker scanned the small yard and its perimeter of tall shrubs. Sparrows chattered and busied themselves in the trees. To the left and right the roofs of the neighbors' houses surfaced above the greenery. Riker looked hard for the telltale shape of a person—a man in black leather—crouching behind the woody screen, watching the house. Seeing no one, he shrugged. Maybe they were out there, maybe not.

Down in the kitchen, Ghazal was making *mamouniuyeh* with pine nuts and hunks of white cheese. Riker ate heartily.

"I'm going to Beta Syria," announced Ghazal. "I'll be back within two hours."

Leaving Riker in the house, she drove her Land Rover south to the Beta Syria facility in Jableh. She pulled up to the gate. The armed guard approached her car.

"My name is Ghazal Banir," she said as she handed the guard her identification. "I'm the Party communications manager. I need to see Sami Noman immediately."

After scrutinizing her identification, the guard waved her through.

At the front door of the lab she announced herself in the same way, and was admitted into the lobby.

After a few minutes Sami Noman came out of the suiting room of the lab. He was scowling.

"I was told that you wanted to see me," he said. "What's this all about?"

"I've talked to Bani Mahadi," said Ghazal in a tone of authority. "I've been sent here to document the patriotic work the Fire Sword team is doing at Beta

Syria. This program is a cornerstone of the rebirth of Syrian hegemony, and will be the most powerful statement ever made against the Great Satan. The effects of Fire Sword will dwarf the 9/11 plot. It's my job to record, for posterity, the valiant efforts being made by you and your staff. At the appropriate time, our president will make public these images, so that the whole world will know of the power of the Syrian people. Now then, where is the room where I can put on the proper protective equipment?"

"Wait a minute," said Noman. "I haven't heard anything about this. Why wasn't I notified?"

"The decision was made this morning," asserted Ghazal. "I ask you again to direct me to the suiting room."

"You have a camera?" said Noman.

"Smartphone," said Ghazal. "Hi-resolution video."

Still scowling, Noman turned and walked to the door of the suiting room.

Ten minutes later, garbed head to toe in blue plastic, gloves, booties, and helmet with face mask, Ghazal entered the working laboratory.

A dozen technicians, all in similar biosafety level three suits, were working at the long tables. Most were injecting eggs using small hypodermic needles, while at a different table a few were removing the tops of eggs and extracting the allantoic fluid.

"Is the smallpox virus present in this fluid?" asked Ghazal as she filmed a technician insert a few drops into a standard commercial freezer pack.

"Absolutely," replied the technician, his voice muffled by the mask and respirator. "These eggs are the very first to be harvested. We have verified that the smallpox virus is being produced inside. From each egg a sample has been taken and placed under the electron microscope. The evidence is conclusive."

Ghazal turned to Noman, who was shadowing her. "Let me see the proof under the microscope."

"I don't think that's necessary," said Noman.

"It's absolutely necessary," said Ghazal. "We must

be able to prove to the world that we have done what we said we have done. An action of this magnitude and importance must be documented. And don't forget—your name will become legendary as well."

"All right," conceded Noman. "Come this way." He led her to the big electron microscope. "We're preparing a sample now. First a tiny amount of the fluid is flash frozen, then placed in a vacuum."

"Why in a vacuum?" asked Ghazal as she filmed.

"Instead of ordinary visible light," said Noman, "an electron microscope uses a beam of electrons as a source of illumination. Because the wavelength of an electron is much shorter than that of visible light photons, the electron microscope has a higher resolving power than a light microscope and can reveal the structure of smaller objects. These beams of electrons—and the electrons that are reflected back into the viewing screen—would be knocked off course by the relatively large molecules of air. So, in order to get a clear picture, you need to get rid of the air."

"Are you seeing any smallpox particles now?" asked Ghazal as she filmed the microscope's screen.

"Yes," replied the technician, anonymous in his biosafety suit. "See? The lozenges with the dumbbell shapes inside? That's unmistakably smallpox."

"Amazing," said Ghazal. "And to imagine that these tiny weapons will be unleashed against the Great Satan! It's truly glorious to consider."

"Yes—glorious," echoed Noman.

"And then the virus particles are packed into these ordinary freezer packs? How long can they last in there?"

"Indefinitely," replied Noman.

"Then you've got to get them into the United Sates," said Ghazal. "How do you intend to do that?"

From behind his mask Noman gave her a hard look. "That has not been determined yet."

"I understand," she replied as she put away her phone. She sensed that it was time to leave. "Thank you very much for your time. I'm sure Fire Sword will be an unprecedented success."

"What's going to happen with the video file you've made?" asked Noman.

"It's not my decision," replied Ghazal. "I'm sure that it will remain top secret until such time as the president's inner circle chooses to use it to our best advantage."

"Of course," said Noman.

Ghazal returned to the suiting room with Noman. Fifteen minutes later they stepped out into the lobby.

There she was surprised to see two men waiting. One was middle-aged and wearing an expensive tailored suit, like a successful businessman. The other was younger, rougher, with jeans and a polo shirt.

Instinctively Ghazal stuck out her hand. "Hi—I'm Ghazal Faoud. I'm with the Party, in communications."

The man in the business suit took her hand warmly. "Hosni Raseen. I'm an investor."

"Oh—and what do you invest in?" asked Ghazal with a disarming smile.

"Lately, in films," replied Raseen.

"That sounds terribly risky," said Ghazal.

Raseen shrugged. "You win some, you lose some. I enjoy the challenge."

"If you'll excuse us," said Noman abruptly to Ghazal. "We're on a tight schedule. We need to get you inoculated." Taking Raseen by the arm, he steered Raseen and the young man towards the suiting room.

"It was nice to meet you," called Ghazal as she took out her phone. Pretending to make a call, she held the phone near her ear and began to record video. "I just met someone named Hosni Raseen," she said under her breath as she captured a few seconds of video of the two men. "He said he was an investor in films. Noman is giving him and his young friend the vaccine."

Noticing that the armed guard was watching her, she put away her phone. Under his watchful eye she left the building and got into her Land Rover.

When she arrived home, Riker was waiting for her

in the living room.

"Mission accomplished," she said as she went to her laptop. She quickly downloaded the video file from her phone onto the computer. Then she inserted a thumb drive, to which she transferred the videos. She handed the thumb drive to Riker. "Here's your proof," she said.

"What about Noman?" asked Riker. "What will happen when he finds out that your visit was the result not of an official order but simply of your sweet talking Bani Mahadi?"

"I've thought about that," she said. "I have a cousin who lives in Paris. I think that it might be a very good time for me to leave this place and start a new life. I've got some money stashed away in a Swiss bank account. It will be enough to provide a modest income until I can find work." She looked around the comfortable living room with its paintings on the walls and cherished mementos on the shelves. "It's a lovely place here, and I will miss it, but life is change, isn't it? You change or you die."

Riker's phone rang. He listened for a moment before saying "okay" and hanging up. "That was Amena," he said. "She's made contact with her friend with the boat. It's time for me to leave. But how about you? What are you going to do?"

"I'm going to drive myself to the border. I can use my Party position to get into Lebanon, just like Akram Aflaq did. But I can't bring along an American doctor who is wanted by the GSD. The border security agents will thoroughly search my car. Your best bet is to make your getaway by boat."

"Okay," said Riker.

He waited in the living room while Ghazal packed a suitcase. The last item she put in was a small photo of her and her late husband. It was in a silver frame. As she clicked the suitcase closed she said to Riker, "I've always believed that if you've got more stuff than can fit into one suitcase, you've got too much stuff. Of course, real life makes it difficult to live up to that ideal—but once in a while, that very same real life *forces* you to do it." She looked around the living room. "I've many wonderful memories here, and now it's time to make new memories somewhere else."

She and Riker went out the front door, which she locked behind her. "Hopefully I'll be able to sell this house before the government seizes it," she said wistfully. They walked to the garage, where Ghazal stored her Land Rover. She backed the car out of the garage, turned it around in the driveway, and after one last look at her villa drove down the tree-shaded driveway to the road.

"Amena gave me the name of the Hotel de Charme, a cheap dive used by traveling salespeople, truckers, and prostitutes," said Riker. "It's on the outskirts of town, on the new Highway 1. I'm supposed to wait there until tonight, when it will be less dangerous to make an escape by boat."

"I know the area," said Ghazal as she drove north. "The hotel is next door to the big Al Jameh gas station, where all the truckers stop."

Fifteen minutes later, Ghazal wheeled the Land Rover up to the front door of the Hotel de Charme. The plain, two-story brick structure looked like a dormitory at a community college. Double rows of blank windows stared at the street. Before Riker opened the car door, two women sauntered out of the hotel.

"It's amazing," said Riker to Ghazal, "but wherever you go in the world, from New York to Tokyo, hookers all have that same look. I don't know what it is, exactly, but it's unmistakable."

"It's that certain *je ne sais quoi*," said Ghazal.

"Thanks for all you've done," said Riker as he stepped onto the asphalt. He breathed the aroma of diesel fuel wafting over from the gas station next door. "Good luck," he said to Ghazal before he closed the door. "If you're ever in Florida, give me a shout."

"Likewise," said Ghazal. "If you come to Paris, I'll take you to the Folies Bergère."

Riker watched as she pulled onto the highway. He

then pushed open the glass door underneath the garish and weatherbeaten sign that spelled out Hotel de Charme in metal letters. He approached the desk, behind which a sullen man was sitting, reading a newspaper. Without more than one or two glances in Riker's direction the man accepted his cash payment of ten thousand Syrian pounds—about fifty bucks—for one night. With his key in hand, Riker ascended the cheaply carpeted steps to the second floor, where he found himself standing in a long straight hallway that ran the length of the building. The air smelled of smoke and sweat and spices. Room 209 was halfway down the hall. He opened the door. The room was a plain box, furnished with a sagging double bed with an electric massage attachment, a bedside table with brass lamp, an upholstered chair, cable television, and a bureau with mirror. Going to the window, he pulled aside the scratchy polyester curtain to reveal a view of the highway and, to the left, the Al Jameh gas station. It was the busiest place Riker had yet seen in Latakia, with a steady stream of cars and trucks lined up for gas, snacks, and the restrooms. In contrast to the depressing lethargy of downtown Latakia, the gas station was fairly crackling with energy. In this sorry land paralyzed by civil war, thought Riker, at least some people were still doing all the mundane, crappy things that humans do every day.

Sitting on the edge of the bed, Riker took the remote and clicked on the television. Syrian channels were mostly owned and controlled by the Syrian Arab Television and Radio Broadcasting Commission (SATRBC), an arm of the Ministry of Information. Since the start of the Syrian Civil War, to combat the criticisms broadcast from other popular media outlets such as Al Arabiya and Al Jazeera that were viewed throughout the Arab world and internationally, the government had been pumping out a steady stream of propaganda sandwiched between mindless entertainment programs. After clicking around, Riker found Ugarit TV, a channel based in Latakia that aired service, political, and social programs. There was a news broadcast. A pretty young woman in a yellow dress was sitting at a desk in front of a big Syrian flag, reading a story. To her right was a split-screen showing a video of President Bashar al-Assad talking to a group of young people in his presidential office. Everyone was smiling and relaxed.

The newscaster said, "On Wednesday, President Bashar al-Assad issued Law Number Eleven for this year, establishing a scientific agency for supporting creative individuals. The agency will be named the Distinction and Creativity Agency. The agency will scout for distinguished creative talents and provide them with support, as well as providing education for students who excel in basic education using special curricula and programs. It seeks to direct and unite the sides that find, sponsor, encourage, and care for talented, gifted, and creative individuals. The agency will be based in Damascus, and will be affiliated with the Ministry of Higher Education while still enjoying financial and administrative independence."

A nice thing to do in the middle of a civil war— establish a new government agency to encourage students to be creative.

The pretty girl in the yellow dress dutifully read another story: "Yesterday, the People's Assembly session, chaired by Speaker Mohammad Jihad la-Laham, discussed the performance of the Ministry of Water Resources during the current circumstances, and its efforts to provide water for all areas. The Assembly members affirmed the importance of rehabilitating dams and other water infrastructure, which were damaged by terrorists in the areas to which Syrian Arab Army restored stability and security, as well as implementing sanitation projects in some areas."

The People's Assembly? The "current circumstances"? What a joke!

After a few hours of this nonsense, Riker shut off the television. The steady stream of state propaganda and shows with bad popular singers was eating at his brain.

From the hallway came violent sounds—a woman shouting, and then a man. Riker went to the door and listened. The man and woman were arguing in Arabic, which Riker didn't understand, but it sounded personal. This went on for a few seconds. The man yelled something, and then there was silence. Riker was turning away from the door when he heard a shout. It came from the man, and the tone was unmistakable: deep and shocking pain. Riker unbolted the door and opened it a crack.

Lying face down on the cheap carpet of the hallway was a man wearing a black leather jacket and dark slacks. A knife was sticking out of his back.

28.

Over the prostrate man stood a woman. A hooker, by her oversexed appearance. The door to room 206, across the hall, was ajar.

The man—a *mukhabarat*—wasn't moving.

Christ! Why did this prostitute have to stab a goddamn member of the secret police on the same floor of the crummy hotel that I'm trying to hide in?

With the instinct that every doctor possesses, Riker moved swiftly.

Using hand gestures, he told the woman to run. With a last sneering look at her victim, she sauntered to the stairway and was gone.

The *mukhabarat* lay on the floor with the knife in his back. Riker bent over him. He knew that even a small wound to the chest or back could be deadly if it went deep. Knives can puncture lungs, slice organs, and cause internal bleeding and swelling that disrupts organ function.

Fortunately, the knife hadn't gone in very far—a good three inches of the blade remained exposed. Bleeding appeared to be minimal. The *mukhabarat's* leather jacket had probably saved his life by inhibiting penetration.

The man groaned. No blood came from his mouth—another good sign.

While using one hand to apply pressure around the wound, Riker carefully tested the stability of the knife. It became instantly clear to him that the blade had become lodged between two of the man's ribs. The point of the blade hadn't gone far enough to damage any organs or sever any major blood vessels.

The guy was in shock, but he wasn't going to die.

By now, other doors along the hallway had opened. Faces peered at the scene on the floor. Riker felt himself becoming increasingly self-conscious.

"Doctor!" he called. "Is there a doctor?"

The people in the doors began talking amongst themselves. None of them ventured out into the hallway.

"Does anybody speak English?" said Riker.

A man held up his hand.

"What are you waiting for?" said Riker. "Get a damned doctor up here!"

The man nervously nodded and then ran to the stairs. A moment later he returned with the hotel clerk. The clerk looked at the scene in the hallway, cursed, and took out his phone. After punching a number he spoke in Arabic. Then he hung up.

"What did he say?" demanded Riker of the nervous guy.

"That there had been an accident at the hotel," the guy replied.

"Okay," said Riker.

The *mukhabarat* groaned and tried to get up. Riker held him down.

"Tell him to stay down and that help is on the way," Riker told the nervous guy.

The nervous guy spoke to the *mukhabarat* in Arabic. Under his hands, Riker felt the man relax.

The group waited in the hallway. Riker overheard someone say "American" in Arabic. *How ironic,* he thought, *if I were arrested because I stayed to help save the life of a member of the hated secret police.*

Then he thought of the thousands of lives that were at risk in America, and the knowledge that he—and only he—needed to carry back across the Atlantic to save those lives.

He had to get out of the hotel.

"You!" he said as he pointed to the nervous guy. He motioned him to come closer.

The nervous guy edged near.

"I must leave," said Riker. "You take over. Put your hands here. Press down. Okay?"

The guy did as Riker instructed.

"Whatever you do, *do not* pull out the knife!" said

Riker. "Leave it exactly where it is. Do you understand?"

"Yes."

"Don't worry—you'll be a hero," said Riker as he removed his hands from the victim's back.

The nervous guy nodded. He did not smile.

Riker stood up. Everyone in the hallway was looking at him. Any moment, an ambulance—and the police—would come screeching into the driveway of the Hotel de Charme. He would be exposed and arrested.

He turned. At the end of the hallway was a door with a glowing red sign over it. Without a word he walked to the door, opened it, and stepped into a cinderblock stairwell. After descending the single flight of metal stairs he pushed open another door and walked out into the parking lot.

Under the dismal overcast sky, Riker casually strolled over to the Al Jameh gas station. As he walked he pulled out his phone. He tapped Amena's number.

She answered.

"Listen, I had a problem at the hotel," he said. "I had to leave. I'm going to the gas station, but I probably shouldn't stay there either. Too many cops will be around. I'll tell you more when I see you. It's almost sunset. When can we leave? Not for another two hours? Okay. I'll just keep moving until you pick me up."

He went into the convenience store section of the gas station. The shelves were mostly bare, but there was a rack with a few baseball caps for sale. New York Yankees? No, too American. Nike? Ditto. Ah, here was one—a red and white cap with the logo of the Syria National Football Team. For decades they had competed for the World Cup, but had never reached the finals. Riker then went to the sunglasses rack, which was also nearly empty. He picked up an unfashionable pair of aviators with yellow lenses that made the world look as if it had been drenched in lemonade. He then went to the newsstand and picked up a copy of *Al Ba'ath*, the party newspaper.

After paying at the cash register, Riker donned the glasses and jammed the cap low over his forehead. He glanced into the little cracked mirror on the sunglasses rack. He looked like a rural trucker who had just returned from a trip to the nineteen eighties. With his newspaper in hand, he stepped outside of the building and looked over at the Hotel de Charme. An ambulance was waiting by the front door, and there was a police car. It wouldn't be long before the second-floor guests told the police about the English-speaking doctor who had treated the victim before suddenly walking away. The first place the cops would come would be to the gas station.

He took out his phone and punched Amena's number. He told her he had to get away from the neighborhood.

"Okay," she said. "About a kilometer away from the gas station, as you walk towards downtown, there's a diner called Kiss Kabob. Wait there for me."

Riker hung up and started walking. The street led through an industrial area of slab-sided warehouses and weedy parking lots full of old trucks. Crossing a rusty rail spur, he entered a commercial neighborhood of gas stations, shabby mom-and-pop stores, and greasy spoon eateries.

Kiss Kabob was the nicest looking place on the block, with fresh paint on the brick façade and a colorful wooden sign over the door. He went inside. The place had a counter with stools, a few small tables, and four or five booths. A young woman stood behind the counter, drying glasses. There were two middle-aged women sitting at a table. The setup reminded Riker of those funky diners that young entrepreneurs start in low-rent neighborhoods.

Wishing to minimize direct contact with the girl—it would be madness to assume she was politically progressive—Riker took a seat in a booth. After a few minutes the girl came around the counter and approached him. Handing him a menu, she addressed him in Arabic.

Riker smiled and quickly pointed to a photo of a chicken kabob.

"Do you speak English?" asked the girl.

"Uh, yes," Riker said.

"American?"

"No—Canadian," he replied.

She smiled. "I'd love to go to Canada."

"Well, maybe someday you will."

The girl returned to her counter and stuck the order ticket on a little clip next to the window to the kitchen. A young man peered out of the kitchen, took the order, and disappeared.

Riker glanced at his watch. It was after eight o'clock. The inside of the restaurant was now brighter than the gloomy sky outside. A few scattered streetlights had come on.

The girl delivered his plate—mercifully, without engaging him in further chitchat. The kabobs were excellent—tender and perfectly seasoned. Riker was pleased that what he hoped would be his last meal in Syria was a good one, served by a young person who, despite the miserable pit into which her country had fallen, still had hope for the future.

A vehicle pulled up in front of the restaurant. Riker glanced over the top of the little café curtain and saw through the window that it was a Latakia police car. He watched as an overweight cop got out of the car and huffed towards the front door. The cop came into the restaurant and, after a perfunctory glance around, went to the counter, on which, to support his heavy bulk, he rested his elbows.

The girl smiled at him and they talked for a few minutes. She did not look at Riker. Then the guy in the kitchen put a bulky paper bag on the sill of the window before hitting the little bell, which went "ping." The girl picked up the bag, stapled shut at the top with the order ticket, and handed it to the cop. He thanked her, turned, and with a quick glance in Riker's direction, waddled his way to the door.

Riker peered over the café curtain and watched as the cop got back into his cruiser and drove away. Riker had seen no money change hands.

The two women paid their bill and left. Riker was the only customer left, and the guy from the kitchen was now behind the counter, fiddling with the coffee machine. Riker got the impression that they were getting ready to close.

Where was Amena?

The girl came over to him. "Will there be anything else?"

Riker said, "No, I'm fine, thank you. Just the bill."

She put it on the table. "Thank you for coming."

Riker had been nursing his cup of cold tea. He looked at his watch. Eight forty-five. He couldn't stall much longer. After taking the last swallow of tea, he stood up and went to the counter, where there was a cash register. He paid his bill.

"Thank you," said the girl. "We hope to see you again."

"I hope so too," said Riker. He went to the door and stepped outside.

It was now fully nighttime. The overcast sky blotted out the moon. The city was quiet, and in the distance Riker could hear the low rumble of trucks on the highway.

A pair of headlights came down the street. Riker watched as it came closer. It was a Mercedes.

A moment later Amena's car came to a stop. He opened the front passenger door and got in.

Amena was behind the wheel. Without thinking, Riker leaned over and kissed her. "It's good to see you," he said. "You're like an angel. A beautiful angel."

She smiled. "And you are my handsome hero. But enough of that—we need to hurry. Joram is waiting."

She drove north up to Sports City Boulevard and turned into the Fishing and Tourism Marina. Near the end of a long, narrow jetty constructed of piled stones, she pulled over and parked.

Riker got out of the car. The salty air was still and

the low clouds made it feel as though a heavy blanket hovered overhead. He and Amena walked to the edge of the jetty, which was built out as a pier. Tied to the pilings was a fishing boat. It was about forty feet long, with a steel hull and, mounted on the flat deck of the stern, a big horizontal drum for reeling in the seine nets that caught midwater fish like mackerel, sardines, and hake. On the prow was painted the name Lucky Lady.

"Joram!" Amena called.

From the rusty wheelhouse a man emerged. He had a big black moustache and a shock of black hair, and he wore a dirty yellow weatherproof parka.

He gave Amena a little wave. "Ah, so there you are," he said. "What kept you?"

"I was afraid I was being followed, so I took a roundabout way to pick up Dr. Riker."

Joram eyed Riker. "So you're our passenger?"

"Yes," replied Riker. "I'm very grateful you're taking me to Lebanon."

"Do you have the cash?"

Riker nodded, and gave him fifty thousand Syrian pounds.

"All right, let's shove off," said Joram after he had counted and pocketed the cash.

Riker turned to Amena. "I want you to come with me to America," he said. "It's too dangerous here. It's going to be a very long time before Syria returns to normal—if it ever does. You can start a new life. I'll help you."

"Martin, I would love to come with you," she replied. "You're very special to me. I will never forget our time together. But I have to stay. This is where I was born, and my father and mother are buried here. You understand, don't you? I hope that some day, when this war is over, I can come visit you in Florida. But until then, this is where I belong."

She kissed him tenderly on the cheek.

"Now get going," she said.

Riker stepped onto the wooden deck of the boat.

Joram shook his hand. "Have you ever been on a fishing boat before?"

"In fact, yes—when I was in college I spent summers working on a shrimp boat in the Gulf of Mexico."

"Ah—well then, you should feel right at home," said Joram with a big smile that revealed an urgent need for the services of a dentist. He turned and opened the door to the wheelhouse. "Qasim! Please come here!"

A young man emerged—skinny, with big brown eyes and a mop of curly hair. He looked like a friendly hound dog.

"This is Dr. Martin Riker," said Joram. "We are giving him a lift down the coast, to Tripoli, in Lebanon. After we drop him off, we'll go to the fishing banks."

"Tripoli is about a hundred and twenty kilometers from here, right?" said Riker. "That's about seventy-five miles. How fast can you go? Ten knots?"

"Maybe twelve," replied Joram. "To avoid the Lebanese navy we'll have to hug the coastline, which will add to our time."

"So it should take us about seven hours to get there," said Riker.

Joram nodded. He then went into the wheelhouse. Riker heard the low rumble of the twin diesel engines, and the deck under his feet began to vibrate. Qasim cast off the ropes. Riker waved to Amena. She smiled and blew him a kiss before turning away and walking back to her car.

Riker joined Joram in the wheelhouse. The Lucky Lady eased away from the pier.

29.

Under the moonless sky, the Lucky Lady made her way towards the breakwater and, beyond it, the open sea. "We need to go very slowly here in the harbor," said Joram. "You have to keep your wake down, and you never know when some guy in a dory will appear out of nowhere."

"How long have you been fishing?" asked Riker.

"My entire life," replied Joram. "My father owned a boat, and from the time I was a little kid he put me to work on them. I learned how to repair the nets, clean the gear, maintain the engines, navigate the waters—everything. He also taught me the most valuable lessons of all, which are how to get a fair price for your catch and how to avoid getting into trouble with the government. But fishing has never been a big business in Syria. The Syrian fishing industry, if it can be called that, has always been the smallest in the eastern Mediterranean. Even though most of the species of fish in the Levant basin of the Mediterranean are found off the Syrian coast, the catch has never been very big. This is because the continental shelf off the coast is narrow—rarely wider than four miles—and interrupted by undersea canyons that plunge to nearly a mile deep. As a result, there is little for fish to feed on, and hence, few fish. Somehow, I and a few others have managed to survive in this desolate part of the sea."

Through the pitted windshield Riker could see the long low shape of the breakwater, with its blinking light at the end. The engines chugged reassuringly, and with every minute that passed Riker knew he was that much closer to going home and smashing the deadly Fire Sword plot. He patted his pants pocket and felt the small shape of the flash drive. It was safely there, carrying the shocking secrets of the smallpox lab at

Beta Syria.

A few minutes later they passed the breakwater light and entered the open sea. Riker turned around for one last look at the skyline of Latakia. While he was glad to see it left behind in the wake of the boat, he couldn't help but think of the dangers faced by Amena, Hussein, and the many other people who only wanted an end to oppression and war.

At that moment Joram muttered to himself in Arabic as he peered intently through the glass.

"What is it?" asked Riker.

"A damned Syrian navy patrol boat," said Joram. "He's headed this way."

Looking through the windshield, Riker saw the green and red lights. They were perhaps a mile away.

"Qasim!" called Joram.

The kid quickly appeared in the wheelhouse.

"Take Dr. Riker down to the storage locker. Hide him there until we can get rid of these guys."

Grabbing Riker by the arm, Qasim said, "Quickly! Follow me!"

Qasim led him out of the wheelhouse, through a door, and down a steep ladder. Riker found himself in a cramped saloon, with a small table flanked by cushioned benches. They passed through the narrow galley and came to another door. Qasim opened the door and they descended a short, steep ladder into a storage area that smelled of oil, rust, and fish. Here the throb of the engine was loud, and Qasim had to shout to be heard. He pulled open a hatch to reveal a tangled mass of nets. Quickly he pulled out a pile of netting. The stench of rotten fish filled the gangway.

"Get in!" he ordered.

"Hurry up!" called Joram down from the wheelhouse. "They're coming alongside!"

Crouching low, Riker squeezed through the narrow opening of the hatch and, shoving aside a tangle of nets and floats, burrowed his way into the locker. Behind him, Qasim crammed in the heap of stinking nets until Riker was pinned against the bulkhead.

Then, like a traveler who must sit on his suitcase in order to close it, Qasim mashed the door shut and latched it.

Riker was plunged into complete, rancid darkness. He could barely breathe, and the air that he got into his lungs smelled like the glop that fills up the dumpster behind the fish shack.

Outside, the Syrian craft pulled next to the Lucky Lady. It was a Russian-made Zhuk class patrol boat, seventy-eight feet long and equipped with two machine guns. The two boats were quickly lashed together. The Syrian boarding party—two seamen and a first lieutenant—stepped onto the deck of the Lucky Lady.

The lieutenant, a short man with a round face and round eyes, demanded to be taken to the wheelhouse. Qasim opened the door for him, and he entered the narrow space.

"Joram Habdan—what are you doing out here in the middle of the night?" the lieutenant demanded.

"Well, if it isn't my old friend Lieutenant Lobat," smiled Joram. "You haven't bothered me in weeks! Where have you been? I suppose you've got a lot of important things to do, and can't always be concerned with an old fisherman like me."

"Answer my question," replied Lieutenant Lobat.

"I'm going out to catch mackerel."

"At night?"

"The fish don't care if it's day or night. Do you think they have little hotels they go to when the sun goes down? No. They're still out there, swimming around, ready to be caught."

"We need to search this sorry excuse for a boat," said Lieutenant Lobat.

Joram shrugged. "Be my guest. Anything in particular you're looking for?"

"An American doctor," replied Lieutenant Lobat. "He's an extremely dangerous enemy of the state."

Joram turned to Qasim. "Please show these gentlemen around. I hope this won't take long. I've got fish to catch."

While one of the Syrian seamen remained in the wheelhouse, the lieutenant and the other seaman followed Qasim out onto the deck. They searched the external storage lockers before Lieutenant Lobat ordered Qasim to lead them below. They went down to the saloon, and then to the living quarters—Joram's tiny private stateroom and the crews' quarters with its three narrow bunks. Lockers were opened and mattresses and bedding tossed on the deck. The group then made its way through the galley and down to the hold and the engine room. The big ice chests were opened and the fish cleaning area inspected.

"What's in there?" demanded the lieutenant, pointing to a hatch.

"It's where we store extra nets," replied Qasim.

"Open it."

Qasim went to the hatch, unlocked it, and pulled it open.

Taking a flashlight, the lieutenant peered inside at the stinking heap of nets.

From where he was huddled in the darkness deep inside the compartment, Riker could see the eager fingers of light reaching out to him through the openings in the twisted cords.

"Pull some of this stuff out," demanded the lieutenant.

Qasim took out a small hunk of netting and Styrofoam floats, which he dumped at the lieutenant's feet.

The lieutenant's eyes began to water from the stench. He bent low again and, with his flashlight, probed the dense cordage.

"Okay," he announced as he stood upright. "Put it back."

Qasim mashed the netting back into the compartment, closed the hatch, and locked it. Once again, Riker was plunged into rancid darkness—but this time with a massive sense of relief.

The party made their way to the deck.

"Did you find your escaped doctor?" asked Joram.

"You may go on your way," replied the lieutenant. "When do you expect to return?"

"Maybe tomorrow, maybe the next day," replied Joram with a shrug. "It depends on whether we catch any fish."

The Syrian boarding party returned to the patrol boat. The lines were cast off and the boat eased away into the night.

Joram pushed the throttle and the Lucky Lady chugged ahead. When the Syrian patrol boat was out of sight, Joram turned to Qasim. "Why don't you release our guest from his prison? I'm sure he's ready to rejoin the living."

Down below, Riker was waiting in the darkness, mashed up against the bulkhead, barely able to breathe the foul air. The sound of the engines told him that the Lucky Lady was under way. But in what direction? Was she headed for the open sea, or was she being escorted back to Latakia by the patrol boat?

Through the dense tangle of nets Riker saw the flash of light of the hatch door being opened. He tensed his muscles, ready to put up a fight. He felt the nets being pulled away and the pressure against his body eased.

"Dr. Riker!" came the voice of Qasim. "They're gone! You can come out now."

Peering through the nets, Riker saw the welcoming face of Qasim. With a vigorous shove, he pushed away a pile of cordage and crawled out of the compartment. For a moment he kneeled on the deck, gasping for air. Then he got to his feet while Qasim repacked the compartment and closed the hatch.

"My God, I stink to high heaven," said Riker.

"There's a shower next to the captain's quarters," replied. "If you can stand the cold water, you're welcome to it."

Given the choice between freezing for a few minutes and stinking for hours, Riker chose the icy cure.

Fifteen minutes later he entered the wheelhouse.

"You smell only a little bit rancid," said Joram with a smile, "just like any ordinary fisherman who's been out working on a boat."

Joram followed the coast so closely that Riker could make out the lights of individual houses on the shore. As they passed the busy port of Tartus, Joram warned Riker that he may have to return to his smelly hideout, but no Syrian patrol boats appeared to challenge the Lucky Lady. "You never know," shrugged Joram. "Sometimes they're all over you like seagulls on a garbage scow. Other times they're asleep. You take your blessings when you get them."

As the cold dawn glimmered in the east, the lights winked out and the contours of the landscape emerged. Joram guided the Lucky Lady into a small harbor, where there were a few boats tied among a group of docks presided over by a sturdy red fishing shack.

"This is the town of Al Aabde," said Joram as the Lucky Lady gently bumped against one of the rickety wooden docks. "We're about ten kilometers north of Tripoli. My friend Assal owns this marina. Ah—there he is now."

A skinny man with white hair and beard emerged from the fishing shack. With a friendly wave he hobbled down the dock towards the Lucky Lady.

"He was wounded during the wars in Lebanon in the nineteen-eighties," said Joram. "A piece of shrapnel from a Syrian bomb took a bite out of his leg. But now Lebanon is at peace—and we hope that it can last." Joram went outside the wheelhouse to the deck. Riker followed him.

"Assal, how are you?" said Joram as he tossed the old man a line.

"Heaven willing, I'm still walking the earth," he replied with a big smile that revealed a set of brand new dentures. Riker thought to himself that if he ever got false teeth, he'd tell the dentist to make them look slightly funky, like real teeth. It was weird seeing a guy with a wrinkled face and white hair sporting a set of perfect choppers.

Riker stepped onto the dock. The morning air was crisp and cool. He turned to say goodbye to Joram. "Thanks for getting me out of Syria. I wish you the best of luck—both for you and for your country."

"May the peace of Allah be with you, too," said the captain. Riker helped Assal cast off the lines, and the Lucky Lady turned to the open sea.

Riker walked with Assal along the dock towards the fishing shack. "I need to get to Beirut," he said. "The American embassy."

Assal smiled with his gleaming teeth. "For a small fee, anything is possible!"

"Yes," said Riker. "Anything is possible."

30.

In the laboratory at Beta Syria, Sami Noman, garbed head to toe in his blue biohazard suit, carefully placed the lethal freezer pack into the carton marked "Adana Four Star Black Caviar—Product of Turkey." He nestled the freezer pack into the grey foam among the other packs and the tins of caviar so that it was firmly held. After placing another piece of grey foam securely on top, he closed the flaps of the box and sealed it with packaging tape.

He stood up, and, carrying the box, went into the changing room. After taking off his biohazard suit and washing his face and hands, he brought the box out of the room and into his office, where Zafar, Mahadi, and Mansour were waiting. After placing the carton on the table, he stood back.

"That's it?" asked Zafar, nodding at the carton. "That's our first shipment?"

"Yes," replied Noman. "In this box—in just one freezer pack—there is enough smallpox virus to infect thousands of people and trigger an epidemic in the United States."

"How long will the virus last in the freezer pack?" asked Mahadi.

"It could last a week or even longer," Noman. "Plenty of time to get the virus to the target."

"Has the target been determined with certainty?" asked Mansour.

"Not yet," said Zafar. "We are considering *The New York Times*, *The Washington Post,* and *The Wall Street Journal*. Our choice will be determined by our final assessment of the logistics of placing the smallpox culture into a barrel of printing ink. This could happen at any stage in the supply chain—from the manufacturing of the ink, the transport, the storage at the newspaper printing plant, or even during the moment before the ink is poured into the printing press. We have several operatives on the East Coast of the United States, and we're assessing the best tactic to use to achieve our objective."

"In addition," added Noman, "The production of the virus will continue here at Beta Syria. This is in case we're able to strike on multiple occasions—if, for example, the source of the outbreak is not quickly identified and we determine that a second or third strike is possible. We are also creating a backup supply in case this one is intercepted. Just because we are shipping this carton does not mean our work here is complete. Far from it."

"Very good," said Zafar. "There is another piece of business that we need to attend to: the American, Martin Riker. As you know, two nights ago the car in which he was being transported ran off the road and crashed. The car exploded and burned. The bodies of the heroic driver and the GSD agent were recovered. They died almost instantly. The body of Martin Riker was not found. An intensive search of the area was made but he was not captured. I don't need to tell you that this is extremely serious. If he has survived, which I believe he did, and he's been able to slip out of the country, then he will of course tell what he knows to the American authorities.

"Amena Qabbani has been interrogated. On that particular evening, she was at home—we can verify this because her house was being watched—and the next day, Thursday, she was at work. She left work around eight o'clock last night. Unfortunately, for about an hour the agent who was shadowing her lost her. We re-established contact with her when she returned home at nine o'clock. When confronted by our agent, she said that she had been out shopping.

"Meanwhile, the woman from the communications office of the Ba'ath Party—someone who should have impeccable credentials—has utterly vanished. What do you know about this, Bani?"

"What do you mean?" stammered Mahadi.

"The woman, Ghazal Faoud, used your name to gain access to this facility," said Zafar coolly. "She used a smartphone to film the operation. We've verified that there was no such project ordered by Party headquarters. And now Faoud has disappeared. She emptied out her bank account and has vanished. Can you explain this?"

"I know absolutely nothing about it!" protested Mahadi.

At that moment three *mukhabarat* entered the office. Two carried automatic weapons. They stood behind Mahadi.

"Bani," said Zafar, "the strange disappearances of Akram Aflaq and Ghazal Faoud have your fingerprints on them. Taken together, these two incidents have raised serious questions."

"That's crazy!" said Mahadi.

"These gentlemen need to take you downtown for some questioning," replied Zafar. "I'm sure that if you fully cooperate, you will have no problems. Okay?"

Shaking and ashen, Mahadi rose to his feet. One of the agents swiftly bound his hands behind his back with a plastic zip tie. With his head held high in a futile show of defiance, Mahadi had no choice but to allow himself to be escorted from the room.

Zafar rose. "Sami and Nizar, please follow me."

With puzzled expressions, the two men stood up and followed Zafar out of the office. Going through the lobby and out the front door, they saw that the agents hadn't taken Mahadi to one of the cars that were waiting in the parking lot. In fact, they were nowhere to be seen. Without making a comment, Zafar led the two men around the side of the building. Just ahead, they saw the three *mukhabarat* turn the corner with Mahadi between them. A moment later all of them were at the back of the building, where there were no windows, just a loading dock and a dumpster.

A man was waiting there. He was dressed like the others—black leather jacket and dark slacks—but with one difference: he wore a black ski mask.

Without hesitation, the executioner put a gun to the back of Mahadi's head and told him to kneel on the broken asphalt. Mahadi complied. The executioner pulled the trigger. With a sharp "pop" from the gun, Mahadi slumped forward onto the ground. The executioner leaned over and the gun popped again. Mahadi's body jerked once and was still. Blood and brains seeped from his shattered skull.

The executioner stepped back and holstered his pistol.

The three *mukhabarat* hoisted the corpse and tossed it into the dumpster.

"The disposal company will be here in a few hours to cart away the dumpster," said Zafar. "By sunset, the body will be incinerated. Let this be a lesson to all of us of the seriousness of our mission. We cannot have any more mistakes. The stakes are too high."

The seven men walked around to the front of the building. The three *mukhabarat* and the executioner got into a black ZiL and drove away. Zafar, Noman, and Mansour entered the lobby.

Mansour and Noman said nothing. Silently they took their seats at the conference table in the office.

"Now then," said Zafar, "I hope that we can proceed with Operation Fire Sword without any more stupid mistakes. The unfortunate fact is that we still have several problems, chief among them the apparent escape of Martin Riker. We can only assume that the video taken by Ghazal Faoud will also find its way to the Americans. To counteract these problems, we have someone tracking Riker, and we expect to pick up his trail. When we do, we will move swiftly to eliminate him, either here in the Middle East or in the United States. The same goes for Ghazal Faoud." He turned and put his hand on the carton of caviar. "It is therefore all the more imperative that we execute our plan swiftly. I have arranged for a Turkish sympathizer to take this carton to Mersin, on the southern coast of Turkey, and thence to Istanbul. From there it will be sent to Berlin, and on to the United States. The transit will take three days. Therefore, it's possible that Operation Fire Sword could be set into motion as early as Tuesday morning, the eighth of December. That could be the day that smallpox begins to wreak its havoc on the American people."

"The beauty is that the attack will not manifest itself until twelve to fourteen days later," said Mansour. "This is when the symptoms of the disease will begin to appear."

"It would be just before Christmas," smiled Zafar. "It would be a spectacular holiday gift to the Great Satan."

There was a knock on the door.

"Ah—that would be our courier," said Zafar.

The door opened and a man entered. He was about forty years old, very fit, and wearing a grey business suit.

"May I introduce Ahmet Demir," said Zafar as the man shook hands all around. "For reasons that are too lengthy to go into now, Ahmet shares our hatred of the United States and its long history of imperialistic meddling in the affairs of sovereign nations. However, Ahmet has one singular advantage over us: As a member of the Turkish diplomatic corps, he enjoys much more freedom of travel than we do. We are grateful to him for stepping forward and providing us with his services."

Zafar picked up the box and handed it to Demir. "I entrust this to you, my friend, and look forward to celebrating with you the ultimate achievement of Operation Fire Sword."

Demir accepted the carton with its lethal contents. "We will not fail," he said. "The Americans will regret the day they chose to oppose us."

31.

As he stirred his tea with a silver spoon, Dr. Luka Radznev let his eyes drink in the quiet beauty of Lake Seliger. He had worked hard to pay for this charming dacha, with its roaring fireplace, rustic stone walls, and wide-timbered floors cushioned by soft Persian rugs. Located a few hours from Moscow, Lake Selig had long been the ideal place to get away from the hectic city, relax in nature, and regain spiritual balance. Nestled between the Tver and Novgorod Oblasts, Lake Seliger—one of the largest lakes in Russia—had been formed eons ago by a glacier. Dr. Radznev's nineteenth-century dacha was comfortably situated among rustic churches, strikingly beautiful manors, native Russian wooden houses decorated with multicolored tiles, and the old theater, one of the first in the Russian empire open to the general public.

Dr. Radznev turned away from the snowy scene at the window and went to his desk. Putting down his teacup and saucer, he opened his laptop to see if the internet provided any breaking news about a smallpox epidemic in the United States. His clients in Syria— Zafar, Mansour, and the others—had been maddeningly vague about the exact timetable of the attack. He had told them that it was important to tip off the Russian diplomats and businesspeople in New York and Washington that they needed to get smallpox vaccinations, and in fact Dr. Radznev had, himself, attempted to suggest this to the Russian Foreign Ministry without exactly coming out and saying why. While many Russians, including the very wealthy Ilana Yaltsin, would cheer Operation Fire Sword, it was likely that others, including people in the inner circles of the Kremlin, would be opposed. Dr. Radznev shook his head. Some people had no imagination! Why, the most powerful weapon on earth was sitting right there at Vector; and while bureaucrats moaned about the many enemies of Russia and how the nations of NATO had encircled Russia with deadly missiles aimed at Moscow, these same career windbags did nothing to change the situation. At least Zafar and his band of Syrians had the courage to take decisive action!

Dr. Radznev had been happy to pocket two million dollars of Ilana Yaltsin's money in exchange for no more smallpox material than would fill a test tube. If another country or group wanted to make the same deal, it would be no problem—there was plenty more smallpox where that came from, as well as other nasty stuff, like anthrax.

In fact, Dr. Radznev had another potential client lined up. He had gotten a call from a man who said that he represented someone in East Asia whom Dr. Radznev took to believe was the dictator of North Korea, Kim Jong Il; and that this person had taken an interest in acquiring a quantity of the smallpox virus. For the North Korean dictator, Dr. Radznev thought he might jack up the price to four million dollars. After all, the North Korean government was rolling in cash, simply because they didn't spend any money on nuisances like food and electricity for the twenty-five million citizens of North Korea who were so unlucky as to be neither employed by the military nor part of Kim's secretive inner circle.

Dr. Radznev glanced at his watch. It was nearly eleven o'clock in the morning—time to leave and meet his contact.

After putting on his overcoat and fur hat, he went to his garage and fired up his Mercedes—no crummy Russian car for him, thank you. The drive into the town of Ostashkov took only fifteen minutes, and Dr. Radznev quickly found his destination—the charming Café Pushkin, on the lake near the old Orthodox Cathedral, with its five green onion domes topped by ornate metal crosses. Dr. Radznev took a seat in a booth in the back, where he and his companion could talk in private.

Exactly at eleven o'clock a man entered the café. He was thin, with a protruding Adam's apple and wide eyes that made him look a bit like a startled chicken. He spotted Dr. Radznev and came over to the booth.

"May I sit down?" the man said.

"May I know your name?" asked Dr. Radznev.

"Spasky," said the man.

"Yes, please do, Mr. Spasky," replied Dr. Radznev. "What will you have? The *kalduny* are delicious. They're stuffed with tender veal, cabbage, and sour cream."

"No thank you," said Spasky. He lowered his voice. "I'd like to get right down to business. As I mentioned on the phone, I represent a highly placed buyer in the Pacific Rim."

"I must interrupt you," said Dr. Radznev with a smile. "I need to know the exact identity of the person or organization to whom I am selling this material."

Spasky regarded Dr. Radznev with his unblinking round eyes. "I represent the State Security Department of the Democratic People's Republic of North Korea, which, as I'm sure you know, is an autonomous agency of the North Korean government reporting directly to the Supreme Leader."

"Very well," said Dr. Radznev.

"And now it is my turn to ask a question," said Spasky. "How am I to know that the material is genuine? I can't exactly test it out on myself, can I?"

Dr. Radznev smiled. "Absolutely not—I do not recommend testing it on yourself or anyone else. To verify the presence of any virus in a growth medium, you need an electron microscope. If neither you nor your client has easy access to one, you can buy a good one for five thousand American dollars. The other thing you can do is watch the newspapers in the next few weeks. You will see a tremendous outbreak of the disease in the United States. Of course, they will eventually bring it under control, but it will cause much suffering before they do."

"This was your material?" asked Spasky.

"Absolutely," said Dr. Radznev.

"And it came from Vector?"

Dr. Radznev shrugged. "You should know that there are only two places in the world where you can get this virus. And I assure you I didn't get it from the Centers for Disease Control in Atlanta."

"No—of course not," replied Spasky. "And your price?"

"Two million American dollars in my Swiss bank account as a deposit, and two million upon delivery."

"What's the time frame?"

"After I receive the deposit, delivery in one week."

Spasky sat back in the booth. He took a sip of his coffee and his Adam's apple bobbed up and down. He set the coffee mug on the table. "Why don't we take a walk outside, where we can finalize the details?"

To Dr. Radznev, the idea of marching around in the snow when the temperature was near zero seemed supremely unpleasant, especially when the booth at the café was quite warm and private; but for five million dollars he'd be willing to jump naked into the freezing water of Lake Seliger.

The men put on their coats. After Dr. Radznev paid the bill, they walked outside.

"Let's go to the park," suggested Spasky.

They walked along a quiet street. Halfway down the block, Dr. Radznev, comfortable in his surroundings and thinking of his five-million-dollar paycheck, failed to be concerned when a black van pulled up alongside them. The side door to the van slid open. Two men got out and, without a word, approached Dr. Radznev from the rear. Grabbing him forcefully by the arms, they halted him in his tracks.

Spasky pulled a pistol from his pocket and turned to face Dr. Radznev. "If you fight, I'll shoot you," he said.

The two men marched Dr. Radznev to the side of the van, where they zip-tied his hands behind his back before expertly frisking him.

"What's this all about?" stammered Dr. Radznev.

But his protest was half-hearted: he knew exactly what it was about.

After he was hustled into the back seat of the black van with a man on each side of him, Spasky got into the front passenger seat.

"Okay, let's go," he said he said to the driver.

Twenty minutes later the van pulled into the driveway of a private airport on the outskirts of Ostashkov. A Kamov military helicopter waited there, its twin rotors idling. The group transferred from the van to the helicopter; then, with a scream of its turboshaft engines, the chopper took off into the cloudy sky.

Within two hours of his arrest on the street in Ostashkov, Dr. Radznev was marched into the Lubyanka, the fearsome Neo-Baroque monolith of yellow brick located in the heart of Moscow which served as a notorious prison and home of two state agencies: the headquarters of the Border Guard Service of Russia and one directorate of the feared FSB—the Federal Security Service of the Russian Federation. Dr. Radznev was taken to the basement, from where, in the old days of Stalin, it was said that you could see Siberia. There he was put into an interrogation room, chained to a chair and table, and left to wait.

A man entered the room. He had a broken nose, like a boxer, and he wore his grey hair in a severe military buzzcut. In his black suit, white shirt, and grey tie, he looked like a mortician from the toughest neighborhood in Moscow.

"Good afternoon, Dr. Radznev," he said. "I'm Special Agent Karpol. I represent the people of the Russian Federation."

Sitting down opposite Dr. Radznev, he opened a folder and examined some documents. After a moment he slid one of them across the table to Dr. Radznev.

"This is your confession," he said. "Please read it carefully. We will discuss it when you're finished."

With his manacled hands, Dr. Radznev picked up

the papers. The confession revealed everything—how he had bribed a technician at Vector, taken the vials of smallpox to the Russian naval installation in Tartus, and then delivered them to Mansour, Noman, and Mahadi at Beta Syria. It was even written that the proposed target was the United States of America, and that an American named Dr. Martin Riker had been involved in overseeing the cultivating of the smallpox at Beta Syria.

It was also noted that Dr. Radznev had, in the past week, bought the dacha by Lake Seliger for the equivalent of five hundred thousand dollars in cash, and the Mercedes for forty thousand.

"You will notice," said Karpol, "That your confession does not specify exactly who provided the funds for the smallpox material. We don't think it was the Syrian government. They can barely afford to buy ammunition for the surplus Kalishnikovs that we sell to them. So, Dr. Radznev, who gave the Syrians the money to pay you?"

Dr. Radznev continued to study the confession. Aside from Ilana Yaltsin, there was another name conspicuously lacking: Zafar. Was it possible the FSB had missed him?

He looked into the cold eyes of Special Agent Karpol. "The person who provided the funds," he said, "is a Russian patriot, whose reasons for contributing were purely personal. This person should be spared. But there is someone else whom you should know about—someone who should interest you very much. He is at the highest levels of the Syrian government."

"I'm listening," said Karpol.

"What do I get in return?"

"Perhaps the opportunity to live your life in prison, rather than facing the firing squad."

Not a bad deal, thought Dr. Radznev. After a decade or two, who knows what could happen? Maybe someone new would seize power in the Kremlin, and Dr. Radznev's so-called crime would be hailed by the new dictator as a prescient act of heroism. In Russia, that kind of stuff happened all the time. Yesterday's political criminal was tomorrow's warrior for the people. Something that you did in the past that was deemed to go against the interests of the state could, in years to come, suddenly be proclaimed to have been exactly the opposite.

"Okay," said Radznev. "I will give you another name, which will change the significance of Operation Fire Sword."

"Go on."

"The operation is being directed by a man named Zafar."

"The cleric?" said Karpol.

"Yes," said Dr. Radznev.

"We know that Zafar was a spiritual leader at Homs Military Academy when Bashar al-Assad was a cadet there," said Karpol. "We're not aware that he currently has influence in Damascus."

"Well, you're aware of it now. Everyone on the team—Mansour, Noman, Mahadi—obeys Zafar. He has the final decision on every aspect of the operation, including choosing the target. It was my impression that he has direct access to Mount Mezzeh."

"You're implying that this was not a rogue operation by a bunch of overzealous agents of the Syrian GSD, but that it was approved at the highest levels of the al-Assad regime."

"It was never my belief that it was anything but."

Special Agent Karpol sat back in his chair. "Of course we'll need to independently verify what you're saying. This would be a very serious charge to make against Bashar al-Assad."

"I take it that you don't approve of smallpox being used for a terrorist attack against the United States," said Dr. Radznev.

Karpol looked Dr. Radznev in the eye. "I can assure you that if it were in the national interest of the Russian Federation to weaponize smallpox and use it to attack an enemy, we'd do it. At the present time, it is not in our national interest. Hence your recent actions not only represent the crimes of theft and bribery, but of treason."

"Yes, I understand, and I fully and freely confess," said Dr. Radznev.

"I have a very important question to ask you," said Karpol. "To your knowledge, where is the smallpox cultivation being carried out?"

"At the Beta Syria laboratory, near Jableh," answered Dr. Radznev. "You know that already."

"Yes," said Karpol. "I'm just confirming it. Anywhere else? Or is that the only place?"

"I'm absolutely certain that's the only place," said Dr. Radznev. "You need specialized equipment to handle a dangerous virus. There's no reason for them to set up a lab anywhere else."

Karpol showed Dr. Radznev a Google Maps photo of the Beta Syria lab in Jableh. "Is this the place?" he asked.

"Yes, absolutely," replied Dr. Radznev. "That's the facility where they're producing the smallpox virus."

"Okay," said Karpol. He stood up and went to the door, and opened it. He spoke to someone in the hall. A moment later a technician entered with a video camera on a tripod, which he set up so that it captured the image of Dr. Radznev sitting at the table.

"Dr. Radznev," said Special Agent Karpol, "Are you ready to freely sign your confession of the crimes you have committed against the Russian Federation?"

"Yes," nodded Dr. Radznev.

Karpol handed Dr. Radznev a pen, which he took. He signed the confession and slid the paper across the table to Karpol. The agent put it into the folder. He then stood up. "Tomorrow, the judge will pass sentence upon you," he said.

"Based on the information I gave you, you'll recommend leniency?" asked Dr. Radznev.

"What information?" replied Karpol coldly.

"About Zafar being the mastermind of project Fire Sword!" said Dr. Radznev.

"We already knew that," said Karpol as he turned

towards the door. "You told us nothing new. You are going to the firing squad."

"But wait," pleaded Dr. Radznev, rattling the chains that confined him. "I have more! If you spare my life, I'll tell you who paid two million dollars for the virus!"

Karpol stopped. He gestured to the video camera operator to turn off his machine. When this had been done, Karpol said, "I'll give you a chance. Give me the name."

"It was Ilana Yaltsin," said Dr. Radznev. "She's the daughter of Alexander Dimitrov, the oil billionaire. She paid for it. But you can't touch her—she has friends at the highest levels of the Kremlin."

"How did you, a doctor from Siberia, make contact with someone like Ilana Yaltsin?" asked Karpol.

"There was an intermediary," said Dr. Radznev. "Henri Kaminsky. He introduced her to me. He's a highly placed control officer in the Foreign Intelligence Service—the SVR."

"So he is," said Karpol. "So he is. All right—I will recommend that your life be spared until we can sort this out."

With those words he gathered his papers and left the room. Dr. Radznev was left sitting, manacled to his chair, wondering how his plan could have gone so wrong.

32.

At three o'clock on Friday afternoon, Lufthansa Flight 2356, direct from Berlin, landed at Reagan International Airport in Washington, D.C. Among the four hundred passengers on the Boeing 747 was Dr. Martin Riker.

At customs, he dutifully got in line. After a few minutes he arrived at the screening table. The customs officer—"D. Snyder," according to her nametag—examined his passport. She punched the information into her computer. After a moment she motioned to an agent standing behind her. The agent looked at the computer, took Riker's passport, and said, "Dr. Riker, please come with me."

Riker knew he had no choice. After giving up his cell phone and travel bag, he allowed himself to be taken to an interview room. He sat down at the plain white table.

A few minutes later a man entered, wearing the blue uniform and gold badge of a Customs officer. He was carrying a laptop and holding Riker's passport. He sat down.

"Dr. Martin Riker?" he asked.

"Yes, that's me."

"My name is Officer Ridley, and I'd like to ask you a few questions."

"Will this take long? I've got an appointment—"

"I understand," said Ridley. "As I'm sure you know, the Terrorist Screening Center is a department within the FBI that maintains the U.S. government's consolidated Terrorist Watchlist, which supports the ability of front line screening agencies to positively identify known or suspected terrorists trying to obtain visas, enter the country, board aircraft, or engage in other activity."

"Yes, yes, I know all of that," replied Riker. "Why

am I here?"

"We've detained you because your name is on the list," said Ridley in the bland tone of the professional bureaucrat. "Can you tell me why your name might be on the list?"

"How should I know?" replied Riker. "I suppose it's because a week ago I went to Syria. I can explain."

"All right, why did you go to Syria?"

"To investigate the possibility of the Syrian government being engaged in a program of biological warfare."

"To investigate, or assist?"

"What the hell are you talking about?" demanded Riker.

Ridley rotated the laptop so that Riker could see it. "Did you write this?"

Peering at the screen, Riker read the text. It was a blog posting under his name in which he extolled the virtues of the Syrian regime of Bashar al-Assad and criticized American meddling in the Middle East.

"For this, you guys put me on the Terrorist Watchlist?" asked Riker incredulously.

Ridley scrolled through some files. "You entered Syria through the port city of Latakia and stayed at the Shahbandar Hotel," said Ripley. "You met with various people. On Sunday afternoon, the twenty-ninth of November, you were arrested, taken to Sedaboud Prison, and then released just a few hours later."

"How do you know this stuff?" asked Riker.

Ignoring Riker's question, Ridley continued to scroll through the files. Without taking his eyes off the screen, he said, "Why were you released? Generally, Americans who are arrested in places like Syria are used as bargaining chips, and aren't set free until a deal is made. On the following Wednesday you were brought to Sedaboud again, this time with a woman. Her name is Amena Qabbani. Again, you were quickly released, while she remained in custody. To what do you attribute your amazing good fortune?"

"I had friends in high places," replied Riker.

"Listen, I can clear this up very quickly. I've come to Washington to see Angela Powell. She's a case officer for the Defense Clandestine Service. As I said, I was in Syria to investigate the possibility of a terror attack using a biological weapon. And you'd better let me go so that I can finish the job and save us all from a very bad experience."

Ridley stood up. "If you will excuse me for a moment, Dr. Riker," he said as he took his laptop and Riker's passport. He went out the door, closing it behind him.

Riker sat and waited. In his mind he could see the technicians at Beta Syria patiently injecting new eggs with smallpox particles and harvesting the ones that had incubated, over and over again, building up their stockpile of the deadly virus, patiently planning their attack, and every hour getting closer to making it a reality.

Perhaps Operation Fire Sword had already been set into motion. Riker calculated that by now the Syrians should have been able to harvest enough of the virus to pack several million particles into a freezer pack, put it into the Adana Four Star Black Caviar box, and send it to their agent in the United States.

If only he knew who that agent was!

A minutes ticked by. Riker fumed that the same phony internet blog posts that had convinced the Syrians to trust him were now being used by his own government to implicate him. Will bureaucrats never learn?

Ridley returned. He placed Riker's passport and cell phone on the table. "You're free to go," he said. "Ms. Powell confirmed your story. We apologize for any inconvenience."

"Okay," said Riker as he collected his things.

He hurried from the room and, with a heightened sense of urgency, rushed to the car service desk.

Having battled its way through Friday rush hour traffic, Riker's Uber car turned off MacDill Boulevard SE and pulled up to the entrance of the gleaming

Defense Intelligence Agency building, across the Potomac from the airport. After passing through security—and mercifully not being detained—he went to the sixth-floor office of Angela Powell. When he walked through the door, she rose, shook his hand, and asked him to sit down.

"You've had a busy week," she said as she settled into her big leather chair. "I'd say you lived a charmed life, with not one, but two visits to Sedaboud Prison. Most people who check into Sedaboud never check out."

"Everybody seems to know a lot about what happened to me in Syria," said Riker.

"We have our unnamed sources," she replied.

"Would one of them be a taxi driver?"

"Maybe," she said with a smile. "The important thing is that you've managed to return safely. Now then—please brief me on what you discovered."

"The short version of the story," said Riker, "is this: A group of Syrians who are connected to the regime of Bashar al-Assad are, with or without his personal approval, planning a biological attack on the United States. The goal of Operation Fire Sword is to contaminate the ink used by a major newspaper with particles of the smallpox virus. People who read or handle the newspaper will inhale the virus, and a portion of them will become infected. Since the incubation period is between twelve and fourteen days, when the disease erupts in the general population it will be virtually impossible to trace it back to the newspapers because most of the individual infected copies will have been thrown away or recycled. It's a breathtakingly simple yet deadly scheme."

"Deadly pages," mused Powell. "You're right—it's a plan that is both ambitious and conceptually elegant. What's the timetable?"

"It's my belief that the attack could be launched within days. The last time I was at Beta Syria, which was on Wednesday night, the virus cultivation operation was fully under way. I saw a carton of Adana

Four Star Black Caviar. It is into this carton that the freezer pack containing the virus will be packed and shipped to the United States. The carton will contain half a dozen freezer packs, only one of which will contain the virus. Obviously they will have to mark it somehow, or record an inventory number, to ensure the agent uses the correct pack. This is all simple logistical stuff. The bottom line is that they have enough smallpox virus to fill a freezer pack right now. It could already be on its way here."

"What's the target?"

"The plans that I heard involved *The New York Times*. They also mentioned *The Washington Post* and *The Wall Street Journal*."

"Those newspapers have a combined circulation of nearly five million people," said Powell. "I think we have enough to escalate to the next level. Let's go to my boss with this."

She picked up the phone. "Larry? Have you got a few minutes? Dr. Riker is here. Yes, the man who went to Syria. Okay, we'll be right over." She turned to Riker. "We're going to take this to Larry Winters, the associate director of domestic counterterrorism for the East Coast."

Five minutes later they were seated in a bigger office with a better view of the Capitol Building.

They watched as Larry Winters, enthroned behind his big desk of burled walnut, collected some papers and stacked them neatly next to his computer. Then he took off his heavy tortoise-shell eyeglasses and cleaned the lenses with a tissue. He dropped the tissue into the wastepaper basket. After putting on his glasses again and clearing his throat lightly, he picked up the printout of the internal email that Powell had just sent him. His bushy grey eyebrows formed a stubborn "V" as his dark eyes scanned the page. His fleshy mouth turned down at the corners.

Setting the paper on the green baize blotter, he directed his eyes at Riker. "It's your contention, Dr. Riker, that the Russians have sold smallpox virus particles to a Syrian cleric and his group of conspirators, and that this group plans"—he peered at the paper on his desk and stabbed at it with his blunt finger—"to somehow introduce the virus into the printer's ink used by a major American newspaper, and that by doing so they will infect readers of the newspaper with smallpox?"

"Yes, that's absolutely correct," said Riker.

Winters stared hard at him. "You'll forgive me if I think this is somewhat far-fetched," he said.

"You can think what you want," replied Riker, "but the evidence is right here." He handed Winters the thumb drive that Ghazal had given him.

"What's this?" demanded Winters.

"It's a video of the technicians at work at the Beta Syria lab, near Latakia," replied Riker. "Go ahead, look at it. It's not infected."

Winters's eyebrows furrowed more vigorously as he plugged the thumb drive into his computer. After a few clicks, he watched the screen intently.

The video lasted four minutes. When it was finished, Winters clicked it off and pulled the thumb drive out of his computer. He tossed it on the desk.

"I'm sorry, but it's not conclusive," he said. "It could have been filmed anywhere."

"But it shows the Syrians cultivating smallpox!" insisted Riker. "A woman risked her life to take this video! And they tried to kill me, too!"

Winters sat back in his swivel chair. "Dr. Riker, I want you to understand something. This nation is facing countless threats from terrorists, both as organized units and as individual actors. Bombings and mass shootings have become a way of life. To counter these threats we have developed significant assets, and, with some unfortunate exceptions, we're doing pretty well. You say the Russians sold smallpox to the Syrians. That's a very serious charge. Do you have any idea what the blowback would be if we were to accuse the Russians of something like that? It would take us to the brink of World War Three."

"Who cares how the Syrians got the stuff!" countered Riker. "The fact is, they've got it and they intend to use it. Operation Fire Sword is very real."

"Dr. Riker," said Winters, "what do you expect is going to happen? Do you want us to order three of the biggest newspapers in the United States to shut down? Can you imagine the loss of income and economic hardship? I'm sorry, but there's just not enough here to warrant my getting involved. We don't want to give potential terrorists what they want, which is to create a firestorm of panic in the American people. Now if you'll excuse me, I have an appointment. Thank you for your time."

Once they had returned to the privacy of Powell's office, Riker sat down dejectedly. "He gave us the bum's rush," he said. "Is he *crazy*? Doesn't he see how obvious this is?"

"What he sees," said Powell, "is something unfamiliar that defies what the company believes. As the associate director of domestic counterterrorism for the East Coast who is a year from collecting a fat retirement package, Larry Winters has one concern: cover his ass. It's easier to say 'no' and hope that this threat is no more substantial than hundreds of other wild schemes that are floating around on the internet. Last week Larry asked me about a report that terrorists wanted to hijack the Goodyear blimp, fill it with explosive hydrogen gas, and blow it up over a football game. He's seen every outlandish scheme you can think of, and ninety-nine percent of them are fantasies."

"How about the other one percent that are real?" said Riker. "This is the one percent. Unless we take action, a lot of people are going to die horrible deaths."

"We have only one choice," said Powell. "You need to go directly to *The New York Times*. If Larry Winters doesn't believe that this plan is both real and plausible, I'll bet the guy in charge of printing operations will. He knows how vulnerable the paper is, and how easy it would be to intercept a barrel of ink and contaminate it."

33.

It was after ten o'clock on Friday night when Riker, having disembarked from the American Airlines jet that had flown to LaGuardia in Queens from Reagan Airport in Washington, guided his rental car out of the Hertz lot onto Grand Central Parkway, heading east. With Flushing Bay on his left, he exited onto the Whitestone Expressway north. Then a quick cruise to 20th Avenue, and after a double-back under the expressway and a quick jog south, he entered the parking lot of the vast *New York Times* College Point printing facility. The building was easy to spot: Painted in huge black Old English letters rakishly across the façade was "The New York Times."

Riker found an empty parking space. As was his habit—something he had done for most of his life as a licensed driver—he backed his car into the space. When he wanted to leave from someplace, he liked being able to just get into his car and go, having taken care of the backing-up part of the procedure upon arrival rather than when leaving, when most people did it.

He went inside the building and approached the receptionist—Mabel, according to her nametag.

"Mabel, my name is Dr. Martin Riker," he said. "I need to see the manager of printing operations, Dave Dewey."

"Mr. Dewey is on the floor," replied Mabel. "They're about ready to start the presses. Does he know what this is about?"

"I called him from Washington," replied Riker. "It's a matter of a possible threat to the security of the newspaper and its readers."

"I'll see if I can reach him," said Mabel with a distinct lack of enthusiasm. She picked up her phone and punched a number. After a few moments she said,

"Dave? There's a Dr. Riker here to see you. He says he called you about some sort of security issue." There was a pause. "Okay, I'll send him in. You'll pick him up by the main door? Okay."

She hung up and pointed to a set of double doors. "I'll buzz you in, and you'll go through those doors and down the hall to another set of doors. That's the main floor. Wait by those doors and Dave will pick you up."

"Pick me up?" asked Riker.

"In his golf cart," replied Mabel.

Following Mabel's instructions, Riker found himself standing inside a vast space filled with towering printing presses, huge rolls of paper, conveyor belts, and—most significantly to Riker—fifty-gallon drums of printing ink, in four colors, ready to supply the whirring rollers of the hungry presses.

A few minutes later a man arrived, driving a white golf cart.

"Dr. Riker?" he asked. "I'm Dave Dewey. Hop in, and I'll show you around."

Riker got in the golf cart and they set off down the long center aisle.

"This facility encompasses over five hundred thousand square feet," said Dewey. "That's why we use golf carts and tricycles to get around. Tonight, like every weeknight, we'll print more than three hundred thousand newspapers. Saturday night it's double that number. By exactly three twenty-five tomorrow morning, every single paper needs to have been bundled and loaded onto one of our trucks. The trucks—we have dozens of them—fan out to distribution points, from which the copies will be delivered to newsstands, office buildings, grocery stores and bodegas from Albany to Trenton.

"We have seven different presses. Each one operates for between six and eleven hours per night. The paper we use comes from four different paper mills—two in Quebec, one in Tennessee, and one in Ontario. Each roll is fifty inches in diameter and weighs just over one ton. We keep a supply of them in a big storage facility in the Bronx, and we have over two thousand rolls stored here as well. Conveyor belts—which in this building total fourteen miles in length—deliver them to the paper-handler area, where the rolls are flipped sideways, ready to be loaded into press reels that feed them through slits in the ceiling."

"How about the ink?" said Riker. "You must buy it by the barrel, right?"

"Yes," replied Dewey as he drove expertly among the towering machines. The place was full of employees either bent over their tasks or pedaling the big adult-sized tricycles to get from one place to another. Riker got the impression that golf carts were reserved for people in upper management. "In offset printing," continued Dewey, "it's all about getting the right amount of ink on the rollers. An offset printing press is really nothing more than an assembly of rollers. They contact each other, and by doing so, ink is transferred from one roller to another, and eventually onto the paper. The ink is poured into what we call an ink fountain. I don't know why it's called that, because it's just a long open trough that contains the ink that's picked up by the ink roller. Each press has another fountain, or trough, and a set of rollers for the water."

"Water?"

"Sure," said Dewey. "Our offset printing is a form of lithography, which is predicated on the principle that oil and water don't mix. The plate cylinder—the one that has the text and images to be printed—is first coated with a thin film of water. Then it's coated with the ink, which adheres only to the areas on the plate that are to be printed. On the plate cylinder, the tiny particles of ink are surrounded by water molecules that help keep the ink where it needs to be. I should clarify something—the stuff we use is not really plain water; it's an acidic aqueous solution with isopropyl alcohol, glycol ethers, butyl cellusolve, and a bunch of other chemicals."

"Does the water solution get onto the newsprint?"

"Yep. In some processes, to evaporate the water off

the paper, the finished product is heated. We don't do that. We use a cold process, whereby the ink and water become dry by a combination of evaporation and absorption."

Dewey stopped the golf cart. "Let's go in my office and you can tell me about this supposed plot."

Once inside the office—a glassed-in cube giving Dewey a view of the immense presses—Riker sat down. Dewey picked up his phone and punched a number. "Pete?" he said. "Do you have a minute to stop by my office? Thanks." He hung up and then looked at his computer for a moment. "Sorry," he said with a frown. "It looks like we have a half-mile section of conveyor belt not working. Okay—the guys are fixing it. Now, where were we?"

Riker recited his story, and emphasized that the Syrian plotters were deadly serious and had almost certainly dispatched the first pack of smallpox to its target—which was likely to be *The New York Times*. The plan was to contaminate the ink used to print the newspaper, thereby spreading the virus particles throughout a wide cross-section of the general population, including people in positions of power. "Because," added Riker, "Just about anyone who has any influence reads *The New York Times*."

Dewey drummed his fingers on his desktop. "Dr. Riker, we run a pretty tight ship. Security is a top priority. Don't you think that there are countless terrorists and terrorist groups that would like to take down *The New York Times*? This is a massive operation. I have three hundred and fifty people working here, in this facility, and there are thousands more in other areas around the city and around the country. What do you want me to do?"

"You need to be vigilant for anything that seems to be out of the ordinary, and especially any evidence of tampering with the ink."

"That's something we do routinely," replied Dewey.

At that moment a man came to the door. Dewey waved him in. The man came in and closed the door behind him. "Dr. Riker," said Dewey, "I'd like you to meet Pete DiCenza, head of security here at College Park. He's the guy who handles the threats we receive every day."

DiCenza shook Riker's hand, but his expression was one of detached amusement.

His face said, *Here's another nut with a conspiracy theory.*

Riker felt like he was pissing into the wind. But could he blame them? Here he was, a guy off the street—with good professional credentials, yes, but in New York City just about everyone has impressive credentials—with a farfetched story about just having escaped from Syria on a fishing boat after witnessing a gang cultivate smallpox to use in an attack against the United States.

DiCenza quizzed him. Was he certain the target was *The New York Times*?

No.

Was there a specific date or time?

No.

Did he have a clue as to the identity of the person who might attempt such an attack?

No.

"I thank you for coming in, Dr. Riker," said Dewey as he rose from his chair. "If you'll excuse us, we're gearing up to print tomorrow's paper, and I've got some problems to fix. Pete will drive you back to the reception area."

"Sorry we can't be more responsive," said DiCenza as he drove Riker along the vast corridor of printing presses with their conveyor belts snaking overhead. "You gotta understand—we get threats all the time. We can't freak out every time a new one comes in."

As Riker walked past Mabel, she gave him a little smile and said, "Have a nice evening."

Riker went to his car. Dejectedly, he sat for a moment. He had run into a brick wall. If the DIA and *The New York Times* weren't going to listen to him, he'd just have to figure out how to uncover the plot on his own.

It might even mean going back to Syria.

It was then that something caught his eye. Under the cold glare of the tall pole lights in the parking lot, a nondescript sedan cruised slowly along the aisle where Riker had parked his car. Riker happened to notice that the rear window of the car—it was a four-door vehicle—was being lowered. As the car drew closer the tip of the barrel of a gun emerged from the open window.

Instinctively, Riker ducked and wedged himself tightly to the floor of the car.

Suddenly the windshield exploded in chunks of glass as bullets slammed into the car seats and headrests. As Riker shielded his face, staccato pops of semi-automatic weapon fire matched the slap of lead hitting steel and the whine of fragments of glass and plastic as they rocketed through the air. The car shuddered under the impact of one bullet after another.

As suddenly as it had begun, the firing stopped. The only sound was the hiss of steam escaping from the punctured radiator. Riker waited under his blanket of glass and plastic shards. He heard no other noises. Gingerly he unfolded himself and raised his head just high enough to peek through the gaping windshield. The attacking car was gone.

Riker carefully crawled up onto what was left of the driver's seat and opened the door. He stepped out onto the pavement and brushed the chunks of glass off his clothing and out of his hair.

A man ran up to him. "Hey mister—are you all right?" he asked breathlessly.

"Yeah, I'm fine, thanks," replied Riker. "Did you see what happened?"

"Sure I did," said the man. "I was coming out to my car when I heard gunfire. I ducked behind another car. I looked up and the attackers were driving right past me! It was a grey Toyota Corolla—I recognized it because I used to own one. They drove away, towards the highway."

Riker and the man walked to the front of Riker's rented car. Bullet holes riddled its nose, and the windshield and back window were blown out. Steam rose from under the battered hood.

"Looks like the engine saved my life," said Riker.

A siren wailed in the distance, quickly becoming louder. More people hurried out of the vast *New York Times* building, and a small group began to form around Riker.

"Are you sure you don't need a doctor?" a woman asked.

"Really—I'm all right, thank you," said Riker.

A police car arrived. The uniformed officer asked what had happened, and Riker stepped forward and told him what he knew.

"Any reason why someone would target you, Dr. Riker?" asked the cop.

"I've just returned from Syria, where I made some enemies," he replied.

"Okay, folks, let's go back inside," said a familiar voice. Pete DiCenza was making his way through the crowd. "It's under control now, so you can all go back to work." He looked at Riker's car. "What the hell happened here?"

"Drive-by shooting," replied Riker. "I was the target. Luckily I saw them and had time to take cover. The people at Hertz won't be pleased about their car."

"Are you injured?" asked DiCenza.

"No, I'm good."

"Let's go inside and look at the tapes."

"The tapes?"

"Absolutely," replied DiCenza. "We've got cameras covering every inch of this facility. C'mon, let's go to the security office."

A few minutes later DiCenza and Riker were scrolling through the videotapes of the security cameras mounted in the parking lot. "Okay—here we are," said DiCenza as he zoomed in on Riker walking to his car. Then, at the top of the screen, a grey Toyota

Corolla could be seen pulling out of its parking place at the end of the aisle. The Toyota drove down the lane and paused in front of Riker's car. Suddenly a cloud of smoke erupted from the rear window of the Toyota just as the windshield of Riker's car erupted in a shower of glass. The firing continued for about four or five seconds—long enough for Riker's car to be reduced to a pockmarked tin can with its windows and headlights blown out. Then the Toyota sped away.

"Let's see if we can zoom in on the guy's license plate," said DiCenza. After a few seconds of manipulating the image he said, "Yes, there it is. A New Jersey plate. It figures, right? Let's see—H45 6B7. Now we'll run it through the system."

"You can do that?"

"Don't forget, we're *The New York Times*. Here it is: the car belongs to Irving Gruber, in Clifton, New Jersey. The car was reported stolen this afternoon from the Ikea parking lot in Brooklyn. Seems like Irving and the missus were visiting their daughter, who lives in Williamsburg, and they went to Ikea to buy her a new kitchen table. Tough break for the Grubers. At least no one got hurt—just massively inconvenienced."

"Can you get a view of the driver?" asked Riker.

"Sorry—too much glare from the lights," replied DiCenza. "And it looks like the driver was wearing a ski mask to obscure his face. They probably knew that the parking lot is covered by cameras."

DiCenza shut off the video. "It's likely that the car will eventually be recovered—the guys who stole it will probably just abandon it on the street somewhere. You can make book that they wore gloves and didn't leave any evidence behind." He turned to Riker. "You say you think these guys are Syrians?"

"I'm sure of it," replied Riker. "Just one week ago, before I went to Syria to investigate the smallpox victim who had come from there, I was enjoying a nice early retirement in Naples, Florida. I had worked for the Centers for Disease Control and Prevention in

Atlanta, but you don't make enemies by saving people from Ebola and malaria. No, I'm certain that these guys were sent by Zafar to eliminate me."

"By who?"

"A Syrian cleric who's the mastermind behind Operation Fire Sword. He doesn't mess around. He's a fanatic who will do anything to make his twisted vision a reality. Believe me, he and his cohorts have the means, the opportunity, and the motive to pull off an attack using cultivated smallpox. They could also hire a couple of sympathizers to try to take me out."

"I remember my parents telling me about smallpox," said DiCenza. "When they were kids in the late nineteen fifties, everyone was inoculated against smallpox. Then it stopped being a threat."

"Because it was eradicated," said Riker, "very few people receive inoculations today. It's not available to the general public. In the United States, only military personnel who are assigned to South Korea, as well as forward naval operations, get the vaccine. Public health authorities claim that in the event of an outbreak there's enough vaccine to administer to the general public, but the problem is that you need to administer the vaccine within three days of exposure to the virus. But symptoms don't appear for twelve to fourteen days after exposure. So if a massive attack occurred, the vaccine would be too late to help the hundreds—or thousands—of people who had already been infected."

"Okay, I believe we have a problem," said DiCenza. "What do you want me to do?"

"Give me full access to the building and your staff, twenty-four-seven."

"Because our union rules are strict, " said DiCenza, "that's not going to be easy. An employee from one department can't just go wandering around to another department. A pressman can't hang out on the loading dock or in the security office. An admin assistant can't go clambering around the catwalks over the presses."

"A few years ago I read an article in a magazine

about the inner workings of *The New York Times*," replied Riker. "The reporter went everywhere, from the newsrooms to the warehouse where you store the rolls of newsprint. What I want you to do is put out a memo that a guy named Gary Howard is writing a book about the paper and will be spending time here at College Point, getting to know the operation and talking to employees. Most people enjoy talking about what they do on the job, and the union won't care because I wouldn't be threatening their authority."

"Why call yourself Gary Howard?" asked DiCenza.

"Because the bad guys know that Dr. Riker is here. I'm going to have to do this undercover."

"Okay," said DiCenza. "I'll get you set up with a photo ID and I'll put out a memo to all staff. Welcome to *The New York Times*, Mr. Howard."

34.

At six o'clock on Saturday evening, Dr. Martin Riker entered the security office of the College Point printing plant. After having his mug shot taken, he slipped his new laminated ID tag around his neck. He then stuck his head in the door of Pete DiCenza's office.

From behind his desk, DiCenza peered at the tag. "Gary Howard! I'm pleased to meet you." He stood up. "I've got a vacant office I can give you where you can keep your stuff. Do you plan on being here all night? Remember, we're printing the Sunday edition. It's all hands on deck."

"I'll be here all night, every night," replied Riker. "I need to figure out at what point in the printing process the system is vulnerable."

"How about our ink supplier?" asked DiCenza. "Couldn't they dump the stuff in a barrel of ink, and put the lid back on?"

"Yes, they could," replied Riker. "My colleagues at the DIA have sent a guy to your wholesaler in New Jersey. They're setting up a system to install special seals on the barrels that will show if a barrel has been tampered with. While contaminating a fifty-gallon barrel would probably be effective in spreading the virus, I think that because we're talking about a quantity of material no more than the contents of a freezer pack, they'd get a lot more bang for their buck if they could dump it directly into the ink fountain on the press.

"Before I hit the floor, I need to know if you have any new employees that have come on board within the past two weeks."

DiCenza went to his computer and scrolled through the employee database. "Yes, in fact we have three new employees.

"Richard Scarry was hired two weeks ago. He's an

assistant in the plate room. That's where the digital files from our headquarters in Manhattan are etched onto the aluminum plates, from which the pages are printed.

"Elaine Gormley arrived last week. She's in human resources. While the main human resources office is in Manhattan, we have a satellite office in this building. It's staffed by two people—Gormley and Rosemary Hopkins, who's been with us for twelve years.

"The third newcomer is a guy named Mohammad Parsi. He's an assistant press operator. He has access to the inks." DiCenza turned to Riker. "We'd better get him out of here."

"Why?" asked Riker.

DiCenza frowned. "It's obvious—he's Muslim. We can't take a chance!"

"I think it may be a bit premature to draw conclusions," replied Riker, who in the course of his global travels had developed warm relationships with hundreds of people of the Islamic faith in the Middle East, Africa, and Southeast Asia. "I'll tell you what— why don't you hold off on forming any opinions about Mr. Parsi until I've had a chance to talk to him. Okay?"

"All right," shrugged DiCenza. "But I'm gonna keep an eye on him." He clicked off the screen. "Last night I sent out an email blast to all of our employees, telling them that Gary Howard was going to be spending a week or two here, and that they should feel comfortable talking to you about anything that's not proprietary information. You should be able to strike up a conversation with just about anybody. And by the way—you can borrow a tricycle from the ones we have outside this office. It will save you a couple of hours of walking."

A few minutes later, Riker was pedaling his way towards press number six, which was on the other side of the building. The presses hadn't started yet, and the place was quiet except for the hum and whirr of golf carts and tricycles.

He arrived at press number six. The huge machine

sat idle, with the long ribbon of newsprint from the big roll suspended on its spool a floor below, in the basement, already locked into place.

High up on the catwalk a man was making an adjustment. Without hesitation Riker ascended the narrow steel ladder.

"Hi there," he said to the man. "You got a minute?"

The man put down his computer pad. "Can I help you?"

"My name's Gary Howard. I'm writing a book about the history of *The New York Times*."

"Oh, yeah," said the man. "I got the email. You want to hang around and watch while we print the newspaper?"

"More than that," said Riker. "I want to talk to people who work here, and really get to know the heart and soul of the paper. Not just the mechanical stuff, but why it's been such an important part of American life for over one hundred and sixty years."

"Oh—this is some sort of company public relations project, right?"

"No, not at all. I'm not part of the company. I'm independent. I want to hear everything—positive and negative." He glanced at the man's nametag. "You're Mohammad, right? Pleased to meet you. Are you new here?"

"Yes—I'm Mohammad Parsi. I was hired last week."

"But you look like you're not exactly a novice."

Parsi smiled. "You're right. Back home, I worked for the *Jakarta Post* as a pressman. We have a circulation of only forty thousand, but the presses they use are similar."

"What brought you to America?"

"My mother died a few months ago. My father had already passed away. My sister has lived in Brooklyn for five years with her American husband, so I thought, why not? With no more family in Indonesia, I might as well join Gita and her husband."

"I understand," said Riker. "I'm sorry about your parents. It must have been tough to leave home and emigrate to a new country. Do you feel like you're accepted here?"

"Do you mean because I'm a Muslim?" Parsi smiled. "I get along with everyone. Back home I was involved with Jaringan Islam Liberal."

"I've heard of it," said Riker. "The mission statement is something like, 'We're a community to study and bring forth a discourse on Islamic vision that is tolerant, open, and supportive for the strengthening of Indonesian democratization.' Something like that, am I right?"

"Yes. It's an organization dedicated to building bridges between different faiths."

Riker directed his gaze to the big machine that loomed next to them. "So, you know how this thing works?"

"Absolutely."

"What can you tell a guy who knows absolutely nothing about it?"

"The principle of offset printing is very simple," said Parsi. "It just gets complicated when you try to do it very fast and with four colors. As you can see, the big roll—or web, as we call it—of paper is already in place. We're just waiting for the plates to be delivered. Nothing can be done until the editorial office in Manhattan sends the digital files to the plate room, and the plates—one for each color for each page, totaling some six thousand or more for a fat Sunday paper—have been created and rushed to the presses for installation. After receiving the plates that have been assigned to us, we attach them to the plate cylinder, which rotates against three other cylinders: the ink cylinder, which picks up the ink from the ink fountain; the water cylinder; and the offset, or blanket, cylinder. It's this latter cylinder that transfers the inked words and images from the plate cylinder to the paper. The press that you're looking at consists of four of these complex roller assemblies, one for each color—cyan, magenta, yellow, and finally black.

"The tricky part is getting all the plates to line up

absolutely perfectly. At the top left corner of each page is a tiny box only a millimeter wide. This is the registration box. When we print a page, the box needs to be perfectly black, with no colors showing at the edges. When we see a color peeking out at the edge of the box, we need to fine-tune the alignment of that particular color. Then we make some more test printings of the paper. Eventually we get what's called a 'good first copy,' and we can run the press and make newspapers."

"How about the ink?" asked Riker.

"It comes in barrels. We pry the lid off a barrel and pour it into the appropriate ink fountain, which is also called a reservoir or trough; there are a bunch of different names for the same component. In the old days, the ink cylinder sat halfway submerged in this long trough, and it picked up the ink and transferred it to a set of smaller inking rollers. Nowadays the ink delivery is digitally controlled, but the principles are still the same. The more inking rollers you have, the smoother the distribution of ink. The last inking roller in the set transfers the ink to the plate cylinder, then to the blanket or offset cylinder, and then to the paper."

"So the ink fountain is exposed? It's just out there in the open?"

Parsi shrugged. "They came with covers, but we don't always use them. We need to refill the fountains fairly often."

"Like every night?"

"For a typical weekday edition, yes," said Parsi.

Parsi nodded towards an approaching golf cart. "Here comes the first batch of plates. If you'll excuse me, I need to move quickly."

Riker stood aside and watched as the plates were carefully attached to the four plate rollers—one for each color. After a few minutes of adjustments, Parsi signaled that the press was ready to run.

He pushed a button and the huge machine roared to life.

"Wow," said Riker, "It's very loud."

Parsi nodded. "It's been measured at eighty-five decibels, which is below the OSHA monitoring requirements but still loud enough to cause hearing loss over time."

Suddenly the press stopped. The pressmen, including Parsi, grabbed the pages that had been printed. The registration marks in the corner showed that the colors weren't lined up exactly right.

After more adjusting, the process was repeated. The samples were inspected and more adjustments made. Finally the press began to run and the finished pages flowed along the conveyor belts to be cut, assembled, and bound.

Eventually the production settled into a rhythm and Riker could talk to Parsi again.

"What time do you think you'll be out of here?" he asked.

"For a Sunday paper, this one is about average in size, and there were no last-minute changes after the deadline; so I'd say we'll get done by four o'clock this morning. What I'm worried about is Sunday night."

"Why?"

"Because at eight o'clock this morning a film crew is coming in to shoot a scene for an action film. They'll be here all day. They're supposed to be out by four o'clock in the afternoon, but sometimes they try to push it."

"A film crew?" asked Riker. "They make movies in here?"

"Once in a while," replied Parsi. "I suppose the company likes the million-dollar location fees. The plant has had a steady stream of smaller productions— movies that you've never heard of, and industrial training films. The last major feature film that shot here was *The Bourne Legacy,* in 2012. They transformed this production floor into a pharmaceutical manufacturing plant, where the crew shot a scene with four hundred extras each morning for several days. During the scene, the two stars were trying to escape from the manufacturing facility. They were pursued by security, and the male star—the guy played by Jeremy Renner—shot out a lighting control panel on the factory floor. I was still living in Indonesia, but I saw the movie in the local theatre. Little did I know that I'd be working here some day! I recently rented the DVD and watched it. It was cool to see this place on the screen. This press—number six—was in one of the shots."

Riker thanked Parsi for his time and climbed down from the press. He got on his tricycle and pedaled back to DeCenza's office. He found him behind his desk.

"I'd like to talk to you about the film crew coming here tomorrow," said Riker.

"Yeah, it's going to be a headache. Star Magna Films is making a movie called *Lethal Last Chance*. It's a cop movie, with lots of car chases and stuff like that. Apparently the bad guy finds his way here, and the cops chase him around the place before they corner him and shoot him."

"The film company is bringing in extras, right?"

"Yes. It'll be the production crew—the lighting guys, camera guys, and all the rest—plus two hundred extras, who play the factory workers."

"And they'll be on the presses?"

"Sure, they have to be."

"Who will be your security guy in charge?"

"That would be Richard Laskey."

"I'm going to get some rest. Please let Laskey know I'll be here at eight tomorrow morning when the film crew arrives."

"I'll walk you to the door," said DiCenza.

With DiCenza standing by the front door, Riker left the building. As he stepped out into the cold night air, flurries brushed his face. As he approached his car—to replace the Ford that had gotten shot up he had rented a beefy Chevy Tahoe, with lots of iron between him and a shooter—he scanned the parking lot. He started the engine and turned on the headlights. No other cars moved. He eased his way out of the lot, and twenty minutes later checked into his room at the LaGuardia

Plaza Hotel.

Sitting at the little desk, he went online. He remembered that in Ghazal's video of her tour of Beta Syria, she had briefly met a man named Hosni Raseen, and that he had mentioned he invested in films. Riker searched for Star Magna Films. He didn't find much; over the past few years the company had produced only a handful of cheap comedies and slasher films. The budgets for these films were no more than twenty million dollars each. Now, they were suddenly able to rent the printing plant of the *The New York Times* for a day of shooting.

Riker searched in vain for any connection between Hosni Raseen, who was apparently a successful Saudi businessman, with Star Magna Films. Raseen's online presence was minimal. He kept a very low profile.

Riker punched the direct number for Angela Powell. Of course she wouldn't answer on a Saturday night, but she had people who checked her messages every few hours.

"Angela—it's Riker,' he told her voicemail. "I'm in New York, at the College Point printing plant. You guys have much more powerful research tools than I do. Can you find a connection between Hosni Raseen, a wealthy Saudi investor, and a film company called Star Magna Films? I appreciate your help. Thanks."

Tired and needing sleep, Riker fell into bed after setting his wakeup call for seven o'clock.

35.

The morning came with a coating of fresh snow on the ground. At breakfast in the hotel coffee shop, Riker picked up a copy of the Sunday *New York Times*. He was casually skimming the pages and enjoying his newfound insight into how the paper had been printed only a few hours earlier when an item on page one of the international news section made him stop and read more closely.

Russian Jet Strikes Pharmaceutical Plant in Syria

WASHINGTON, D.C.: Sources in Syria have reported that on Saturday afternoon a Russian MiG-29 fighter plane fired several air-to-ground missiles at the defunct Beta Syria Pharmaceutical facility in Jableh, a coastal town near the city of Latakia. The former factory was completely destroyed.

According to Defense Department sources, reconnaissance photos taken by a U.S. surveillance satellite suggest that the missiles were incendiary, meaning their purpose was to ignite the target and cause it to burn, rather than simply destroy it, as would a conventional bomb. "Infra-red photos indicate the heat from this fire was unusually intense," said a Pentagon source. Photos show a dark plume of smoke rising high into the sky from the burning building.

Russian officials have made no comment on the attack, and have neither confirmed nor denied that it had been ordered. Syrian officials have not commented either. It is not known if there were any casualties; it is likely that had there been anyone in the building, the intense heat of the fire would have destroyed any human remains.

While Russian jets have been pounding targets in rebel-held territories for weeks, this strike was highly unusual because it occurred deep inside Syrian territory still controlled by the regime of President Bashar al-Assad. Why the Beta Syria facility, once a thriving regional business but now shuttered, was targeted is not known.

It was almost two o'clock in the afternoon in Syria. Riker pulled out his phone. He punched Amena's number.

"Hello?" she said.

When he heard her voice, Riker could not help but smile.

"Amena—this is Martin. I'm calling from New York."

"You made it!" she exclaimed. "I'm so relieved. Joram told me he had dropped you off at Assal's marina in Al Aabde. I'm glad that you're safe."

"How about you?" asked Riker.

"I'm okay," she replied. "By disappearing, you and Ghazal are taking all the heat. Mahadi has vanished, too, and Mansour has been spreading the word that Mahadi is a traitor. They're leaving me alone, at least for the time being. But we'll see—around here, we all live minute by minute."

"Did you hear the news?"

"About what?"

"Yesterday a Russian jet destroyed the Beta Syria facility. Burned it to the ground."

"No—the state news agency hasn't reported it, and they probably won't. What happened? Did the Russian government figure out that Dr. Radznev stole the virus from Vector?"

"That's what it looks like. The Russians didn't approve of Operation Fire Sword, so they crushed it. But what we need to know is this: How much of the smallpox virus were they able to ship out before the place was torched?"

"At least one freezer pack," she replied, "but possibly more. Production was going full steam. Now that I know what the Russians did, I can discreetly ask around and see who was in the building when it was destroyed. They had at least twenty technicians in there, plus the armed guards and the bosses, like Noman and Mansour. They may all have been killed."

"Okay—one more question. Have you ever heard of a rich Saudi businessman named Hosni Raseen?"

"No, I haven't," she replied.

"All right, thanks," said Riker. "I have to go. Stay safe."

"You too, Martin."

Riker drove to the College Hill plant. When he arrived at fifteen minutes before eight, the film crew was beginning to load in their gear. Trucks were parked around the main entrance, and a row of porta-potties had been set up off to one side. Crew members were carrying in cables, rolling in road cases, and hauling boxes of lights and other gear into the building.

Riker strolled over to one of the truck drivers, whom he assumed was a teamster and not directly associated with the production company. "Say, what's going on here?" Riker asked casually.

"Movie crew," replied the teamster curtly.

"Wow, they sure have a lot of stuff," said Riker. "The road cases are labeled 'Star Magna Films.' To be able to rent this building, Star Magna must be a big company from Hollywood, huh?"

The teamster shrugged. "I drive for a lot of film companies. Before this job, I had never heard of these guys. I think they're based in New Jersey. But they pay me, so I drive."

"I hear you," said Riker. "You gotta make a living. No one's giving it to you free."

Blending in with the flow of traffic, Riker walked in the front door, unchallenged. As a result of the place being taken over by Star Magna Films, the normal security systems seemed to have vanished.

Riker made his way to the security office, where he found Richard Laskey at his desk, eating a donut and drinking coffee. Riker introduced himself.

"Oh yeah—you're the doctor who's looking for terrorists," said Laskey with a sugary smile. "Well, be my guest. The place is yours. I've got a few guys on the floor keeping an eye on things. But we don't expect any trouble."

Riker felt like asking Laskey, "Did Star Magna *bribe* you to stay out of their way?" but he held his tongue. Heck, as far as the film company was concerned, keeping Richard Laskey happy was just another incidental company expense.

"By the way, do you have a list of the cast and crew?" asked Riker.

"Sure do," said Laskey. After opening a file on his computer, he hit the print button. Across the room, the printer came to life.

"Coming out now," said Laskey.

"Does this list include the extras?"

"Nah—the casting agency said they couldn't finalize the list until this morning. Lots of times, people sign up to be extras and then just don't show up."

"Thanks." Riker took the list, folded it, and put it in his pocket.

Riker drifted down to the main floor. The crew was setting up the first shot, which was near the entrance. Now the first extras began to arrive. They were herded into a roped-off area of the plant floor, which had been equipped with folding chairs and a table with refreshments and beverages. A woman sat at a table, checking them in as they arrived. The woman had frizzy red hair and big jangly earrings. Her nametag said "Odeon."

"Hi there," said Riker. He introduced himself and told her that he was a writer working on a book about *The New York Times*, and would she mind if he hung around with the extras?

"No problem," said Odeon. She looked at him. "You know, I could use another guy your age. Do you want to be in some scenes? We pay a hundred bucks for the day."

"Because I've never been in a movie, it's a tempting

offer," replied Riker. "But I think I need to be able to move around when I want. I don't take direction very well."

"Suit yourself," she said.

"The setting for these scenes—is this place supposed to be a printing plant, or some other type of factory?" asked Riker.

"To keep costs down, the script was re-written to make this location a printing plant at a big newspaper—*The New York Enquirer*. On the front of the building, the name will be changed with computer generated imagery."

"So you'll have extras on the catwalks above the presses, in the places that real employees would be?"

"That's what the producers want."

"By the way, has your casting company worked very often with Star Magna Films?"

"No," replied Odeon. "We did a small slasher film for them last year. There were only three shooting days with extras, and the job was barely worth our time. The principal actors were all non-union. Then suddenly last week they came and said they were shooting here, and they had a big budget, and they needed two hundred extras to play factory workers. It was weird because these shoots are usually planned weeks in advance. But we scrambled, and here we are."

After thanking Odeon, Riker ambled among the extras. They were a varied bunch—men, women, young, old—but they all looked as if they could conceivably work in a printing plant.

Some wardrobe people appeared with racks of grey overalls. "Okay, folks," announced the woman in charge, "We need to get all of you fitted for work clothes. You can put them on over your regular clothes, or if you prefer, we have changing booths over by the window."

An assistant director came and called for the first group of extras. Riker watched as they were positioned in various places among the big printing presses. The scene would include presses one, two, and three. That gave the terrorist—if he or she were among these actors—three opportunities to contaminate the black ink, which, because it was the last layer of ink to be applied, was the best choice.

Riker watched the extras closely. Among this first group, only one person, a young woman, was positioned near an ink fountain. This was on press number two. The scene was filmed four or five times. The lead actor—the bad guy—ran through the area, firing his gun at his pursuer. As the action unfolded the extras ducked to avoid the gunfire. In its entirety, the shot lasted about five seconds; and by Riker's reckoning it took an hour to set it up and film it.

When the director was satisfied, the lights were broken down and reset in new positions. The next shot involved the bad guy hiding behind one of the presses and firing his gun—loaded with blanks—at the good guy, who was also taking shelter. Meanwhile, the extras, clad in their ink-stained overalls, cowered in fear. Riker watched the woman by the ink fountain on press number two. She took no interest in the long trough next to her, and Riker never saw her put her hands near it.

Lunch break was called. The extras had their own craft services table at a remove from the one used by the principal actors and the crew. Riker helped himself to a plate of chicken *cacciatore* and Caesar salad. It wasn't half bad.

The next shot was set up using presses five and six. A new batch of extras was assigned to their places. For this shot, both press number five and number six featured an actor positioned near the black ink fountain. The extra assigned to press number five was a bald, middle-aged black guy with a big belly. The extra on press number six was a young Middle Eastern guy. Both seemed relaxed, and they followed the instructions of the assistant director.

In this scene, the production crew had rigged up a big stack of phony ink barrels, held together by plastic strap on a wooden pallet. The bad guy cut the strap and the barrels rolled along the broad main aisle of the plant, forcing the good guy to dodge and weave. The scene lasted about five seconds, and they did it four times. Each time they did it, the crew had to collect all the barrels—which were in reality empty—and re-stack them on the pallet. Everyone spent a lot of time relaxing and waiting for the scene to be reset.

Everyone except Martin Riker. Like a guard at a supermax prison, he intently watched the extras positioned on the presses, looking for the slightest suspicious gesture, the one furtive motion that would suggest that the terrorist was tampering with the ink fountains. He dared not look away—not for a split second. His keen eyes darted from one actor to another, watching their hands, their eyes, the movement of their bodies. Did that guy's hand stray too near the ink roller? Why was that woman turning her back? Why was the other guy bending over—was he getting something out of his boot?

This attack wasn't like a bomb, which would announce itself to the world with a literal bang. A bomb is a highly visible crime, a garish advertisement of the perpetrator; and the bigger it is, the better. Bombs are brazen public events, designed for immediate shock. No, this was the opposite. It was a crime that could be equally destructive to human life as any bomb, but to succeed the perpetrator must act in complete secrecy. His version of a bomb—a small package of virus particles—had to be set without anyone noticing, and the effects would emerge not with a blinding flash but slowly, over time. At first, the smallpox epidemic might not even be identified as an act of terror, thereby blunting the force of the response. Perhaps the perpetrators would publicly claim responsibility only after the full magnitude of the attack had been felt.

This attack could only succeed by being pulled off in complete secrecy. The message would come later.

A break was called. The extras filed back to the holding area while the principle actors went to their comfortable trailers parked outside.

The Middle Eastern guy sat down near Riker.

"How are you doing?" asked Riker as he got up and went to sit down next to the guy. "Do you like being an extra?"

The guy shrugged. "I like it well enough."

"Gary Howard," said Riker as he extended his hand. "I'm a writer. Doing a book about *The New York Times*. Fascinating business."

"Pleased to meet you," the guy replied. His eyes, under their heavy lids, glanced at Riker and then slid away.

"How often do you work—as an actor, I mean?" asked Riker.

"Once in a while. It's like a hobby."

"Maybe someday I'll see you up on the big screen, huh?" said Riker.

The guy gave a thin smile. "Maybe."

The assistant director called the extras to their places. Without saying anything else to Riker, the Middle Eastern guy got up and walked to the place the assistant director showed him. Riker went over to Odeon, who was sitting behind her table, eating a chicken salad sandwich.

"See that extra who's climbing the ladder to press number three?" asked Riker. "He told me his name, but I can't for the life of me remember it. I should have written it down."

Odeon glanced at the Middle Eastern guy. "That's Tariq Mero. He's new. This is his first time with our company. Good-looking guy. He could get lots of work if he wanted it."

The next scene was set up. As Riker watched closely, the bad guy, waving a pistol, scrambled up onto press number two. The extras hunkered down. The bad guy fired his pistol at an imaginary target. Bang! Bang! Bang! Three shots in rapid succession, with realistic puffs of smoke billowing from the muzzle of the pistol.

Suddenly the lights in the plant went out. The vast

space was plunged into darkness.

What the hell! thought Riker.

After ten seconds of darkness, the director yelled, "Cut! Okay, lights on!"

The plant was again flooded with light.

Riker scanned the presses. The bald black guy on number one was getting to his feet. The woman on number two had stood up, and was watching the actor who played the bad guy clamber down the ladder to the floor. On press number three, Tariq Mero was standing, looking over the railing, with his hands in his pockets.

"What was that scene about?" Riker asked Odeon.

She shuffled through her scene list. "Kurtis—the bad guy—shoots out the main lighting panel. After a few scenes in the dark, which the producers say they're going to film back in Los Angeles, the cops get the lights on again. Jack Slayer—the good guy—takes a shot at Kurtis, who falls from the top of the press and dies. That will be the end of our work here."

Riker's phone rang. Moving away from Odeon, he took the call.

"I got your message," said Angela Powell. "My assistant did some research on Hosni Raseen and Star Magna Films. He's recently become a major investor in the company. Until he came along, Star Magna was a third-rate purveyor of straight-to-DVD junk. *Lethal Last Chance* is their first big film. They're on an incredibly fast production schedule—they started filming only two weeks after getting the script and hiring the director. The scenes at *The New York Times* are the first ones they're shooting."

Riker remembered Ghazal's video from Beta Syria. The end of the video had shown two men in the lobby—Hosni Raseen and another. Riker pulled up the video on his phone. He saw the lab, with the technicians carefully preparing their eggs of death. There was Noman, in his biohazard suit. And then the last clip: Hosni Raseen and the other man were talking to Noman. The younger man's face was turned away from the camera. After a moment Noman led them to the suiting room by Noman. Their backs remained to the camera.

Just as they were about to walk through the open door of the suiting room, the younger man, the one wearing jeans and a polo shirt, turned and glanced in the direction of the camera. Then he looked away.

Riker felt an electric shock pulse through his body. The young man was Tariq Mero. He was here, now, standing next to the ink fountain on press number two, which in few short hours would come to life, and the lethal ink would flow onto the pages, and the deadly pages would fly into the hands of readers for hundreds of miles around.

The director called for places.

"Scene seven, take two!" called an assistant director.

Jamming his phone into his pocket, Riker started walking towards press number three.

"Action!"

Kurtis began his climb up the ladder of press number two. Riker watched as Tariq Mero, high on the catwalk of number three, reached into the deep pocket of his overalls. He pulled out a small blue object.

Riker broke out into a run.

"Hey—who is that guy?" yelled the director. All eyes turned to Riker.

"You there—get out of the shot!" called one of the lighting guys.

Riker grabbed the ladder to press number three and scrambled up. Through the grating he could see the blue freezer pack in Mero's hand. With a screwdriver he was prying off the plastic cap.

From a few yards away Kurtis, oblivious to the commotion, played out his scene. He raised his pistol and fired—Bang! Bang! Bang!—at the imaginary target.

Riker had nearly reached the catwalk. As he reached the last rung he suddenly felt a massive weight on his fingers. Mero's boot had smashed down on his hand.

The lights went out and the factory was plunged into darkness. Riker twisted his hand free. Reaching the catwalk, he lunged blindly forward. His outstretched hands connected with a body. An arm shoved him roughly backwards and he felt himself losing his balance. Grabbing the railing, he teetered on the edge. He pulled himself forward and, leading with his shoulder like a football player, again connected with the body. This time he was ready to attack, and with his right fist landed a solid blow to the kidneys. Mero groaned and lashed back with his fist. Riker stayed on balance and took a shot in the dark at Mero's chin. Feeling a satisfying "crack," the shock to his knuckles told him he had connected. Mero stumbled backwards, and suddenly a light flashed and the mighty printing press sprang to life.

A fist hit Riker a glancing blow to his shoulder. Quickly pivoting, he grabbed the arm to which it was attached and leveraged its owner off his feet. The heavy body slid sideways and suddenly the air was split by an animal scream.

As the arm slipped from his grasp, Riker felt the massive machine lurch under his feet.

The lights in the factory ignited.

In the sudden glare, Riker saw that Mero had fallen between two of the huge rollers. Grabbing the protruding arm of the mangled body, he tried to pull Mero free, but he was jammed too tightly between the revolving drums. Riker let go of the limp arm and ran to the emergency shutoff button.

The press stopped.

For Mero, it was too late. Half of his body had been crushed and his blood ran in rivulets down the side of the machine.

A film production assistant climbed up the ladder.

"Get back!" shouted Riker. "This area is contaminated with smallpox! Get everyone clear of here!"

The production assistant hurried back down the

ladder.

Riker scanned the grating of the catwalk. He found what he was looking for: the small blue plastic cap that Mero had pried off the freezer pack.

The freezer pack itself was nowhere to be found. After opening it, Mero had simply dropped it into the ink fountain. The ink in the reservoir was now loaded with the smallpox virus.

Riker pulled out his phone. On the other end, Angela Powell picked up.

"Tariq Mero is dead," said Riker. "He dumped a container of smallpox into the reservoir of one of the presses here at *The New York Times*. Hosni Raseen was the banker who paid for the American leg of Operation Fire Sword."

"He's in New York, no doubt to witness first-hand what his money has paid for," replied Powell. "We'll pick him up before he flees the country."

Riker hung up.

Richard Laskey appeared on the ladder. "What the hell is going on here?" he thundered.

"What's going on is that a terrorist has contaminated this printing press with smallpox, which is a highly dangerous and contagious disease," replied Riker. "You need to seal this building. It will be taken over by the Centers of Disease Control and Prevention, which will oversee the cleanup and removal of the smallpox virus. It's likely that everyone who was in this facility today will need to be decontaminated and then vaccinated against smallpox. Okay?"

"How about him?" said Laskey, pointing to what was left of Mero.

"He's not going anywhere," replied Riker. "He's been inoculated against smallpox, but his blood may contain the virus. We're not going to touch him. We're going to leave him there until a properly equipped team from the CDC can scrape him off the rollers."

Following Laskey, Riker descended the ladder. He stood at its base.

The film director walked up to him. "This is a

terrible disaster. Just horrible. But we've got a film to make. Can't we just keep shooting in some other part of the building? This place is huge!"

"Sorry—it's a wrap," replied Riker. "Furthermore, I'm sorry to say that this entire production is shutting down. Your number one investor is going to jail for a very long time. Unless you can find a new angel, there will be no more *Lethal Last Chance*."

After the director had stormed off, Riker took out his phone. It was nearly midnight in Syria, but he didn't care. He punched Amena's number.

She answered.

"We got them," said Riker. "Operation Fire Sword has been smashed."

"That's incredible news," said Amena. "But I can't really talk now."

Riker's heart fell. "Oh—are you with someone?"

"Yes—about two hundred other people," she laughed. "I'm in Istanbul. I've just boarded a flight to London."

"Why? What's going on?"

"It's getting too hot for me at home," replied Amena. "A colleague tipped me off. If I stayed, they'd arrest me. It was time to go."

"Go where?" asked Riker.

"I've always wanted to visit Naples, Florida," she replied. "I've heard the people there are very nice, and the weather is beautiful."

"I suppose you'll need a guide to show you around town."

"Do you know of anyone?"

"I think I could fix you up."

"Then it's a deal. I have to go—they want us to turn off our cell phones. I'll text you with my arrival time in Tampa."

"I'm looking forward to seeing you. Have a safe trip."

Riker put his phone in his pocket. There was nothing more for him to do but wait for the arrival of the first responders in their biohazard suits, and for them to once again eradicate smallpox from the face of the earth.

Except, of course, for the two stockpiles in Atlanta and Novosibirsk.

Stockpiles that had been proven to be vulnerable. As long as the smallpox virus existed, someone— somewhere—could be plotting to use it in another attack.

Riker picked up his phone and punched a number.

"Angela? Riker here. We've stopped this plot—but the danger still exists."

About the Authors

Dr. Leslie Norins brings decades of medical research and medical publishing experience to *Deadly Pages*, his fictional thriller about smallpox bioterrorism.

After training with a Nobel Prize winner, he directed a major laboratory at the U.S. Centers for Disease Control in Atlanta, Georgia.

Then, as a medical publisher, for over thirty years he created and grew more than eighty medical newsletters, providing news and advice for hundreds of thousands of healthcare professionals in specialized niches throughout the U.S. and the world. Trade publications have called him "legendary" and "the dean of medical newsletters."

Dr. Norins received his B.A. from Johns Hopkins University and his M.D. from Duke University School of Medicine. His Ph.D. is from the University of Melbourne, where he was a postdoctoral fellow of Sir Macfarlane Burnet, Nobel Laureate, at the Walter and Eliza Hall Institute of Medical Research. He was elected a Fellow of the Infectious Disease Society of America, and has served on committees of the National Institutes of Health and the World Health Organization.

A native of Baltimore, Dr. Norins resides with his wife in Naples, Florida.

Novelist and book editor Thomas Hauck has published numerous works of fiction, including *Pistonhead*, the story of a rock musician; *The Body on the Rocks*, a collection of crime stories set in his home town of Gloucester, Massachusetts; and the Kevin Lone international thriller series.